Down from

Basswood

Down from Basswood

Voices of the Border Country

By

Lynn Maria Laitala

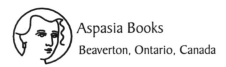

Aspasia Books
Beaverton, Ontario, Canada

Down from Basswood
ISBN 0-9689054-4-7

Published in 2001 by
ASPASIA BOOKS
R.R.1
Beaverton, Ontario
L0K 1A0 Canada

aspasia@aspasiabooks.com
www.aspasiabooks.com

Painting on cover by Carl Gowboy "Morning Chores"
Cover design by Anneli West of Four Corners Communications

*Aspasia Books gratefully acknowledges the support
of the Finlandia Foundation*

National Library of Canada Cataloguing in Publication Data

Laitala, Lynn Maria, 1947–
    Down from Basswood : voices of the border country

ISBN 0-9689054-4-7

    1. Finns – United States – Fiction. I. Title.

PS3612.A49D69 2001   813'.6   C2001-904098-9

Contents

Chapter 1

The Windigo: Charlie Bouchay's Story

W hat could I have done to turn back the change that swept my land, brought by the men who came to cut the forests? My father said that we should teach these new white men the ways of this place. After all, Europeans had been coming to Basswood for hundreds of years, trading cloth and iron in exchange for furs, and we learned each other's ways. Now there are as many French and Scottish names among us as Chippewa. I told my father that the new men weren't interested in furs, or Indians either. They only wanted the timber. They cut more trees than any man could use in a lifetime, than any village or town could use in a hundred years. They consumed the trees from Basswood with the hunger of Windigo.

Windigo is the most terrible of the Chippewa monsters. He burns with greed, regarding others merely as food to feed an appetite so voracious that he eats the lips from his own face. Whenever a child acts selfishly, his mother scolds: "Windigo will get you."

We grow to understand that Windigo isn't a monster of the forest but a beast within, waiting to claim your heart. We guard against him in ourselves, and try to protect others from his evil.

How could I do what my father asked—teach the new white men—when far away from Basswood, the spirit of Windigo signed papers and made decisions that stripped trees from our land and made men into beasts?

The lumberjacks lived in filth and ate rotten food. When they got their paychecks they went to town and drank until they lost their reason, dragging back to camp like whipped dogs. Men were killed and maimed on the job. No one cared.

But because my father wanted me to talk to the new white men, I went to the logging camp on Hoist Bay and contracted to sell them fresh meat. And whenever I was hunting for the camp, I mourned Annie and Busticogen.

Annie was my aunt. She and Busticogen were chiefs of the Deer Creek Reservation.

They went everywhere together—up to Nett Lake to harvest wild rice in the fall, to the sugar bush in the spring to make maple sugar. They hunted and trapped together, and like me, they sold fresh meat to the lumber camps. Late one afternoon when the cold stung the eyes and every breath pierced the lungs, Annie and Busticogen struggled through deep snow toward camp, pulling a toboggan loaded with venison. Only a rosy glow of twilight lingered above the dark silhouettes of the spruce, but they expected to soon stand near a pot-bellied stove, drinking hot tea, thawing toes and fingers in the dark warmth of the bunkhouse.

They turned the last bend in the trail watching for a flicker of lamplight from the windows of the camp, but the woods were cold and black as death itself. They could make out the gray shapes of the camp buildings emerging from the gloom but no light came from the windows, no smoke rose from the chimneys.

Busticogen walked up and banged on the window. A gaunt face appeared behind the grimy glass, eyes sunken and glazed with fever.

"Go away," the man cried. "Smallpox! We are all dead here. Save yourselves!"

Annie went in, found kindling and started a fire in the stove. She and Busticogen went from bed to bed, taking up the hands of the lumberjacks, finding out who was dead and who was not. They carried the corpses outside, laying them near the woodpile.

Busticogen took the blankets from the beds of the dead men and put them over the living while Annie brewed tea and venison broth. They held the men too weak to sit and spooned liquid between their lips.

Most of the men they nursed lived. Annie and Busticogen didn't catch smallpox.

In gratitude, the logging camp boss gave them free passes to ride on any logging railroad. They were heroes of the north, welcome at every camp—until one day, years after the winter of the smallpox, a government official came to the Deer Creek Reservation and told them that the Indians had to leave their homes. He said that an Indian had signed papers authorizing the government to sell the reservation to a logging company.

No one from the reservation had signed any papers. Busticogen and Annie went to see their old friends at the logging camp. The boss had never heard of the new logging company that claimed their land. Next they went to town to talk to the mayor, but he didn't know anything about the Indians losing their reservation, either.

Annie and Busticogen sold their winter's supply of pelts to travel east to find officials from the Bureau of Indian Affairs. They had to explain that someone had made a terrible mistake.

Together Annie and Busticogen rode the train from Cook, Minnesota, to Washington, DC—and together they came back in the baggage car, crated in identical pine boxes.

The official explanation of their deaths from the Indian agent was that Annie and Busticogen had blown out the gaslight in the hotel when they went to bed, not knowing that they had to turn off the gas. In the morning they were dead. The Indians and the lumberjacks believed that they had been murdered.

With the chiefs dead, the Indian agent moved the Deer Creek Indians to the Nett Lake Reservation and a lumber baron took their land.

And there I was, in 1913, working for the Hoist Bay logging camp on Bass-wood Lake, provisioning it with fresh meat like Annie and Busticogen had been doing over near Deer Creek. I thought about them every time I walked into camp. Now that logging had come to Basswood, how long would the Chippewas be allowed to stay?

Most of the lumberjacks paid me little attention but the pale eyes of one man followed me whenever I was at the camp. I was curious about him too. Where had he come from—what made him leave his home and his women? We had no language in common for me to ask.

One night I got in after dark in bitter cold, after trudging for miles through deep, light snow with a broken snowshoe, carrying the hindquarters of a moose on my back. Usually when I stayed in camp I made a shelter of fresh balsam boughs and slept outdoors because the bunkhouse crawled with lice, but that night I was so exhausted I stayed in the bunkhouse.

In dim lamplight, Pale Eyes watched me mend my snowshoe with strips of rawhide.

He moved his chair near me, leaned close to my face, and spoke a word in English.

"Teach," he said.

I pointed to the snowshoe and looked at his face. He nodded. He rose, opened the door and gestured to the silent, snowy woods beyond.

"Teach," he said again.

Chapter 2

Down from Basswood: Mary Bouchay's First Story

Antti's eyes were pale as shadows on snow, yet warm as a cliff baked by the summer sun. Those eyes saw in me something no other eyes have seen.

Charlie brought Antti to our village on Jackfish Bay early in the spring, right at breakup, paddling through floes of ice. From high on the cliff, Ira and I saw the canoe come round the point, riding low in the water.

"It's Papa! It's Papa!" yelled Ira.

"Who's the man in the bow?" I asked.

Ira yipped and squirmed. I hung on to his hand to keep him from tumbling off the icy ledge. We hadn't seen Charlie since Christmas.

"Boujou!" Charlie called out, with a wide grin. "Boujou, Mary. Boujou, Ira. Antti, that is my sister and my son upon the rock!"

Instantly Ira became still. I watched the stranger.

They brought the canoe around the cliff where the woods came to the water's edge. By the time Ira and I scrambled down the rock they'd flung out bales of pelts and lifted the canoe up on shore. Other children ran from the village to meet them.

Charlie picked up Ira. "See what I brought you, Mary?" Charlie said, nodding toward the solemn man at his side. "This is my new partner, Antti. If you were a little older, he'd make a better present."

At the sound of his name Antti smiled. He was dressed in a wool mackinaw and wool pants cut short over high-topped boots, the same as Charlie, but he had those odd pale eyes and a blond mustache, like none I had seen.

"He doesn't speak French, and not much English," Charlie told me in Chippewa.

"What is he then?"

"He says he's *suomalainen*. The others call him Finlander."

"Finlander?"

"*Joo, suomalainen,*" Antti nodded.

We walked together up the hill where Aunt was ready with birch bark bowls of venison stew. Charlie and Antti ate wearily. Ira was pestering Charlie with questions, so I took him with me to break fresh balsam bows. We lay them thickly at the back of the wigwam, and covered them with blankets.

"It's good to have you home, Charlie," Father said when the men lay down to rest on their fresh beds. Later I asked Charlie more about his new partner.

"I met him in the logging camp," Charlie said.

"You can't even really talk to him."

"Good partners don't need to say much."

The next day Charlie and Antti took off for Winton to sell their pelts. They returned with barrels of flour and new traps and bolts of cloth. There was a pair of boots for Ira.

Suckers were running. Charlie and Antti netted suckers, dried and smoked them. When the sap began to flow in the trees, Charlie showed Antti how to strip bark from birches and they built a canoe together. Charlie had a new canoe, a green canvas Old Town. I asked why he was teaching Antti the old way.

"He wants to know how we used to live from nothing but what creation provided," Charlie said.

Our village was high on the cliffs where blueberries grew thick, near lakes where we made maple sugar and harvested wild rice. I looked out over the forests and lakes, rich with plants and animals and fish.

"How can you not live from creation?" I asked Charlie.

Charlie smiled and shook his head.

One bright spring day I watched Antti whittle birch into a knife handle. His face looked gentle as he concentrated on his work. I touched his shoulder. He looked up and smiled. I took his hand and he let me lead him over the hill to the place where the graves were.

"We put our dead here," I said. "See? We bury them, and then build a little house over the grave, for the spirit. The spirit lives there, coming and going around the village for a fortnight. Then it travels west. See the hole where it goes in and out of its house? We put food on that shelf for the spirit, to prepare for its long trip. After the spirit leaves, the house rots away."

Antti peered in the hole of one of the spirit houses.

"There are many new graves," I said. "We leave things that the spirits loved when they were alive, or that they might need as spirits." I picked up a doll from a grave. Antti took it from me and looked at it carefully. Other graves had moccasins, pipes, guns.

"Charlie was my father's second child, and I was his last. Five children born between us are buried here. Some were tiny babies when they died, but three were as full of life as Ira is now. They just got sick and died."

Antti watched me intently.

"See these two spirit houses? The spirits are gone from them now. This one is my mother's grave. That's the grave of Charlie's wife. Last year, on a beautiful day just like today, they were paddling up the bay when a big wind blew up and swamped their canoe. Ira and I watched from the cliff. The icy water drank up their long woolen skirts and pulled them under the waves. Charlie and Father found their bodies after many days. Ira and I became twins by death the day we lost our mothers."

Even though he didn't understand my words, my pain eased a little when I told Antti my sorrow. I took his hand and led him back over the hill to the village.

Often Charlie and Antti took Ira with them on their travels. Charlie called Ira "bourgeois," or big shot, because he sat between them in the middle of the canoe. In the fur trade days the bourgeois were the men who didn't want to work. The Indians laughed at them because paddling is the joy of traveling. Ira squirmed, cramped in the middle, impatient for the time that he would paddle from the bow.

Sometimes Antti came with me when I went on my errands. One shimmering summer day we paddled down the bay to gather spider plants. We pulled the canoe up in a sheltered place and walked down the ancient path. I showed Antti which plants were good for food or medicine. He laughed when I acted out "headache" and "stomach ache" to teach him what the plant was for, and I laughed when he tried to imitate my words. It was easy to talk to him when he understood nothing that I said.

"Last year, and the year before, I was at the boarding school in Vermilion," I told him, as he followed me around, picking plants I pointed to. "They teach English there, and sewing, and how to be a lady. I was very homesick. Some Chippewa children died from being homesick. The government agents make us go. They say they have to keep track of us by numbers so they can pay us for the land they took in the treaty. That was sixty years ago. I don't think we'll see that money."

I showed Antti little red berries that cure side aches. I jogged around in a circle, panting hard. Then I fell down, clutching my side. I popped a berry in my mouth, sat up and smiled. Antti laughed and nodded.

"Charlie took me to the logging camp one time. So many men, no women. I saw the rails through the woods, and the steam engines."

My basket was full. Antti took it and we started back to the canoe.

"Charlie worries about our young men who work in the logging camps. They go to town and get drunk and waste their money with the rest of the lumberjacks.

"I've never seen a man as pale as you," I said, peering at his eyes, paler than the winter sky. Antti smiled, not understanding my words. "Not even at boarding school. My grandfather was French, from Quebec, but he was dark. He worked for Hudson's Bay Company. We sold furs and married with traders for longer than anyone knows. Then the new Americans came to cut the trees. Too bad you don't know French. Father talks to Charlie and me in French, he prefers it. Aunt talks to him in Chippewa, but Father answers her in French. Charlie and I talk English to each other when we don't want Father or Aunt to understand. How strange that you understand none of it."

The low sun reddened the cliffs on the far shore. We'd come to the water's edge. I touched Antti's wrist, to make him still while I listened to the voices of the manitous, the mysteries in the woods. Did Antti hear them, I wondered?

When everyone returned to the village from their winter camps, we were about fifty souls altogether. Children shouted, dogs barked, people came and went visiting other villages. In midsummer, Father decided we should go to the powwow at Vermilion. Charlie and Antti came, too. We paddled to Winton and camped overnight with the Beargrease family by the falls. Next day we left our canoes in the brush by the river and walked to the railroad station. There were other lumberjacks at the depot and Antti talked to them in his own language.

"They sound like frogs," Aunt said, listening to the strange tongue.

We heard the whistle before the train came around the bend and rolled into the station hissing steam. The brakeman put our bundles in the baggage car and helped us up the steps of the passenger car. We sat on brown plush seats and the train moved slowly, backing its way down the tracks to Ely.

I'd ridden the train when the Indian agent took me to boarding school, but this time I enjoyed myself. We passed small houses of miners and the tall steel mine head. Children climbed on fences to wave, and I waved back.

We were hardly out of Ely and into the woods before we reached Tower. We got our bundles from the baggage car and carried them to the river where Father's brothers waited for us with canoes. Father, who loved to travel, bragged to his brothers of the speed of the train as if he had invented the locomotive himself.

People came from hundreds of miles for the Vermilion powwow. They set up wigwams and tents in every yard. Women gossiped and laughed while they fried heaps of fresh fish and crisp golden bread over campfires. I found my friends and cousins and we walked around the village together.

"Look, Mary, there's Joe Keewatin," Frances said.

Joe was hanging from a tree by his knees. I ignored him. He got down from the tree and started following us around with his friend George.

"Joe likes you, Mary," Frances said.

"He smells like cows," I said. At boarding school, Joe had taken care of the cows in the school barn. "Where's your cows, Joe?" I called at him. I turned my back and walked with Frances and Charlene and Anne to the landing to show I didn't care.

At twilight we gathered in a clearing. In the center of the clearing seven men sat around the drum. The head of the village made a speech of welcome. The drummers knelt around the drum and beat in unison, chanting a song for the memory of the people who had perished during the year. The year before Father, Charlie and Ira and I had led the mourners. Now I joined the dance when the circle was full, letting the rhythm of the drum capture my feet, making the long fringe on my shawl swing and shimmer in the torch light. A hundred together, we moved as one, sorrowing for the dead.

Father was dressed in black cotton cloth, with large sleigh bells strapped around his ankles. Charlie wore the outfit Aunt had worked on all winter, made of black velvet covered with the tiniest beads of vibrant colors, patterned in flowers and vines and leaves. The pattern on the vest matched the pattern on the panel that hung from his waist. Each moccasin top was beaded in the same design. After the dance to mourn the dead, the men danced alone, strong and powerful. Next the women danced with solemn grace, and then we danced together again. All night we danced, sometimes arm in arm, sometimes apart. Two pairs of eyes followed me through the night—the dark, steady eyes of young Joe Keewatin, and Antti's pale eyes, like blue flames in the torchlight.

There were more festive days that summer. We had visitors on Jackfish Bay when the blueberries ripened. Joe and his family traveled up from Vermilion, though there were certainly berries for them to pick closer to home. Aunt had taken my hair out of its braids and combed it into a bun on my neck, and Joe treated me more respectfully.

At the end of summer, we traveled in twelve canoes to Mahnomen Lake to harvest wild rice. We set up our birch bark wigwams, and put big iron pots near the doors, ready to parch the rice.

I asked Antti to be my paddler while I riced.

We drifted off shore in our canoes, waiting for the dew to dry off the rice. Finally old Jennie Waboose waved her white handkerchief. We cheered, and started out across the lake.

"This is how it's done, Antti," I told him as he paddled into the rice bed. "Gently bend the stalks with one stick, and then gently brush them with the other." Rice rained into the canoe.

I turned around to get his attention. "You're paddling too hard. Slow and steady." I pretended to hold a paddle and moved it at the right speed. Antti slowed down.

The rice was thick, and the canoe filled with the bearded grain. Rice birds ran atop the lily pads, and fish darted away from the canoe. I sang as I worked, first songs my mother had taught me, and then songs I learned in school. I liked one hymn, about the fair meadows. I thought of the green grassy places behind old beaver dams. Suddenly Antti joined in, singing the same song in his own language. I turned around to look at him in amazement. Beaming, he kept the rhythm of the hymn with the paddle strokes. For the rest of the afternoon we played a game, finding songs we both knew.

Charlie and Antti stayed in the village through the fall, until the whitefish ran. They left us with fish and meat and paddled away to the logging camp.

The snowy, star-filled winter passed quickly for me. In the mornings, Ira and I checked our snares. It was a good year for rabbits. In the evenings I worked on my own powwow outfit and played string games with the little children while we listened to Father's stories.

Charlie and Antti brought sacks of dried fruit when they came at Christmas. They hunted a little before they were gone again.

When the days grew longer and the snow began to thaw, we traveled west over frozen lakes to the sugar bush. We hitched the dogs to toboggans loaded with iron pots, and we snowshoed beside them, pulling toboggans piled high with blankets and rolls of birch bark for the wigwams. Babies rode on top of the packs, bundled up to their noses. Our spirits were high as the sun.

From a distance we saw smoke from a campfire. I was afraid that cruisers from the logging company had come to mark the sugar bush for timber, but when we got there, Charlie and Antti sat by the fire, grinning and whittling taps for the maple trees.

"Antti wanted to make sugar," Charlie said.

Wherever I went, Antti followed me. He carried my sap buckets to the big pot on the toboggan and pulled it back to camp through the deep snow. One time when we were resting on a log, warm in the radiant spring sunshine, I told him about boarding school.

"There were many things that were hard about boarding school," I said. "The hardest part was living indoors. We were always cold, it was always dark. The work never warmed the body or the spirit. People smelled sour. The teachers crushed our spirits. I don't know why they want to crush the spirits of children."

"I understand you better when you talk English," Antti said.

I jumped a foot in the air.

"You understand me?" I asked in English.

"Better when you talk English than Chippewa," he repeated.

I was devastated. I had talked straight from my heart, believing he didn't know what I said. What had he heard?

"How long have you been able to understand me?"

"I've been picking it up right along."

"You never said anything.

"I understand more than I can speak."

"And last summer, did you already understand me?"

"Not always the words," Antti said.

After that morning I was too shy to be near him. When he came to sit by me, I moved away. One day he came into the wigwam while I was alone.

"I miss your talk," he said simply, and I had to relent, but I never felt as free to speak again.

Joe Keewatin visited Jackfish on every possible occasion. His mother and my aunt engaged in serious conversation about me. I kept aloof. I wanted Antti.

If Antti wanted me, he was courting slower than a turtle crosses a cold beach. I grew impatient. It was summer, and we were picking blueberries apart from the others when I decided to move things along. I led Antti into the woods, where we were screened by thick brush.

"I'm not a girl any longer, Antti," I told him.

"No," he said. He reached out to touch my hair. There was a low growl behind me just as I saw the cub up the tree behind Antti. We were between the mother bear and her baby. Mother bear charged. Antti grabbed my hand and we scrambled over rocks and brush and fallen logs, mother bear close behind. She was nearly on us when we reached the edge of the cliff. We went over, clinging to roots and little twisted cedars, dropping to the narrow sandy beach below, bruised and scraped. Mother bear walked back and forth, growling on the ledge above.

My heart pounded so hard I could hardly breathe. I began to laugh. Antti was laughing too. He kissed me just as Charlie came around the point in his canoe.

Later I asked Charlie what Antti's intentions were.

"He's saving money," Charlie said.

"What?"

"He's saving his money. He wants to marry you when he can buy his own land and get you nice things."

"Does he want me to live in a cabin and live like I was taught in boarding school?"

"Well, maybe live in a cabin," Charlie said.

"I don't want that!" I said. "What does he need money for? What do I need that I don't already have?"

"I think it has to do with his honor."

"Oh," I said. I tried to understand. A man's honor is the most important thing he has. I thought about it. Even if I married Joe Keewatin I'd have to live in a cabin. Anyway, the Keewatin family had given up on me.

I had decided to wait for Antti, when the Great Death swept over Basswood and ripped me from my life.

In early winter, a man came home sick from the logging camp. In a few days he was dead. Rapidly, others got sick. The old people and the babies died first. Charlie came home and told us that Death was in the logging camp. They called it the Spanish Flu. Antti was sick but Charlie had left him behind to come home to care for us and bury the dead. Father took ill, then Aunt. Father died.

When Aunt lay dying she said to me, "Don't harden yourself to death, Mary, because then you are hardened to life."

We couldn't bury them properly. There were too many. They had no spirit houses. We put Father and Aunt in one grave with some others. Half of the village had died.

Then Charlie got sick. Charlie.

Charlie died. Ira and I were digging his grave when the Indian agent came.

"I've come to take the survivors to safety," he said.

"How did you know about the Death?" I asked.

"It's all over the world and it's hitting Indians hard. We figured this village would be nearly wiped out."

"There's half of us left. People aren't getting sick anymore. We'll be all right."

"I'm authorized to remove you for your own protection."

"We won't leave."

The agent nodded at the other government men, standing below him on the lake. I saw their rifles.

"We thought you might resist. These are government orders."

"I have to bury my brother."

"No time. Tell your people to pick up their things. We're moving out now."

Ira swung at the man. The agent cracked him on the side of his head with his rifle butt. "Don't you think that there's enough dead here already?" he asked.

I was too numb to resist. We all were, except Ira. Ira ran into the woods. I ran after and caught him.

"I need you," I told him. "You're all the kin I have left."

They took us to Lac La Croix in Canada, even though we had our treaty numbers from the United States. Ira and I lived at the edge of the village until Joe Keewatin appeared one summer day.

"I've come to take you and Ira home to Vermilion, Mary," Joe said.

"How did you know we were here?"

"I didn't, but the agents bragged how easy it was to take the people from Jackfish, so I knew Charlie and your father must be dead. I had to find out what happened to you."

Ira and I went home with Joe. I became Mrs. Keewatin, and lived in a cabin. Joe worked in the woods. Two of our children survived.

There were times when I couldn't imagine that life would go on, but it did.

Joy came back to me in my old age. The manitous, the mysteries, were always there in the woods, though for many, many years I couldn't hear them.

Each summer we travel back to visit the graves on Jackfish Bay. The first year we went home, there was a strange new spirit house like no one had ever seen. It was built of squared logs, tightly fitted, with dove-tailed corners. It told me that Antti had lived, he had come home, and he had buried Charlie.

I left a cooking pot for Aunt and laid two ricing sticks for Father on their grave. I gave Charlie back the rifle that I had taken with me to Lac La Croix.

The spirit house stood over Charlie's grave for many years. Charlie's spirit had gone from it, but Antti's lingered on.

Chapter 3

River Farm: Timo Lahti's Story

There were strange noises coming from the old log barn. Thunk. Thud. It took a moment for my eyes to become accustomed to the gloom. In grim, concentrated silence, Father and Urho fought. Blood ran from Father's nose and a cut above his eye. I watched in horror as Father knocked Urho down and picked up a pitchfork.

"Father!" I screamed. His hand lowered.

"Not as long as I live!" Father shouted at Urho. He threw down the pitchfork and pushed past me. I left Urho alone in the barn so he wouldn't be shamed by my sympathy.

I never learned what the fight was about, but it changed my life forever. The midnight sun shone through the windows of the sleeping cabin when Urho told his plans.

"There's opportunity in America," he said. "You can be your own boss. I'm going."

We three younger brothers listened warily. Urho had his moods.

"Listen Timo," he said to me, "you're the youngest son. You don't have a future here in Finland. There's cheap land in America. Come with me. You might as well come along too, Antti," he said. "You don't like farming that much anyway."

Then he looked at Taavi, our other brother. A year younger than Urho, Taavi was his opposite in temper. Urho had overshadowed him all his life. "Taavi gets the farm," Urho said.

And that's how it was. I was sixteen. I danced on the boat from Liverpool. In New York we caught a train to Michigan, but there wasn't work so we traveled on to Minnesota's Iron Range. Red ore dust covered everything. We earned up to $2.50 for a day of shoveling dirt.

In Finland they said that American streets were lined with gold, but in Hibbing they were made of mud and lined with drunks. That's not what I'd come to America for. I wanted my own farm on a pretty lake, with a house set among birch trees, and sleek horses and fat cattle grazing in the pasture.

Most of all I wanted a beautiful wife—strong and kind. We'd work together on the farm. There would always be enough to eat, and our children would be happy.

There were hardly any girls at all in Hibbing. Antti had his eye on the girl who waited on us in the boardinghouse. When Urho noticed he taunted him about it.

"What do you see in that Aina? She's nothing but a meek little servant," he said. But when Antti started walking with Aina in the evening after supper chores, Urho started courting her, too. It was his nature to take what someone else wanted, whether he wanted it himself or not. Antti had never won a fight with Urho, so when Urho went after Aina, Antti took off for the lumber camps up north.

I'd had enough of the mining pits myself. I heard there was good money working the harvest in Dakota so I went out west in a threshing gang. That's where I found my gold, in a Finnish community near Frederick. Golden hair and golden smile, Kaija was the beautiful woman of my dreams. She was dressed in black from head to toe, her mother was mean and her father silent, but Kaija glowed with joy and spirit. She cooked for the harvest crew. At every meal I said something to her to make her notice me. When the threshers moved on, I promised Kaija that I'd be back.

"Remember me," I said.

When the harvest ended, I went back to northern Minnesota to look for Antti. I was asking for news of him in a bar in Ely when I met Seppo.

"I need a man to help me clear my land. Can you work?" Seppo asked me.

"I can work," I said. "I can cut trees and pull stumps. I can plow and I can seed. I can build with board or log. I can forge iron. I know cows, and I talk to horses in their own language."

Seppo took me home with him.

A pretty little river ran through the middle of Seppo's land, but otherwise there was nothing to recommend it. It had a small shack and a tiny clearing with the stumps still in the ground.

"How long have you been working on your land?" I asked.

"I've been here six years now, and just look at it. Sometimes I sit down on a stump and say to myself, 'no use, no use.'"

"What do you want me to do first?"

Seppo looked around, discouraged. "Whatever you want," he said.

I set to work chinking the cracks between the logs of the cabin. After a proper house is built this will make a fine chicken coop, I thought.

While Seppo always had money to buy alcohol, he had no money to pay me. I bought us food with my threshing money. Every night he drank, and then cried about how miserable he was in the godforsaken woods.

"Why don't you go back to Finland?" I asked.

"I don't have enough money."

"Why don't you earn money to go back?"

Seppo thought for a while. "No use," he said finally. "No use."

Seppo had gotten an old horse from a logging camp. Before the ground froze solid I grubbed and hacked and tugged out enough stumps to make the horse a little pasture, and then I built a brush fence and a lean-to shelter. I scythed marsh grass on the banks of the river and put up a tall stack of hay. Next I built a log bridge across a narrow place in the river, and set to work cutting big pines on the other side. I marked the logs and skidded them down to the river with the horse. Come spring, we'd float them to the mill for the first cash crop.

Sometimes Seppo came out with his axe, sat on a stump and watched. I tried to get him to work with me on a two-man crosscut saw, but he complained about his sore shoulder.

Every night I dropped into exhausted sleep, and every night Seppo woke me with his crying, drunk and homesick.

"Seppo," I said one night, "If you had a ticket, would you go home to Finland?"

"Right now," he said. "I'd be on that boat right now."

"Would you sell me this land for the price of a ticket?"

"Right now," he said. "I'd sell you this land right now."

I left him a sack of beans and a chunk of salt pork and went to look for work at the logging camp on Burntside Lake. As luck would have it, the blacksmith had just walked off the job and the camp boss believed me when I told him that I knew how to forge iron.

In the spring I went back to the farm to plant potatoes and work on the stumps. Seppo had already sold the timber I'd cut in the fall and drunk up the money.

It rained every day. The horse and I were tormented by black flies and mosquitoes. I put grease in the horse's ears and hung kerosene soaked rags from his harness to keep away the bugs. We kept at our work, day after day, dragging stumps onto a pile. One evening, after a week of no rain, I told Seppo to come see what I had done. He crossed the bridge and looked around at the newly bare field but said nothing.

I doused the stump pile with kerosene and lit it. The fire raged up to the sky.

Seppo started to cry.

"We always had a bonfire in Finland to celebrate the midnight sun. Now here I sit in this wretched wilderness."

When harvest season came I headed west with the threshers, filled with anticipation and apprehension. I could show Kaija what kind of man I was. I'd survived a year in America, and soon I would have my own farm. I was seventeen.

The threshing crew traveled from farm to farm, gangs of men and horses and machines. Finally we reached the Koivisto place. From a distance, I saw golden Kaija standing on the porch, shading her eyes, searching the faces of the men coming up the road. When our eyes met she turned and hurried into the house.

That night I crept out of the barn where the men slept and walked toward the house. Kaija stood waiting, silhouetted against the prairie sky.

"Kaija," I called softly. It sounded like a shout in the stillness of the evening. She came to me. I took her hand and we walked onto the prairie. We lay on the grass and looked at the stars. I told her my dreams.

"It'll be three or four years before I can bring a woman to my farm," I said.

"Hurry," she said, kissing me.

With my logging camp wages and the harvest wages, I had enough money to buy Seppo's tickets. In Duluth I purchased railroad passage to New York, and steamer passage to Finland. In Ely, I found Seppo in his favorite bar. I showed him the tickets and he started to cry. We signed some papers at the courthouse and the land was mine. The next day Seppo packed his suitcase, put on his black wool traveling suit and walked the six miles to Ely to catch the morning train.

I didn't have any money left, so the horse and I went back to the Burntside camp, and I lost a winter's work on the farm. The time to

21

cut trees and skid logs is when the ground is frozen. Back on my land in the spring, I worked in mud, dreamed mud when I slept, and woke to struggle back into mud-caked clothes. The wet spring turned into a dry summer with heat that never let up, but the horse and I didn't quit either. When I got tired, I thought of Kaija's silhouette in the dark Dakota evening, and my lips tingled with the memory of her kiss. "Hurry," she'd said. It kept me at my work.

I cut trees for my own buildings now. Mornings I chopped and limbed the trees and afternoons I squared them and stacked them to season. I wished for Antti. Antti could hew a log so flat and smooth you couldn't see the axe marks.

I walked my land. The house should go just here, where you could see the bend in the river, near this clump of birch, just like my dream. Here I would build my blacksmith shop. There would be the sauna on the bank of the river.

I built the sauna first.

Harvest time came nearly too quickly. I'd wanted to get more done before I returned to Kaija.

"Aren't you lonely, working by yourself in the woods?" she asked as we lay under our prairie sky.

"No," I said. I wasn't lonely because I thought of her all the time.

Kaija told me that her family was very religious. They didn't allow dancing or fun, or pretty clothes.

"Do you want to wear pretty clothes?" I asked.

She laughed. "I'd never feel comfortable wearing fancy dresses," she said. "Last year I worked for a woman in town who made me wear a maid's apron. I wore it home one time. 'Look there, the devil perches on your shoulder,' my mother said, pointing at the ruffles."

"Do you think God punishes people for being happy?" I asked.

She thought for a while. "The world is so beautiful, the sky is so beautiful. God must want us to enjoy His work. My parents are too angry to see God's beauty around them."

"Will your parents be angry when you leave them?"

"Yes. I'm sorry, because I love them, but I don't want their angry life."

"What would happen if they found us together?"

"Too terrible to even think about." She leaned over and gave me one of her sweet kisses. I could see her smile in the darkness.

Only a few yellow leaves clung to the poplars when I got back to Ely. I bought beans, flour and fat in town and borrowed Teituri

22

Lepisto's boat to row my supplies across Long Lake and up the Burntside River. My first glimpse of home was the tall pines that I'd left standing like an island on the cutover land.

I stopped at neighbor Reino's house to get my horse.

"Come in, come in. Coffee's on," Reino cried. Anxious as I was to get home, I couldn't turn him down.

Reino poured the coffee and sipped awhile before he told me the grave news.

"Somebody is living in your cabin," he said.

"Who is it?"

"I don't know, I just hear his axe. Once I saw a man walking down the trail." I set down my cup and made for the door.

"Can't you stay for supper?" Reino called after me.

When I turned down the path, I saw things were worse than I'd imagined. There was a new building going up near the old horse lean-to. This intruder meant to stay on!

He was working even now, chopping away. I took my *puukko* from its sheath and ducked into the trees, approaching stealthily. The stocky man worked with his back to me, expertly squaring the logs with his broad axe. The cut surface was as smooth as planed wood, without a mark on it. I sat down with a laugh and found that I was shaking from fear.

"Antti!" I shouted. He turned as I ran from the woods and set aside his axe. Stiffly, he accepted my embrace.

"Come in and eat," he said. "I have a rabbit stewing."

He made biscuits while I told him about the harvest.

"What have you been doing here in America?" I asked. "I asked everyone I met if they had seen you, but you'd disappeared."

"I wasn't far. Just up on Basswood Lake. A man came to the logging camp last winter and said you were looking for me, so I knew you were here."

"You winter in the camps, then, like me. What do you do in the summertime?"

"I've been living with the Indians."

I was impressed. "Wild Indians?"

Antti laughed. "Yah, wild Indians."

Two men never worked like we did that winter. Antti kept us fed with venison, fish and even beaver from his trapline. We built from my store of seasoned logs, and cut more.

In the spring Antti went to town to sell his winter pelts and came back with two of the prettiest colts I'd ever seen—jet black, with arching necks, deep chests, and solid feet. I saw them coming down the trail—one horse charging on ahead, the other lagging behind, Antti hanging on to both, grinning a giant grin.

"What are you going to do with those horses?" I asked.

"I got no use for horses! I got them for you."

I couldn't believe it.

"They aren't such a good deal," Antti said. "I got them cheap from the man who takes care of the horses for St. Croix Lumber. One's too hot, he said, and the other's stupid. But I figure you can train anything."

I stroked the neck of the hot-tempered animal.

"Easy, Loistaa," I crooned. The other colt planted his feet and hung back timidly. I took his rope from Antti.

"Thanks," I said.

That night Antti said he was heading back to Basswood.

"Time to go to the sugar camp," he said. He got very shy. "I have a girlfriend," he told me.

"Me, too," I said. "She's in Dakota. I'm going to bring her here when I get enough money."

When I got up the next morning the coffee was cooked and Antti was gone. There was money on the table, and a note: "This is the rest of the money from the pelts I took from your land. Get some cows."

There was more money there than Antti had gotten for a winter's pelts, more than I needed for the cows. It would take me through a year. In the fall I could bring Kaija home.

I bought two heifers, and all spring and summer I worked with the black colts.

Training those horses took as much patience as any man might hope to have. When I hitched the fiery colt to my old horse, the colt reared and plunged and tried to run off. The good old horse paid no attention. Day after day we struggled. I nearly gave up. Then one day he walked calmly for a moment before he renewed his fight to be free.

"A horse that can't get trained is food for the vultures," I told my beautiful prancing horse.

Someone had beaten Kivi, the other horse. He trembled when I brushed him and whirled in terror from a raised hand.

Finally he allowed me to curry him and to pick up his feet. He allowed me to put on the harness, but when I hitched him to the old horse, Kivi planted his feet in the earth. The old horse calmly dragged Kivi along beside him.

24

It was late summer before either colt walked beside the old horse nicely, turned right and left, and stood calmly when I told them to stop. It was time to hitch them to each other.

Away from the calm presence of the old horse, Loistaa again plunged and reared, dragging Kivi along. The first day I walked behind the horses ten miles or more, driving them up and down the path, before Loistaa settled down and walked like a gentleman.

I had to teach them to step together. I shortened Loistaa's lines and gently tapped Kivi's rump with a willow stick. Tap, tap, tap.

"Keep up there, Kivi."

The summer was nearly gone. I hadn't hitched the colts to the wagon with its strange weight, its scary creaks and rattles. It was one thing to drive the colts from the ground walking behind, but if they ran away with the wagon, there'd be a terrible wreck.

It was time to leave for the harvest and I planned to bring Kaija home. But that wasn't enough for me any more. Now I wanted to bring Kaija to her new house behind my beautifully matched team.

I could undo all my patient work if I rushed, but I couldn't help myself. I hitched Loistaa and the old horse to the wagon. Loistaa flattened his ears when he heard the rattle of the wagon behind him, but that was all. When it was Kivi's turn to be hitched to the wagon with the old horse he balked for a moment, but then he fell into step.

I should have taken them out one at a time with the old horse every day for a week—better, two weeks—until I was certain they were accustomed to the wagon. But on that very day, knowing it was too soon, I hitched the young horses to the wagon with each other.

Loistaa pawed nervously while I climbed up over the wheel. Kivi trembled. I settled on the seat, lines taut in my hands.

"Okay, boys, walk," I said. They took a ragged step forward. When the wagon rattled Loistaa lurched and Kivi pulled back. For a terrible moment it looked like the old harness would break.

"Easy boys, easy now," I crooned. Their ears swiveled around, listening to my familiar words. Loistaa calmed, Kivi relaxed.

"Okay boys, walk," I said again. They leaned into the harness and walked off together, matching steps.

Tears of pride flowed down my cheeks, mixed with tears of relief. If Loistaa had run off, if the harness had broken, a horse could have been killed. I could have been killed.

Sometimes God is kind.

I drove the team to Reino's house, with the old horse tied behind the wagon. Reino shook his head in disbelief.

"I thought they would never be trained," he said.

"Can you take care of my animals, Reino?" I asked. "I have to go threshing in Dakota."

"Sure."

"I have another favor to ask. Could you keep the old horse after I come back?"

Reino was pleased. "I could do that for you, Timo," he said.

I was in the Duluth depot, waiting for the train, when a drunk staggered in, asking for nickels. I recognized Seppo.

"Seppo! What are you doing here? Why aren't you back in Finland?"

"I don't know you," he said.

"Yes, yes, you do! I'm Timo. I bought you a ticket back to Finland."

"Timo." Seppo took a step back and peered at me. Understanding penetrated the fog in his brain. "Timo. You stole my farm."

"No, no, I paid you for it," I cried, but Seppo staggered on, telling all who would listen that I'd stolen his farm and now he had nothing. I burned with shame.

I worked my way west to Frederick with the threshing crew. The first day on the Koivisto farm I saw Kaija from a distance, but when I went out at dusk she didn't come. All night I tossed and turned in anguish.

The second night she came, running into my arms.

"I couldn't sneak out last night. Mother was watching me," Kaija said.

"My farm is ready! Will you come home with me?"

"Yes!" Kaija said.

Days I worked in the noise and the heat with the threshers and nights I lay under the stars with Kaija. Soon the wheat was threshed and the crew was moving to the next farm.

"Will you leave with me now?" I asked. "We can go right to Minneapolis and be married."

"Come to the house in the morning. We'll tell my mother."

I walked toward the house at dawn, my stomach churning worse than when I'd hitched Loistaa and Kivi to the wagon. Over and over I practiced what I would say: I was a hard worker and had eighty acres of good land, a team, and money in the bank. Kaija's mother didn't let me say any of it. Way out by the barn I heard her shrill screams, growing louder with every step. She didn't hear my knock, so I walked in. Kaija sat at the table, crying. Her mother saw me.

"You common laborer!" she shouted.

"Mother," Kaija said quietly, "I'm pregnant."

For one moment her mother was struck silent. Then she began a high-pitched wail. Kaija rose and took my hand.

"We can go now," she said. We walked out the door and down the road. After a ways, she veered off into the grass and picked up a bundle she'd hidden there.

On the train to Minneapolis we said nothing to each other, we who had so much to say under the stars.

This is what I was thinking: every minute that I cut logs, hewed them, fitted them—grubbed the stumps, plowed the pastures—worked in the camps for money, worked the harvest for money—plowed up rocks and roots from the fields, built fences, trained the team—and more, oh so much more, I had worked for Kaija. And Kaija was pregnant with another man's child.

When we got to Minneapolis I went to the ticket window.

"I want to buy a one-way ticket to Frederick, South Dakota," I said carefully in English.

"You're sending me back?" Kaija asked in disbelief.

"Go back to the father of your baby."

Kaija walked away and sat down on a bench in the waiting room. I brought her the ticket. She jerked it from my hand and turned on me with fury.

"I broke the hearts of the ones who raised me. I left my little brothers and sisters who depend on my love. I lied to my mother that I was pregnant so she would let me leave with you."

She regarded me with cold blue eyes.

"My mother was pregnant with me before she was married," she said. "Her mother hated my father and drove them both out. That's how they came to Dakota, where I was born."

Kaija stared into space a long time.

"What I did to my mother was very cruel. I knew I would be punished. But I didn't imagine that you wouldn't realize that I was lying so I could leave with you." She turned to look at me again. "I've never been with a man," she said.

I heard her words, but I was thinking about Kivi, how carefully I had to work with him once a man had destroyed his trust. How perhaps it would never be fully restored. I put my hand on Kaija's wrist, but she drew it away.

"Let's go," I said, and picked up our bundles. She followed me to gate number three.

Chapter 4

Burntside Spring: Kaija Lahti's Story

They picked at the frozen ground to dig Timo's grave. The Finnish minister talked about fate while the men lowered his coffin into the icy hole.

Three days earlier I was filled with the joy of early spring. Snow was melting from the hillsides and my baby was stirring within me. I made dinner and called out to Timo who was working in the nearby woods, but he didn't come and he didn't answer. I couldn't hear his axe. I found him in the woods crushed beneath a tree that had been hung up in the branches of another tree—the kind they call a "widow maker." I sat with Timo as the life ebbed from him.

"I'm sorry," he said. "Try to keep the farm."

Our neighbor Reino brought Timo's body to town in his iron-wheeled wagon.

"Will you go home to Dakota now, Mrs. Lahti?" he asked.

"I don't know, Reino," I answered. I had no family in northern Minnesota, no friends. Last summer I'd been on my father's farm in North Dakota, cooking for the army of threshers that came to help with the harvest. Timo was one of the workers, and I went home with him to his little farm on the Burntside River in the fall. The woods were glowing in autumn gold. I'd expected a crude new homestead, but Timo had made a beautiful place.

I could see how hard he'd worked, clearing the land, grubbing up stumps, picking up the rocks. He and his brother Antti had built a tight log house with dovetailed corners, overlooking the river. It was large for a homesteader's cabin. When I told him so, Timo grinned.

"I wasn't going to be single for long," he said.

There was a sauna on the riverbank. I plunged into the river from the hot bath, cold water thrilling my heated skin. When I climbed from the river, Timo's look made it tingle anew.

The cows came down to drink at the river, up to their elbows among the cattails, meditating as we splashed about. The great black horses followed, seeking firm footing on the sandy beach.

Timo and Antti left pines and birch trees sheltering the farmyard. Before the ground froze that fall, I planted mountain ash and lilac bushes. I was home on Timo's farm. I never wanted to look at the endless, treeless prairies again. Now Timo was gone. How could I manage alone? What would I do when the baby came?

When my time comes, I thought, maybe I'll have to go back to Dakota, but until then I'll try to stay on the farm.

What is lonelier than a new widow's bed? I filled my days with endless chores, but at night, I still lay wakeful in misery. If only, I thought, if only...

The minister told me to accept God's will, but I could not accept it. In grief and exhaustion I moved toward despair. My body grew awkward; my mind grew hazy and confused. I couldn't farm without a man. Maybe I'd marry one of the neighbors. None were to my liking, but at least I knew who was lazy, who was slow, who drank to excess. I could take my pick.

I could hire a man to work for me, except I couldn't pay him. There was no money. One day as I came blinking into late afternoon sunlight from the dark of the barn, a long shadow lay across my path, cast by a strange man standing in front of the blacksmith shop.

"Hello," I hailed in English.

"*Päivää*," he replied in Finnish. "You're Mrs. Lahti?"

I nodded. "They said in town that a Finnish woman needed a man to work."

I said nothing for a long time. I wanted to cry out, yes, help me, but I was afraid. A woman alone is always in danger. On the other hand, God will send an angel in your darkest hour. Could an angel be unshaven, ragged and tired, like this man? The worst thing you can do is send away an angel God has sent.

"Come in and have coffee," I finally said out loud.

"How did you get here?" I asked as we sat at the table with our cups.

"I walked from town," he said.

"You haven't been in America long," I said.

"About a month. A friend from my village wrote about work in the mines, so I came to be a miner. I tried it but I would sooner work in hell."

That was what Timo had said.

The stranger's name was Matt Keskinen. He said that he'd farmed in Finland, but he had fallen out with his older brother, so he set off for America.

"It's been a disappointment. I won't work in the mine and there isn't work in the woods. I'm a latecomer as far as land is concerned. There's none left that's suitable for farming."

"There's more than enough work here, but I have no money to pay wages," I said.

"I'll work for food and a roof over my head until there's something to sell," he said.

"I can't have a strange man sleeping in my house."

"I'll sleep in the sauna."

"Then please stay," I said, weak with relief. "My name is Kaija."

"Thank you, Mrs. Lahti," he said.

Matt was a hard worker and he treated the animals kindly. He loved to work with the great black horses that had been Timo's pride. One evening I watched Matt wearily drive the team home from the field they were plowing. Frogs were singing along the riverbanks, and the great cloud of sorrow that enveloped me lifted enough for me to realize that Matt must be lonely. I'd hardly spoken to him since he'd come. I walked to the barn in the gathering gloom where he unhitched the team by lantern light.

"You've had a long day, Matt," I said. "I've got your supper waiting."

The big horses stomped their feet and shook their broad backs as Matt lifted off the harness.

"I'll wash up, Mrs. Lahti, as soon as I've bedded these fellows."

He sat drowsily over his coffee after supper.

"Is your bed comfortable in the sauna?" I asked.

"I'm fine," he said.

"You should take a day off now and then to rest. Go to town or something."

"Too much to do in the spring," he said.

"Do you get homesick?" I asked.

"No," he said.

One day Reino brought a letter for Matt. Matt took it into the sauna to read. I was curious, but I didn't ask him what it was about.

Two days later he told me at supper.

"My brother died," he said. "His widow wrote, asking me to come home to Finland and take over the farm."

My heart sank.

"Is it a prosperous farm?" I asked.

"It's a very good farm."

"This can never be a good farm," I said slowly. "The growing season is so short. This farm will always just get by." I thought of my father's great acres of wheat in Dakota.

"That's true."

"What about your brother's widow?" I asked.

Matt was silent a long time, deciding what to tell.

"She was betrothed to me," he said. "Then suddenly she married my brother and became mistress of the farm. As my wife she only would have been a tenant. So I left. Now she writes that my brother treated her badly, and that she still loves me." He sat back in his chair.

"Do you love her yet?" I asked.

"I'm going to check the cows," he said, rising from his chair. "One looked like she was ready to calve."

I'd scarcely begun washing the supper dishes when Matt was back at the door.

"The little one's in labor," he told me, "but it's a breech. We have to help her."

I grabbed my cloak and we ran to the barn.

The little cow was straining. Two tiny hooves had emerged, but they were pointing the wrong way. The calf was twisted inside.

I knelt by the cow's head, trying to soothe her. Matt grabbed the little hooves and pulled when the cow pushed.

"I'm afraid that I'll rupture the cow or break the calf's legs," he said, "but stuck like this, they're both going to die."

He looped a rope around the protruding feet, took a turn once around a post, and hauled while I hung on to the cow's head. Slowly the calf emerged from its mother. The cow rested a minute, and then turned curiously to lick her baby.

The strangely big-headed calf made no attempt to move. Matt rubbed it with clean straw. The calf breathed, but that was all. Matt held its drooping head up to the cow's udder but the calf made no attempt to suck.

"Let's try a bottle," Matt said. I ran to the house for a glass bottle and a clean rag. Matt expertly milked the cow and poured the steamy liquid into the bottle. The calf wouldn't suck. Milk dribbled down her chin. Her breath slowed. Matt held her head in his arms until dawn, trying to get her to eat, when the breathing stopped altogether.

The cow cried for her baby when Matt carried the little corpse from her stall.

"You did all you could," I said. I touched his forearm. "And the cow is all right."

We were both chilled.

"Come up to the house for your breakfast before you bury the calf," I said.

"No, it won't take long," he said.

I rekindled the fire and made coffee before Matt came in, carrying a bucket of new milk.

"I'll make cheese with that," I said. Matt smiled.

He ate his mush silently.

"You're too tired to work today," I said. "Get some rest."

"I never sleep in the daytime."

"You can't work when you're so tired. You'll have an accident."

He must have heard the fear in my voice.

"If I can't work," he said, "then you must take me fishing. You can show me how it's done in America."

"I'm from Dakota," I said. "I've never fished."

"Then I'll show you how I do it in Finland," Matt said.

I brought a loaf of bread for lunch. All day we floated on the river in Timo's little skiff. Matt caught some fish, though fishing was better early in the morning, he said. We brought them home and he made a chowder with milk, the first milk from the farm.

A few nights later Matt knocked on the door in the middle of the night.

"The other cow is calving," he called. By the time I pulled on my cloak and hurried down to the barn, a wet little calf was lying on the straw.

"It's healthy," Matt told me. "A little bull."

It would have been nice if it had been a heifer, but we had two milkers now, and one fine calf.

Matt came up to the house in a jovial mood, and told me stories about his cows at home in Finland. Soon he'd return to his big farm, I thought. In a month my baby would come. What would I do when Matt left?

"I'm not in such a hurry to go back to Finland," Matt said, as if he knew my fears.

A few days later, hanging wash on the line, I felt a warm rush of water between my legs.

33

Oh my God, no, I prayed, I'm not ready.

"Matt!" I cried. Far away I heard him answer.

"I'm coming!" he called again, much nearer. I clung to the clothesline post.

"It's begun," I told Matt when he arrived. "We have to hurry to town."

"Come sit," he said, leading me to the bench. "Tell me when you feel a cramp."

"Now," I said, and a little later, "Again."

"I'm going to heat the sauna," Matt said. "I don't want to birth a baby in the wagon."

"Please take me to town," I said.

"There isn't time," Matt said. "I've birthed many cats and dogs and cows and horses. People aren't so different. We'll do all right."

He built a fire in the sauna stove and carried buckets of water from the river. I brought towels and blankets.

Saunas are good places to have babies. They're clean and warm and it's easy to clean up afterwards. I was relieved that I wasn't going to the hospital. I would be ashamed to see bedsheets stained with my blood. Sometimes women took ill and died when they gave birth in the hospital.

The pains grew strong and I stopped caring for my modesty. Only the baby mattered, and it mattered with the greatest urgency.

I gripped Matt's hand as I labored. When the baby girl finally slipped into the world, Matt caught her gently and wiped her nose and mouth. She gasped and breathed and sobbed a little. He cradled her a moment before giving her to me.

"She's messy," he said, "but perfect." Awe overwhelmed me when I looked at the tiny baby.

Matt took her back and tied the cord with fishline. He cleaned her with soft cloths and warm water, and wrapped us both in the blanket.

"How do you feel?" he asked.

"Elated," I said.

He lifted the corner of the blanket to see the baby nursing. I was still beyond modesty. We laughed at her eagerness.

"How do new babies know what to do?" I asked.

"It's a wonder," Matt said.

I named her Laila.

For a few days Matt did the work in the house, stopping now and then to sit and hold Laila. Reino came to see the new baby. He peered into her basket and touched a little fist reverently.

"Timo should have seen her," he said.

Matt returned to work in the fields. He cuddled Laila and cooed to her when he came in for meals, but our conversation grew stiff and strained. His leaving hung between us. I didn't dare ask when he would go, for fear of hastening his departure.

Laila was a month old when Reino came with another letter for Matt. Again Matt went into the sauna to read it.

I waited for him to come to tell me that he was leaving for Finland, but when he came up the path he carried a beautifully carved cradle.

"I made a proper cradle for Laila," he said.

"How nice," I said. I choked back the question, is this a good-bye present?

"What did your fiancée write you now?" I blurted out instead.

"She sent me a steamer ticket to Finland," he said.

"Then there's nothing to prevent your departure," I said bitterly and went out to churn the butter, leaving Laila asleep in her basket next to the new cradle.

It was Midsummer's Day. The earth was fresh in bloom but I felt caustic as lye. That night I tossed and turned in my bed, stifling screams and tears. A scented breeze from the open window soothed my hot, wretched body and suddenly I knew what was the matter. I wasn't afraid to farm by myself. I could easily get another farmhand.

I wanted Matt.

I stepped into the night dressed only in my long cotton night-gown. A kerosene lamp glowed in the window of the sauna. As I approached the light was blown out and my courage died with it.

I pressed myself against the large birch tree. The fragrance of the pine and sweet poplar aroused my senses. Beneath me the river glistened in the moonlight.

"It's Midsummer's Night." Matt said near my shoulder, causing me to start. "The sun didn't set in Finland today. People are celebrating around bonfires."

He's come to talk of Finland, I thought bitterly.

"You look like a twin for the birch tree in your long white gown," he said. He touched my braid, undone from its knot. I meant to push him from me but he clasped me to him and the harsh words died in my throat.

Mosquitoes hummed around us.

"Please," I said. "Come into the house."

35

Matt carried Laila, sleeping in her cradle, to the far side of the cabin.

The ferocity of my passion blotted out all awareness of the ordinary world, but when I returned to my senses I felt more heavily burdened than before. Matt put his arm around me but I rolled away, turning my back to him.

"I can find another hired man," I told him. "Go back to your midsummer bonfires whenever you like."

Matt tensed. He was silent for a long time. Finally he spoke.

"I don't understand why, but I'll go if you want."

"If I want! I don't want you to leave. But I won't hold you here with pity when you're dreaming of your Finnish fiancée."

"My Finnish fiancée! I'd never go back to her."

"Then why have you grown so quiet and strange?"

"It's you who's quiet and strange! I thought it was something women go through after they have a baby."

"You don't want to go back to Finland?"

"I want to marry you and take care of you and Laila."

I felt lightheaded.

"Kaija, I loved you from the time I came here, but you were a woman in mourning. I didn't want to intrude on your grief."

I rolled back into his arms.

"I didn't know I loved you until tonight," I whispered. "I was coming down to you in the sauna, but I lost my courage."

"You don't want another hired man?"

I pressed my face to his chest and shook my head.

"Then I'll write to my brother's widow and release my claims to her farm. She chose the farm instead of me and that's what she'll get. But I still wanted to be a man of property when I asked you to marry me, so you wouldn't think I was marrying you for your land."

"My stony fields and two cows." I began to giggle. "You marry poverty."

"I'll be rich married to you," he said. Matt held me through the night and my world began anew.

Chapter 5

When Darkness Reigns: Korva's Story

In the winter of 1926-27, Antti and I made ice, cutting chunks two feet thick out of Jackfish Bay, hauling them to shore on the bobsled and packing them under sawdust. It was a hell of a job in thirty below. We were working for the U.S. Army Corps of Engineers, which was making a survey so they could flood the lake country.

"They're going to flood out the wild rice," Antti said. "Well, the crazy won't notice and the wise won't say anything." But he drank heavily and quit halfway through the winter.

Bill Magie was in charge of the survey. Once he brought some government officials to camp on a speeder on the railroad spur from Winton. As I carried their gear into the tents, Magie jerked his head in my direction.

"Finlander," he said.

One of the officials laughed. "Weak minds but strong backs."

Once, long ago, I was respected as a man, with a mind and a soul. I had a sweetheart who waited for me when I went to study at the University of Helsinki.

I was a good student and an obedient citizen of Finland, Grand Duchy of Russia. When the Czar drafted young Finns into the Russian army, I went.

I knew Latin, and spoke Russian as well as Swedish and Finnish, so they trained me to be an engineer and sent me to the Pacific to fight the Japanese. I was wounded in the Battle of Mukden. Over 8000 men were killed, more than 50,000 wounded. It's hard to imagine, when you hear those numbers, that each was a man who once delighted in the freshness of spring. I was one of the lucky ones. I was shipped back to Moscow by rail and wagon, a two-month journey. When I recovered from my wounds, I was put on duty in Moscow. The Revolution of 1905 had begun and the army was supposed to protect the government from the citizens, but I had become cynical about the government. I went out to ask the revolutionaries what their revolution was about.

On the street I met a man named Bogaras. He'd just returned from studying the natives of Siberia to find that his long-awaited revolution had begun. People were rising against the brutality of the Tsar, he explained. It was the dawning of a glorious new epoch when we would govern ourselves.

I smuggled illegal pamphlets and newspapers into the barracks. Why should I fear breaking the law? Obedience had brought me to the Battle of Mukden.

Revolutionary fervor spread among the veterans. My battalion presented the government with a list of demands. We wanted decent living conditions, like one man to a bed. We wanted libraries and access to newspapers. We wanted the right to engage in free political discussion. We wanted our fellow soldiers to be brought home from the East. We asked that officers use polite forms of address to subordinates. It was radical for Russian soldiers to demand to be treated like human beings. It was regarded as a mutiny.

On the streets I got word that Bogaras had been arrested. It took two weeks for his friends to bribe officials to let him go. While he was in jail, the regimental commander arrested the revolutionaries in my garrison. I escaped out a window and deserted the army. I found Bogaras at the train station, embarking for Finland. I gave him the name of my uncle in Viipuri.

"Will you join me in Viipuri?" Bogaras asked.

"I can't go back to Finland," I said.

"Where are you going?"

"Alaska. I know a man who went there to mine for gold."

"Go by way of Siberia," Bogaras said. "I'll make you a map."

He gave me his huge fur coat.

"A Buryat gave it to me," he said. "A good man, Yuan. You'll need it more than I will."

The army discharged the veterans of the Japanese war and the mutiny collapsed. New recruits attacked the citizens of Moscow. As I left the city drunken soldiers were hacking through crowds of unarmed people.

I headed east, traveling by rail and mail cart as far as Lake Baikal, to the city of Irkutsk.

Dozens of languages rang out on the streets of Irkutsk. Sledges drawn by oxen, horse and reindeer bumped over frozen ruts. I was asking how to get north to the Lena River when a huge man grabbed my arm and pulled me around.

"What have you done with Bogaras? Did you murder Bogaras? Why are you wearing his coat?" he roared.

"Ha! You must be Yuan," I said. "Greetings from Bogaras," I said. The Buryat dropped my arm and crushed me in a furry hug. He brought me to an inn where I told him about the revolution over a bottle of vodka. In turn, he was inspired to tell me about the Buryats.

"We were a fierce people. Proud. Mongols. No, before the Mongols were Mongols, many centuries ago when Russia was a part of our empire. Now we're part of theirs, but the tide will change. We have the Russian tax collectors, but there is no ruling class in Siberia. We'll welcome your revolution!" We celebrated with another round of vodka.

Yuan the Buryat made arrangements for me to travel north to the Lena. I found myself lying under a pile of furs, jolting along on the bottom of a tarantas pulled by three horses.

When we changed horses at a rest station, I asked our driver about the crosses I had seen along the road.

"A cross for each traveler killed by a brodnyak," he said, "a convict, escaped from the mines. They'll kill for a crust of bread. When spring comes, they roam the forests. I've heard there are 60,000 at large. Most will be soon dead. Better off dead than in the mine."

I thought of my comrades who had been arrested for the mutiny. Next spring some might be brodnyaks lurking on this road.

We passed through villages with little wooden churches. In each, the finest house belonged to the tax collector.

"Tax collectors, hah," said my driver. "Robbers! They steal everything of value, leaving people scarcely enough to survive."

We traveled across steppes and through forests for a hundred miles. With another guide I traveled by reindeer sledge over the frozen Lena, between great red and green rocky spires, rising six hundred feet tall in rows above the river. Trees clung to sheer rock faces. Mountains ran back to the depths of the continent.

It was a well-traveled route to Yakutsk, an outpost of civilization. Yakutsk had a cathedral and a vodka factory. Russians had been trading with the Yakuts for hundreds of years. When I was looking at the ruins of their ancient fort, a Yakut approached me.

"Are you a Russian?" he asked.

"No. A Finn," I said.

"Ah, a subject people like us," he said. "My name is Amga." He wore fur clothing trimmed with reindeer hide. On his belt hung a hunting knife, its handle inlaid with silver.

"Why are you so far from home?"

When I explained, he invited me to his yurt where his wife and daughters fed me while Amga asked questions about the revolution.

"When the Russians came to trade for furs, we greeted them as friends," Amga said. "We wanted to trade as friends but they wanted conquest. Cossacks built the fort and shot from it with guns. When they couldn't win that way, they left offerings of friendship at the bottom of the fort. When our leaders went to get the gifts, the Cossacks dropped stones from the walls and killed them. Then they stalked Yakuts in the forest, captured and tortured and killed them, killing children in front of parents and parents in front of children. 'If you bring us furs,' they said, 'we will spare you.' So we brought them furs, as we would have done in the beginning, as friends."

He told his history, hundreds of years old, as though it happened yesterday.

Amga had large herds of horses and reindeer.

"I trade reindeer for furs with the Lamut. Come with me, and I'll put you in good hands."

I found myself traveling with the herd, riding on the back of a reindeer. When we camped, the deer fed themselves on moss. We climbed through the mountain passes, stopping only in the worst of blizzards.

The Lamut lived in huts covered with reindeer skin. Men and women were dressed in skins trimmed with beads and fur.

Amga found the home of Tam, his trading partner. "Is this a tax collector?" the Lamut demanded, looking at me. "We already paid taxes twice this year."

"No, no, no. This man is fleeing from the Tsar. He's making his way north to the coast."

"Forgive my poor welcome. I'll help you along," said the Lamut.

Before Amga left, he gave me his knife with the handle of inlaid silver.

"Be wary," he told me. "Don't become a cross on a highway."

"Before we travel," my new guide said, "I need to hunt for those who remain."

"Don't you eat the reindeer you herd?"

"No, they're trained. It makes them too valuable to eat. We trade them for furs. The woods are full of wild meat."

All I had killed with a gun were men. Tam outshot me with his ancient firearm. He brought the game back to the village and gave it to a woman who carefully divided the meat among the villagers, giving Tam a small share.

"Will your family have enough to eat while you're gone?" I asked.

"They'll be taken care of," Tam said. "We can go."

In the remote and primitive country we traveled, I was mistaken for the tax collector in every village. Then, when the Lamut heard that I'd been sent by Bogaras, they tried to sell me their clothing, their tools— even funeral shrouds and the skulls of their ancestors. Bogaras and others like him had traveled the country collecting native relics in the wake of a deadly epidemic. The desperate survivors sold even their cooking pots to raise money for the tax collector, because there weren't enough men left to meet the Tsar's demands for furs.

We traveled along the Kolyma River, each in a sledge pulled by two reindeer. Tam passed me to a Russian creole, who brought me to a reindeer-herding Chukchi, who took me to the sea. Along the river I met Russians and part-Russians who lived like natives, trading furs.

I traveled over steppe and mountain, through taiga and tundra to reach the vast whiteness of the frozen Siberian Sea, to a large village of underground houses of the Chukchi.

My guide brought me to Tarupiaq. When Tarupiaq saw that I had not come with wares to trade for furs, he asked the usual questions. Was I a tax collector or a scientist?

"I'm a traveler," I said.

"Welcome, then," Tarupiaq said. "My home is yours. I'm sorry that I can't offer you better. I wish you could have come when food was abundant and hunger rare, and before the sickness that made skulls so easy for the scientists to collect."

"Why is there no food?"

"Great ships come from somewhere else, and take all the whales."

After we had eaten, Tarupiaq asked if I could put his mind at rest about the scientists who had visited the village.

"They paid us money to put our words on recording machines. They bought the clothes off our backs. They gathered the skulls of our dead," Tarupiaq said. "Why did they do that? They have a perfectly good language of their own. What use is it for them to learn to build houses like the Chukchi when they return to their cities? What is the use of our harpoons where there are no whales? What do they make from the skulls?" The scientists had not been able to explain to his satisfaction and neither could I.

"What did you do with the money the scientists gave you for your things?" I asked.

"We paid the tax collector."

Tarupiaq was delighted to take me to the Bering Strait.

"I have a cousin in Uelen you must visit," he said. "There's time to travel there and back before the thaw."

He outfitted me with new clothing of furs and skins, and we set out. Tarupiaq acted as if there was no greater sport than running behind the sleds the dogs pulled, unless it was running out in front of the dogs to break a trail when the going got rough. I struggled to keep up with his pace. The mail cart, the tarantas, the saddle reindeer and the reindeer sledges had all been luxury conveyances compared to travel by dog team.

The last three days of our journey we had nothing to eat. The weaker we got, the more cheerful Tarupiaq became. We arrived in Uelen in a state of near collapse.

My guide across the Bering Strait was a Chukchi who herded reindeer and I was in luck. He was making a delivery to America.

I said good-bye to Tarupiaq.

"Return to visit us," he said fondly. "Come when we can hunt walrus together."

Once again I traveled by reindeer.

We traveled to the Diomede Islands, and on to Cape Prince of Wales. I had reached America.

The Eskimo at the reindeer station served me tea. He explained that his reindeer herd was a project of the United States Government.

"A missionary told the government that Eskimos were starving after the ships came and took all the whales," he said. "The missionary thought we should learn to herd reindeer like the Chukchi, to give us something else to live on. They hired Chukchi to teach us, which was awkward because we're enemies of the Chukchi. I came here to learn to herd reindeer, so I could teach other Eskimos.

"I like herding reindeer," Akig told me. "I learned to train them. My herd grew to three hundred before the United States army came and took them away."

"Why did they take them away?"

42

"American whaling ships got caught in the ice north of here that fall. The army herded my reindeer north for the sailors to eat."

"Those sailors were American whalers, the ones that come from far away and make the whales scarce?"

"Yes. I tried to say no, don't take my reindeer, but when they appealed in the name of friendship I couldn't refuse."

"Did they replace the reindeer?"

"Yes, but with young untrained animals. My animals were trained. One trained deer is worth ten or twelve untrained ones. It wasn't necessary. The Eskimos who traded at Cape Smythe, where the whalers were stranded, fed them all winter. They would have been fine without my reindeer."

It was a short trip to Nome. Coming from the vast wilds of Siberia, I looked around at the city in disbelief.

Nome had hotels with velvet drapes. Men wore suits of wool and women wore dresses. There was a babble of languages, like Irkutsk, and quickly my ear picked out Finnish on the street. For the first time in years I was among my own countryman. In no time at all we were sharing a bottle of whiskey in a shack at the edge of town.

"You should have seen this place six years ago," Jalmari said. "Gold lay on the beach. Twenty thousand people came, living in tents. Now you have to work hard digging the gold out of the ground so there are only five thousand of us left. We work a claim," he said, nodding at his partners, "but pickings are getting thin. The only mines making any real money are run by corporations. You can get a job with one of them."

I went to work for wages in the land of gold. I asked my new friends what else I could find in America.

"Anywhere you go, you'll find Finns," said Jaakko, who'd crossed the United States from coast to coast. He brought out a map of the United States.

"I have friends fishing in Astoria." Alfred said, showing me the place on the map. "Lots of timber camps around there, too."

"I was in Montana before I came here. Go to Missoula," another man said.

"My brother lives here," Jaakko said, pointing to northern Minnesota. "Work is easy to get anywhere you go, but the pay is always low."

The Finns in Nome were a happy crowd. Men and women partied every night when they weren't guarding their claims. It had been a long time since I was in the company of women.

43

I was attracted to one in particular—Sirkka. She flashed her eyes, joked with the men, and sang haunting songs of the lakes and forests of Finland in a deep, husky voice. One night, while Jalmari was playing his concertina and I danced with Sirkka, Nikolai showed up. No one had told me about Nikolai, who had been working on his far-off claim. He introduced himself by coming up behind me and flicking off my ear with his *puukko* as I danced the *"Vanhan Musta-laisen Kaiho"* waltz.

My blood splashed over Sirkka's dress. Before a thought formed in my brain, I turned and stuck Amga's hunting knife between Nikolai's ribs, up to its silver inlaid hilt.

Nikolai slumped to the floor, his life leaving him in a long sigh. The first real look I had of him, he was dead. My ear dangled from a strip of skin. Sirkka trimmed it off and bound my head with strips of cloth torn from her petticoat. The others stood staring at Nikolai there on the floor. Then Jaakko turned to me and held out a small pouch of gold. "Take it," he said. "It's not much. Most of my gold went for whiskey and other good things."

"I can't take your gold," I said.

"Hah. I'll get more gold. I like it here. I'm not ready to go back to Finland yet."

"I can't," I said, looking down at the dead man.

"Pay me back later. Send money to my brother in Minnesota. Get on your way."

I traveled by night back to the reindeer station, where I found Akig with his herd.

"Life is cheap where men love gold," Akig said, when I told him I had killed Nikolai. "The best place I can take you is the Swedish mission. How is it that among your people they pay men to talk about God?"

The Swedish missionary was happy to take my gold. When an ugly scar sealed up the place where my ear had been, I boarded a ship that brought supplies to the mission and sailed south to the Columbia River, where I found plenty of work in the timber camps in Washington State.

The conditions in the camps were worse than the conditions in the Russian army. We slept two men to a wooden, straw-filled bed full of lice. We had to supply our own blankets. Most of the food was slop. We worked twelve hours a day in bone chilling rain. They paid us once a month, and we went to town and drank it up in two days.

There wasn't a book or a newspaper to read, nothing to do in town but booze and whore. After we cut down a forest, the camp shut down, and we'd go looking for another camp.

I partnered up with a Swede named Gustav. He was with the Industrial Workers of the World—the Wobblies. They were organizing one big union for all the people in the world who worked for wages.

"The government isn't the ruler here," Gustav said. "The Boss is the ruler. He decides the wages, the standard of living—the value of life itself. Every human being deserves to live in a clean, healthy environment. Everyone should live in a community with both sexes, and make a wage that can support a family."

I agreed with everything he said.

"You heard that in this country all men are equal? Hah," said Gustav. "Two percent of the people control sixty percent of the wealth and sixty percent of the people share five percent of the wealth. Who runs the government? The Bosses. When there's a strike, out comes the national guard and the state militia to put it down."

"Just like the soldiers cut down the citizens of Moscow," I said.

The Bosses were afraid of us Wobblies so they had laws passed that made it illegal for us to speak in public. When a Wobbly was arrested for speaking in Spokane, the IWW decided to make him an issue. Gustav read an ad in the Industrial Worker: "Wanted—Men to fill the jails in Spokane."

"Let's go," said Gustav, so we rolled up our blankets and hopped a freight.

I took my turn speaking from the soapbox and ended up in the Spokane jail with 600 other men. One man got sentenced to hard labor at the rock pile because he read the Declaration of Independence in public.

We starved for a month on bread and water. When we protested, they shut the doors of the jail and turned up the steam heat. Then they took us out, one at a time, roughed us up and moved us to an ice-cold cell. They took Gustav out before me and I never saw him again. A lot of men died.

One time a crowd gathered when they marched us down the street to the central police station. The people cheered and tossed us sandwiches wrapped in paper, apples and oranges, even sacks of tobacco. The chief of police took it all away.

I was in jail four months. When they got tired of spending money to keep us locked up, they let us go. I rode the rails to Minnesota, to the timber camps north of Winton. I stopped drinking to save money to pay back Jaakko.

Conditions in the Minnesota timber camps were the same as in the West. Most of the lumberjacks were Finns and Swedes, all IWW The Finns built a hall in Winton with a library where I went to read on paydays. Saturday nights I spoke at the hall. Afterwards I stood against the wall and watched the dance.

I learned English to read the Declaration of Independence for myself. "These truths are self evident. All men are created equal." I wrote articles in Finnish for the *Industrialisti*.

Conditions were so bad on the Mesaba Range that the miners went out on strike before we got them organized. All we could do was raise relief funds for the miners from locals around the country.

Ely miners were intimidated by the thugs and the bosses, but the miners from Winton struck the Section 30 mine so twenty-five armed gunmen came from Ely to warn Mayor Hokkanen he'd get hurt if the Mesaba strike leaders spoke in Winton. Hokkanen laughed at them. Every citizen in Winton was at the meeting the next day.

Just at the time the strike collapsed, the government started drafting young men for the war in Europe. Wobblies don't believe in war—the enemy of the worker is the Boss, the one who makes money selling weapons while the wage slaves get killed. We refused to register for the draft so we were outlawed, hunted down in camps and farms. There was a shortage of labor to work the mines and there weren't scabs enough to break another strike. The war profiteers were afraid the IWW would strike and prevent them from raking in the bucks.

All Finns were persecuted, Wobbly or not. The government rounded us up, put us in prison for months without trial.

I was living in Mrs. Rautio's boardinghouse, working in the woods. I didn't want to go back to jail, I didn't want to go back to war and I didn't want to be deported back to Finland. For a year and a half Mrs. Rautio hid me in her attic. I stayed there winter and summer, day and night, writing my articles.

Sheriffs raided camps and farms throughout northern Minnesota, looking for Finnish men. In Winton, they arrested the workers at the St. Croix mill. All were Finns and IWW. None had registered for the draft.

In other towns throughout the country, women were cheering their young men off to war, but in Winton, when the militia escorted the resisters to the depot, every Finnish woman turned out to the platform, singing songs of solidarity, cheering their men off to jail. I heard them from my attic window.

They had shut down the mill while the men were in jail—after the government had outlawed the IWW to prevent strikes. Mayor Hokkanen went to Duluth to tell the authorities that the mill needed the men's labor. The women raised money at the hall for bail and lawyers' fees. Eventually the men were freed.

After the armistice, the government cracked down harder on Finns and the IWW. They were still hunting us down in 1919, but I couldn't stay in the attic forever. The war was over. I was out drinking with Antti the night a government man came into the saloon, asking questions. He stood right next to me, talking to Mayor Hokkanen, waving copies of the *Industrialisti* in his hand. He asked who was writing those articles.

Hokkanen shrugged. The government man reached past Hokkanen and took my arm, thrusting the newspapers in my face.

"What do you know about this, Mister?" he asked.

"Don't bother with him," Antti said. "He's a half wit. Lost some of his brains when he lost his ear."

The government man looked at the place where my ear should have been. He dropped my arm and turned away.

After they crushed the IWW, I went with the Timber Workers Union and the Finnish Workers Federation. When the country collapsed during the Depression, we got what we wanted because the government knew we'd win our revolution if they didn't give it to us.

What did we win? One to a bed in the timber camps. No lice. Showers. Good food. An eight-hour day. Franklin Roosevelt even gave us Socialist Security.

Yah. That was the workers' paradise.

But in 1927-28, I was still less than a slave, working for Bill Magie and the U.S. Army in their war on the lakes. I was just a strong back.

Antti was right. The dams they were building drowned out the wild rice.

Chapter 6

Building the Hall: Hanna Rautio's Story

A drunk burst out the doors of Bendy's Saloon and sprawled across the boardwalk in front of me. Through the open door I glimpsed rows of bottles lined in front of the mirror and men slumped over the mahogany bar. I strained to see Tarmo among them, but the bartender glowered at me and slammed the door.

Clutching little Helvi by the hand, I stepped down from the walk into the street, avoiding the drunk lying there. A second story window opened and a woman stuck her head out.

Here to start up a little business for yourself, lady?" she jeered. Other women cackled behind her.

For years Tarmo and I had trekked from place to place, job to job, trying to earn enough to survive. We were sojourners in a world that begrudged us our daily bread. Our wanderings had brought us to Winton, the end of the line. The train had to back out. There were seven saloons to deaden men's spirits, but not one church nor library to lift them up. Hundreds of men lived together in crude boardinghouses. There were only five family houses. They belonged to the bosses.

Little Helvi and I walked on up the street, and climbed the steep path to the top of the hill. We looked down at the lumber mills on the shore below and at the rafts of logs that filled the bay. Beyond the logjams the lake ice was black, thawing under the April sun. Circling the village, the open river flowed to Fall Lake. Sap was running. It brightened the color of bare trees.

Hope rose in my heart as I looked down on lakes and rivers and woods. This was not the end of the line. It was my destination.

People talk about those times when men could be bought for a dollar a day. They usually tell about the hunger, but that wasn't the worst thing. When men lose their spirits, you see that the body without spirit is nothing. Maybe, here in Winton, my Tarmo could get his spirit back.

Tarmo had been full of spirit when we married in Finland. He was just a tenant on another man's farm, but he was tall and straight and broad shouldered, with a swinging stride and an easy smile.

We were married in the village church. The music of the wedding dance lifted me into Tarmo's arms as we whirled and soared into our new life.

Then the crops failed. My heart broke to see Tarmo's shoulders sag and his feet drag from weariness and hunger.

Athere's no hope here, Hanna," he said one night. AI want to take a chance somewhere else. One of the men from the village wrote that there's work in St. Petersburg."

I would have followed Tarmo anywhere if it meant seeing him throw his shoulders back and walk with his old step, so I packed our trunk with the linen my mother had woven for my wedding, kissed Mother and Father and little brothers good-bye, and left the woods and fields and the bluest of skies for the great city of St. Petersburg.

Tarmo worked making sheet metal in a factory. I cooked for a rich family. We lived in a tiny room on the top floor of a big house, sharing a kitchen with families of all different nationalities. I watched my pot as carefully as I could, but still my food was stolen by our neighbors. I never thought people could be like that.

One Sunday every month we were let off work. They expected us to go to church, but Tarmo and I couldn't bear to waste our freedom indoors, separated from each other by the church aisle. Instead, we walked the broad avenues holding hands. St. Petersburg was a city of parks, and in every park a band played. We went from park to park, dancing away the Sunday afternoon.

When Nicholas and Alexandra were married, the factories closed for a week of celebration. I still had to cook, but Tarmo and I had a few more hours together, lying in each other's arms in our little garret room, whispering dreams and telling stories of happiness while rowdy party noises rose up from the street. Every worker in

Russia was given a goblet, etched with the likeness of the Czar and Czarina. Ours were a remem-brance of the hours we spent together.

When the factory shut down and Tarmo was put out of work, we moved to Viipuri, where Tarmo found work in another factory. I cooked for a boardinghouse full of men.

There was no place to rent in Viipuri, so we got together with other families and built a house. We shared the kitchen with neighbors who helped one another out instead of stealing from each other. I was pregnant when the factory in Viipuri shut down. Some of our friends went to Belgium to work, but Tarmo wanted to try his luck in America.

He went on ahead. I cooked for the men until Helvi was born, saving money. I sold everything except my wedding linen and the goblets that we had gotten from the Czar and Czarina to buy my ticket.

I traveled with the baby at my breast by train and by ship, from Viipuri to Hanko, to Hull and Liverpool. Between Hull and Liverpool, someone broke into my trunk and stole the goblets.

I could only afford the cheapest ticket to New York, which bought me passage in the hold of the ship. We were stacked in bunks, and the floor sloshed with vomit. I myself couldn't keep food down for the eight days it took to cross from Hull to New York. My milk started to dry up, and the baby cried from hunger.

Ellis Island was a filthy, stinking place. They put us into wire cages. Men were crying, women were crying, children were crying, everybody was crying. A doctor checked us over. Some people were turned back, families were broken apart. I clutched tiny Helvi to me when the doctor came. He glanced at our eyes and waved us on.

Separated from the other Finns, I found myself sick and weak without language in a strange place. I waited there, in fear with my fussing baby, until someone put us on a train. We traveled two days before a conductor looked at my ticket and made me understand that I was on the wrong train. He put us off at a freight depot where there were hundreds of tracks. A kind man showed on his watch how long I would wait: from twelve to twelve and then to six. He brought me bread and fruit and milk. I sat in the dark, watching the lighted windows of passenger trains flash by, filled with people who knew where they were going.

Finally the kind man took me over the tracks to the passenger station and put me on another train, and I traveled back to where I started, where somebody put me on the right train. I never knew where I'd been.

Tarmo had been working as a hired man on a farm in Minnesota, but he didn't earn enough to support a family. He heard there was work in the mines in Ely, but when he got there, there was no work. Pappinen rented him a room. "Pay me when you can," Pappinen said.

When he expected us, Tarmo met every train for seven days. His face lit with joy when I stepped down from the passenger car, carrying the baby he'd never seen. He hung his head with shame when he brought us to yet another tiny room with nothing to eat but the bread of charity.

Every morning Tarmo went to the mine to see if they were hiring. I got a job cooking for a Finnish couple. The wife was a rich girl who'd fallen in love with a poor man, so they ran away to America together. He started a business hauling coal and hay, but the childless wife was useless. She didn't know how to cook or sew or clean. I offered to teach her, but she only wanted to play with my baby. She asked if she could take Helvi on outings. I was glad for Helvi to get out in the fresh air.

One afternoon my mistress didn't come back when it was time for me to nurse Helvi. I waited until my breasts swelled painfully, leaking milk through the fabric of my dress, before I went to look for them.

Helvi's cries came from the cowshed in back of the house. The woman sat on a milking stool in the gloom, singing a lullaby, trying to nurse the wailing baby from her own dry breast.

I started asking around for another job.

One day when Tarmo went to the mine, the boss motioned, okay, and sent him down the slip with an experienced miner.

"You have to listen all the time. Run when you hear the rocks caving in," his partner told him in Finn.

That frightened Tarmo. He'd lost most of his hearing working in the factory in St. Petersburg, so he couldn't hear rocks falling.

The slip dropped into darkness, lighted only by the dim glow of carbide lamps that filled the tunnels with smoke. In some places the tunnel was only four feet high, with ankle deep water that dripped from overhead and seeped through the sides.

Not an hour after they started work, a man was crushed under falling rock. Tarmo helped dig him out and carry his broken body up the tunnel. He screamed in agony as Tarmo passed him to other miners in a steep place. They lay him down near the shaft.

"Get back to work," the boss shouted before the last moan came from the dying man.

"I want to get out of here! Let me out!" Tarmo cried.

"Lower the slip," his partner translated to the boss. "Take this man up."

"Not in the middle of the day. Nobody goes up in the slip in the middle of the shift," the boss said. "You want out, you can climb out." He pointed to the ladder.

Tarmo was down so deep that he couldn't see light at the top. He climbed in total darkness, feet and hands groping for each rung. He lost his sense of time. Had he climbed for hours or for days? He lost his sense of direction, except that up must be harder than down. When he climbed beyond his endurance, he hung from the ladder in despair, willing his hands to let go of the rung and let him plummet straight back to hell. Then he felt a little fresh air move in the shaft and it gave him the strength to reach the top. He lay on the ground near the mine head for a long time before he could move.

Somewhere on that climb out of hell, terror entered Tarmo's soul. That's why he started drinking, trying to numb the terror.

It was April. The lumber mills were opening for the season in Winton, so we went there to find work.

I got a job as housekeeper for Stanley Pierce, boss at the St. Croix Mill. In the winter he and his family went back to Stillwater, and they left us to take care of their place. They didn't want us to live in the house while they were gone so they built a lean-to of boards and tarpaper on the side, just big enough for a bed and a cookstove. One cold night Helvi's hair froze to the wall as she slept.

We'd never lived like that, not in Finland, not in Russia. I wasn't going to live like that in America.

I told Tarmo we had to find a better place to live. He fixed his lifeless gaze on me, took another swig from his bottle, and shrugged. So I went to the mill at closing time and invited some men home for

52

coffee and fresh bread. I entertained them right in Mrs. Pierce's kitchen. I told them that if they got together and built a boardinghouse, I would cook for them.

Twelve men built a three-story house and painted it red. It came right up to the board sidewalk near the railroad tracks. I had fourteen loud and uncouth boarders, often drunk or hung over, though they straightened up and tried to remember their manners around me.

No, I had thirteen loud and uncouth boarders and meek little Jussi. He never spoke, but sometimes late at night, when everyone else was asleep, I heard noises from Jussi's room. I put my ear to his door. It was not a human voice, but the plaintive cries of a fiddle.

Eventually there were seven of us crowded into the two rooms that my family shared on the first floor. It wasn't right to bring so many children into the world, but I could never refuse Tarmo. If there was a little spark in his eyes, I thought life was returning. I would do anything I could to try to fan that spark.

People in Winton said I should throw Tarmo out. They didn't know what a good man he was before he went into the mine. There is some terror in the world that could destroy anyone's spirit and Tarmo met his a thousand feet below the ground.

When Tarmo lost himself, he was alone. When I lost Tarmo, I found solace in the company of women.

We women cared for the men in the boardinghouses, made big gardens outside the village, kept cows in the sheds by the alley, fattened pigs in pens by the alley gate. Even when they were laid off from work, we could feed our men.

Until my own girls were old enough to work, I had Finnish girls to help me. The spunky things came from Finland looking for adventure. What they got was long hours of work in a boardinghouse. Quickly men married them, and then they worked even harder, caring for their families and usually a few boarders besides.

The girls were good company. We got up at four in the morning to start the bread dough, make the pies and doughnuts, and get breakfast for the men. We hauled water from the river and heated it in copper boilers on the kitchen stove to wash the clothes. Six days a week we did laundry, scrubbing away in tubs set on benches.

Sheets and diapers and tablecloths and men's underwear flapped on my line in summer, froze stiff in winter.

After the noon meal, I changed out of my work clothes into my good dress and went visiting, usually down the street to see lively Mrs. Laitinen. She read a great deal and we liked to talk about politics.

Mrs. Laitinen and her husband kept a boardinghouse and a public sauna on the banks of the river. Her daughter Cecelia played with my babies while Mrs. Laitinen and I drank coffee, ate pulla, and talked. Our conversation always turned back to the men. It was heart-breaking to see what had happened to those decent Finnish boys.

AI keep a clean house," Mrs. Laitinen said. AI won't tolerate a man drinking on my premises. Liquor turns men into beasts. It's a tragic waste, the way the men live here. Nothing but work and drink and whores. Their fathers and mothers didn't raise them that way."

"They drink because they're treated like beasts in the mills and logging camps. They left Finland hoping for better things, but most of them can't even hope to get a wife or have a home. They no longer have the joy of working with the earth, or the pleasure of their own skill used for their own purpose," I argued.

"Well, they don't tell it like that. When they sit around the table in my house, they boast about how dangerous a job is, or how much they can lift, or how high they load the bobsleds," she said.

"Of course they do. They still have their pride."

"ut they're turning into a bunch of drunks," Mrs. Laitinen said.

"What can we do?" I asked. "When they're out in the woods for a month at a time, you have to expect them to blow off steam on payday. Or when they get paid at the mill, what else is there for them in this town except to drink?"

"We need a library. We need to give them something so they can use their minds," Mrs. Laitinen said.

"You think that the men will collect their paychecks and settle down for a quiet afternoon of reading? They need something livelier, like dancing. Dances would get them out of the saloons," I said.

"There's not enough women. They'll fight over women," Mrs. Laitinen said.

"Maybe," I said, "but we'll keep it clean, like you say, and not let them come to the dances unless they're sober, and make them wait like gentlemen to take turns dancing with the women."

"Where will we get musicians?" Mrs. Laitinen asked. "It would be easier to raise money and send for books from Finland than to find musicians."

"I'll talk to some of the men," I said.

That evening I knocked on Jussi's door. Bashfully, he answered. Over his shoulder I saw his neatly made iron cot. Clothes hung from a rope strung across the corner. Lying on the table was a fiddle case.

"I hear your fiddle at night," I told him.

"I'm sorry," he said. "I won't play it anymore."

"No, no. I like it. Why don't you play for others?"

"I'm not good enough." He sat down on the cot and I sat on the single chair at the table. "My father was the fiddler in my village. When he played at weddings, people gave him as much respect as they gave the preacher. He could make life come from the fiddle. But I don't play for any ears but my own."

"May I see it?"

He walked to the table and lifted the fiddle from its case. The polished red wood shone in the lamplight. He sat on the cot, running his fingers lightly up and down the strings.

"The happiest time of my life was when I danced to the fiddle at my wedding," I told him. 'Please. Play for me."

He turned away and put the fiddle to his chin. When he drew the bow across the stings the fiddle moaned and then it sobbed. It was music of loss, music of longing. It brought visions of my father whittling a handle for a knife, my grandmother at her loom. I saw my mother playing with my little brother on her lap. I saw the birch trees on the path by the lake where Tarmo and I had walked in youthful hope. I couldn't hold back my tears. I left quietly as Jussi played on.

The next evening I visited him again.

"Jussi," I said. "If we build a proper hall for dancing, would you play the fiddle for us?"

"No, Mrs. Rautio, I only play for myself," he said again.

"Jussi, your music is a gift to share. You shouldn't be selfish and keep it from others."

"Men make fun of me, Mrs. Rautio," he said in anguish. "I'm a small man. I can't lift as much or saw as fast, or wield an axe with the best of them. I'm timid. My music is all I have of my own. I can't let them mock that too."

"They'd never mock you. They'd give you respect."

For a moment he looked hopeful, but then he shook his head. "No, no, I can't take a chance."

"Will you play for me again, at least?"

This time when he played he faced me squarely, so when I opened the door to slip away, he saw the men who had gathered in the hall.

Jussi stopped playing.

"Please," Sarvoja said. "Please, play one more song."

Jussi played.

We had the music. We needed the hall.

Sarvoja talked to the bosses at the mill. He convinced them that the men would be better citizens, stay sober, and not miss so much work if they had a wholesome place to spend their time. The mill donated a piece of land. The women had bake sales and pie socials to raise money for the materials, and Sarvoja organized a building crew.

The hall was ready in June. We decorated it with fragrant pine and cedar. We put purple irises on the tables and hung lanterns around the building.

The women dressed in fresh dresses and twined wildflowers in each other's hair. I'd forgotten we were young. Even Mrs. Laitinen, for all her strong will, was hardly more than twenty.

Women with children and babies went to the mill at closing time. When Jussi came out, I put his fiddle in his hands. He stood up straight, lay the fiddle under his chin, and began to play a march. The wild sweetness of the fiddle called the others from the mill, called to them with memories of home. Jussi led us from the mill into the village, and we danced up one street and down the other after Jussi's fiddle. Tarmo watched from the doorway of Bendy's Saloon.

Jussi led us through the doors of the hall and took his place on the stage, fiddling as we made a grand march around the room.

Sarvoja was the master of ceremonies.

"If you can't find a woman, grab a friend," he cried. "This is going to be a schottische."

We danced until we couldn't breathe and laughed so hard we couldn't catch our breath. We danced mazurkas and waltzes and polkas. We took a break for coffee and sweets and danced some more.

In one corner of the hall a lumberjack showed a little girl the steps to the schottische. Children raced around the edge of the hall, giddy from their parents' joy.

Sarvoja sang, his rich baritone blending with Jussi's fiddle.

> Oh my friend, oh my beloved.
> Will you remember me?
> As long as the blood in my body is warm,
> I will remember you.

Those rough men "who drank and cursed and fought each other in the saloons" broke down and wept, remembering mother, father, sweetheart, all they had left behind. There was magic in Jussi's fiddle.

We formed a circle to sing one last song, and shook hands all around.

Life began again for me. I lived for the hall. Every night I practiced songs with the chorus, or rehearsed plays that we put on before the dance. I organized bake sales to raise money to buy books from Finland, like Mrs. Laitinen said we should. We bought books on every subject: religion, politics, philosophy. We got books by Russians and Englishmen and Frenchmen in translation. Over time we collected more than 600 books.

Mrs. Laitinen was right. I had underestimated the men. Many came straight to the hall library right from the logging camps, craving food for their minds. Of course, not every man preferred the life of the hall to the life of the saloon, but the hall gave them a choice.

Sarvoja had misled the mill bosses. Men came to the hall exhausted from a twelve-hour day at the mill, but when they started to practice and rehearse they found new energy. When their spirits returned, they no longer accepted the idea that they had no worth other than as cheap labor to power the camps and the mills. They began to gather in the hall to talk about decent pay, decent hours, decent conditions. Then Korva came to Winton, bringing news of the Movement, the Industrial Workers of the World.

Korva was an ugly man. A hideous scar covered the place where his ear should have been. Two or three women turned him away from their boarding-houses before he came to my door. Even I looked at him a long time before I said, yes, there was room in my house.

For all his ugliness, we listened when he spoke at the hall. Korva rallied us to the Wobbly cause, speaking of human dignity, speaking to the desire in every man's heart. He talked about a new community, worldwide, where everyone would be equal. He stood on the hall stage and moved us to love of brotherhood like no preacher had done in any parish church. The IWW stood for all humanity.

When the bosses got wind of it, they shut down the hall. They wanted cheap, obedient labor, not spirited men. It was their land, they said. They weren't going to tolerate subversion and sedition on their property.

"Well," said Mrs. Laitinen, "We'll buy our own land, and build another hall."

We did, there on the Winton hill. We kept the movement going with lectures and plays and songs of solidarity.

Winton wasn't a lumber camp anymore. It was a village. The workers weren't beasts any longer. They were men.

When the movement got strong, the companies shut down the mills. They went somewhere else to exploit other land, other men. Even the houses that were built on company land were rolled away to Ely.

There was no work in Winton. Most of the workers packed up and left, just as Tarmo and I had moved time and again. My boarders went, all but Jussi, Korva and Antti. What was I going to do? Where would I go now?

"You don't need to go anywhere," Antti said. "I'm staying here. If I leave I'll have to move on—again and again—if I depend on the companies."

Antti had been living in the woods with the Indians and couldn't stand the idea of giving up his freedom.

"Hell," he said, "We'll live the way people always lived here. There's meat in the woods, a market for furs, plenty of fuel. We'll see that you and your children are warm and fed."

Korva and Jussi nodded in agreement, so it was like Antti said. We stayed on, rich in room in the great empty boardinghouse. I never went hungry or cold. I took in sewing, making alterations for Ely ladies. Sigurd Olson came to Winton to run an outfitting business and I worked for him, sewing sacks for tourists to carry their flour and sugar on camping trips. Mostly we lived from the woods and the garden—and the hall.

The hall saw us through those years, right through World War II. Enough of us stayed on in Winton to dance together and put on plays and concerts. We had learned how important it was to keep the spirit alive.

Tarmo drank himself to death. We buried him in the cemetery in Ely. My boy David ran off into the woods when they were putting his father in the ground. After the funeral David tugged at my sleeve.

"Come and see, Äiti. I found an Indian grave," he said.

I followed him to the side of cemetery hill. Bones stuck out of the hillside where gravel had washed away.

"No, David," I said. "Those aren't Indian bones. That's where they put the men who died in the mine. Those are miners' bones."

That arm bone sticking out of the gravel might have belonged to the man who died the day Tarmo went down the mine.

I'd begged him every Saturday, but Tarmo never came to the hall. He wasn't there when we lifted our voices in song, shed our troubles in a dance, rallied at the call for brotherhood.

In the hall we became a people of grace. It broke my heart that Tarmo was not among us.

Chapter 7

Children of God: Aina Lahti's First Story

The deputy sheriff walked into the Masonovitch house and grabbed Mrs. Masonovitch.

He thought he'd get away with it. No miner had ever stood up to a sheriff or a mining captain before, even if he wanted the use of a miner's wife. If a miner put up a fight, he lost his job and his children starved. Mining captains often claimed privileges with the miners' women.

But this time Mr. Masonovitch and three other miners burst into the room and shot Deputy Sheriff Myron dead.

We were on strike. The whole Iron Range had walked off the job and it gave Mr. Masonovitch courage.

He was charged with murder, along with his friends. Mrs. Masonovitch was hauled off to jail on a murder charge, too, with her baby in her arms. To show where the power was, the officials arrested ten more men—leaders of the strike—even though they were more than fifty miles away when the deputy was shot. Their speeches had incited the Masonovitches to riot, the officials said.

They were deputizing thugs in Duluth and the bullies they sent to the Range made a practice of going after women on the picket line. In Gilbert, a deputy struck Mrs. Penter on the head and dragged her down the street. In Hibbing, Mrs. Zbenich was carrying her three-month-old baby when she was brutally dragged to the patrol wagon and carted off to jail. Most of us strikers were immigrants who'd come to America believing promises of liberty and prosperity. American promoters taunted desperate people throughout Europe with the visions of land and gold. People had sold everything they owned to buy the tickets that brought them to Minnesota and to the horror of the open pit mines.

We had no common language, religion or politics. A handful belonged to the union. For years the miners' suffering had grown in silence before it erupted in the early summer of 1916.

I'd come to America with my brother Arvo, looking for adventure, but the first thing I knew, I was married, had a baby and was keeping house for my husband Urho, and Arvo as well, in a two-room house owned by the mining company. Our neighbors were Italians and subjects from the Austro-Hungarian Empire. I'd learned more words of Italian, Serbian and Croatian than English.

We weren't organized for a strike. We didn't know each other from location to location, or from nationality to nationality. But we all understood that we couldn't survive much longer the way things were.

The conditions in the mine were inhuman and the mining bosses were corrupt, and in the end we couldn't live on the wages. How could you keep a family on $45 a month, when $30 went for groceries? That's what Urho usually brought home after a month's back breaking labor, $45, but he couldn't count on that because of the contract system. The mining captain sent you to a place. You got paid by the ton. Some places were a lot harder going than others. If you wanted a good place, you had to bribe the captain—and Urho never would.

Compared to our neighbors, we were well off. We had only one child to support, and both Urho and Arvo were young and strong.

One neighbor, Mr. Stubich, worked for the company for fifteen years. The company fired him after his body broke down and his production slowed. He was thirty-five years old with seven children and no work.

Mr. Marinelli, another neighbor, hurt his back carrying a sixteen-foot timber in a low place, where he had to crouch to get through. The company doctor said he hadn't been injured on the job, and told Mr. Marinelli to return to work, where he hurt himself worse. He paid another doctor from his own pocket and got some help, but he was off the job for six months with no pay and five children to feed. The companies took money from the miners' paychecks every month for that company doctor, who worked for the company and never helped a single miner.

My husband, Urho, was a leader in the strike. He was the Finnish speaker at the big rally when Elizabeth Gurley Flynn came to the Range. I remember how proud I was that hot summer night. I stood in the crowd of five thousand with Andy on my hip, waiting to hear

Urho speak the words he had practiced at home. He was the third man at the podium.

"The newspapers say that we are alien filth—scum—ungrateful for the opportunities that America offers us.

"It is true that there are many foreign born among us but strangely enough we are entirely welcome when we are willing to submit to industrial serfdom. Only when we demand our 'rights to life, liberty and happiness' so gloriously pictured as American, do we become *undesirable* foreigners.

"If we work cheaply at first, until we are adjusted to a strange new world, we are cursed for cutting down the American standard of living. When we awake to our possibilities in this country and organize to demand more, we are told 'If you don't like this country, go back where you came from.'

"When we live crowded into foul hovels, English speaking people say, 'They are not like us. They are satisfied with a crust of bread and an onion!'

"When we show we are the same flesh and blood, desiring the comforts of life and education for our children, we are met with bullets, clubs and vicious abuse.

"We journeyed across the world, away from our loved ones, in search of freedom that America promised. We have appealed patiently for sympathy and justice, but our appeals fell on the deaf ears of steel magnates too far away to be disturbed by our cries."

The crowd shouted out its agreement—in Slovenian, Croatian, Serbian, Finnish, Italian. Urho's speech transcended barriers of language. There we stood, thirty-five languages among us, united by condition, united in purpose.

Elizabeth Gurley Flynn traveled across America organizing industrial workers. When she took the platform, her strong voice was confident and filled with love. She told us to keep our courage, even though the power of the steel trust was immense, even though the newspapers were against us, even though the governor stood with the steel trust. She was bringing our message to working people throughout the country, and they were with us.

"Your demands are not great," she said. "Everywhere else workers are earning three dollars for a day's work. Harvesters in the Kansas wheat fields earn three dollars. Textile workers in New England earn more than you do. Coal miners are asking for four dollars."

("I worked out in Pennsylvania," Mr. Stubich whispered to me. "That work isn't nearly as bad as here.")

"Throughout the country IWW locals are raising money to aid the Mesaba strikers," Mrs. Flynn said. She named locals in Chicago that had raised money: Jewish, Swedish, Norwegian, Italian, Flemish, Hungarian, Finnish, Spanish, Lithuanian. The list went on.

We went home greatly comforted by her message. It had been terrible to feel isolated, to think that no one knew our plight. When the representative from the Governor came to the Range to investigate the strike, he didn't talk to one miner or even a municipal official—only to the bosses. The newspapers called us violent radicals and revolutionaries. No one would hear our grievances or listen to us as human beings. The violence that I knew about was all directed at us. Early in the strike, John Aller was murdered in his home by Oliver Mining Company gunmen. He was shot in the back three times in front of his three small children. The mining companies thought that killing John would intimidate the rest of us.

John's own priest refused to officiate at his funeral. His wife and friends pleaded first with him, and then with priests of other nationalities. All refused, so great was the power of the companies. We had the funeral rites at the Finnish Socialist Hall in Virginia. Seven thousand strikers accompanied the casket to the cemetery. I led the procession with three other women, carrying a banner that said: MURDERED BY OLIVER GUNMEN. The Virginia Finnish Socialist Band marched at the head of the parade, playing funeral music. Funeral orations were delivered in all the languages of the strikers.

To keep peace with Urho, my brother Arvo wasn't crossing the picket line, but he didn't approve of the strike and he didn't want me participating in it. He rebuked me for carrying the funeral banner.

"Think how ashamed Father would be if he saw you there," he said. Father was a parish pastor in Finland.

"Do you remember, Arvo," I asked, "When Olli Niemi went to America, leaving his wife with ten children and one cow?"

Arvo nodded.

"Do you also remember that when it came time to collect the tithes Mrs. Niemi had nothing to give, so Father took her cow?"

Arvo said nothing.

"I was deeply ashamed of Father," I told him. "Jesus stands with the poor. I want to tell you something, Arvo. When I was in that procession, carrying that banner, I felt God was with me."

"That's blasphemy," Arvo shouted.

"Since you eat at my table every night, keep your opinions to yourself, and leave me to act on my principles," I said.

Mrs. Flynn had inspired me with her courage. She was so eloquent that even one newspaper man changed his mind about the strike after he heard her speak.

"Miss Flynn has been pictured by the corporation newspapers as a fiery anarchist that preached bloodshed and murder throughout the land, as a means of adjusting the difference between capital and labor, but we have found her nothing of the kind, and the mining men and others who were at the meeting with us will verify the statement.

"She is a woman with a big heart, and it is filled to overflowing with sympathy for humanity. She is an earnest woman who has a mission in life, and it is to better the condition of the common people. Surely a worthy mission.

"We could only wish that more preachers, more newspapermen, more business men, more people generally, could hear this woman as she gives her message of hope to the lowly man who has nothing but his labor to sell, who daily sees the cost of living advancing while his wage remains at a standstill. We believe it would bring home to them the fight this woman is making against all the odds in the world, and it might serve as an inspiration that would give it great coloring."

If Miss Flynn could make that newsman change his mind, then our struggle was different from what Urho thought. He said the only language that capitalists could understand was the language of power, but now I wasn't so sure.

Miss Flynn gave me inspiration. Even though my English wasn't very good, I decided to talk to the people in Hibbing to explain the strike—like the preachers and businessmen who the newsman had mentioned.

Surely the clergy would want to understand the people they ministered to.

"Let's talk to your priest," I said to my neighbor, Mrs. Stubich. She hung her head.

"No," she whispered.

"It can't hurt," I said.

64

"It hurts," she said. "It hurts when the priest says, 'why are you Austrian women so dirty?'" She started to cry. "And when the teachers send my children home from school because they are so badly dressed."

I decided to start with the businessmen. I dressed up in my good dress, took little Andy by the hand, and went out to see Mr. Miller, who owned the dry goods store.

"Has anyone spoken to you on behalf of the strikers, Mr. Miller?" I asked.

"The deputies warned me about rioting and looting. That's all I know about the strike. None of the strikers have talked to me."

"Have you seen any rioting and looting?"

"I have not. If you would like to come into the back room, I can offer you a cup of coffee."

I followed him into his office, where he served me coffee in a boardinghouse mug. Andy leaned against me and buried his face in my lap.

"My husband Urho doesn't think that capitalists understand any language but power," I said.

Mr. Miller laughed.

"I'm a small businessman, not John D. Rockefeller," he said. "My business depends on having good relations with my customers, and miners are my customers."

"Do you know what kind of conditions the miners have been working in?" I asked Mr. Miller.

"Well, no, I can't say that I know much about mining."

I began to tell him about my neighbors, injured and jobless.

"Wait, wait," he said, holding up his hand. My heart sank. He was going to send me away.

"Other people should hear this. I'd like to get some of my friends together so you could talk to them."

"My English is too poor," I said.

"I can understand you perfectly well," he said. "Will next Tuesday be all right with you? We always get together on the second Tuesday."

When I told Urho, he didn't like it at all.

"It's a capitalist trick," he said. "I won't let you go."

I wondered if Miss Flynn had a husband who forbade her to speak and organize but I knew better than to argue with Urho, so Monday I folded my good dress under my arm when I went to see Mrs. Stubich.

Tuesday I went over there like I was going for a visit, but I changed clothes and went downtown to talk to the businessmen.

Twenty-five or thirty men came to hear me. Mr. Miller introduced me courteously as the wife of a striking miner.

"Please, let me tell you about some of the conditions that the miners have to work in," I said haltingly. My voice shook with fright.

I told about the pay, the contract system, the company doctor. I told how when Mr. Pettinelli worked in the Lincoln mine the air was so bad a match wouldn't burn. That's why they used carbide lamps. "One time a mule driver was waiting for a load with the mule and the captain shouted—don't stand there with that mule, get him to the shaft so he can get better air! No one was concerned about the air the miners breathed. They had headaches so bad that they didn't last there more than a few months. New immigrants always come to fill their places," I said.

"We're up against terrible odds in the strike. The companies have all the power. The company has served eviction notices to those of us who live in company houses. We have to find new places to live, with no money for rent. Some strikers who own their own houses were given 24 hours to move them off company land and when they couldn't do it, the company tore them down."

The businessmen leaned forward to hear me. I spoke louder. My courage was coming back.

"The best miners on the Range are Joe Relner and his partners in Aurora," I said. I had written out my speech, so that I wouldn't forget the words. "Last May, working in a good place, they produced 2300 tons of ore. That's the most anyone ever produced. The company got $16,000 for that ore. The miners got $100 each.

"In 1915 the steel trust made $130 million in profit. Munitions makers and armament manufacturers are making huge profits selling products made from iron to the warring countries in Europe. Prices are shooting up around the country, but the wages on the Range are the same as they were in 1905."

Mr. Miller stood up and spoke to his friends.

"If just a little more of those profits went into the miners' pockets, they could spend more in our stores," he said.

"Yes," I said. "We would buy fabric to make clothes for our families. We would use store-bought soap. In the winter, we could get our children shoes and warm coats. Oh, there are so many things we need, so many things we would like to buy."

66

Andy was hanging on my skirt, sucking his thumb. The businessmen stared at his bare feet.

Suddenly they started to applaud.

"There's some people over in Virginia who need to hear this," Mr. Miller said.

"What can we do?" asked Mr. Jackson, the livery man.

"Children are going hungry," I said. "We need money to buy food for the miners' store. And we need people who talk English to talk to the newspapers and to the people from the government.

Mr. Jackson took the hat off his head. "Look here, men, I'm passing the hat, don't be afraid to be generous," he called out.

I left the meeting dazed with success.

Urho was home when I got there.

"You can't imagine what happened," I began excitedly, but before I could explain he hit me in the face.

"You went to see the businessmen after I told you not to go," Urho said, and walked out.

The American, English-speaking capitalists downtown had listened to me, but I couldn't be heard in my own language in my own home.

I went over to see Mrs. Stubich and found her crying.

"It's all right," I told her. "You had to tell Urho where I was."

She looked at my welted face. "That's not what I'm crying about," she said. "I went to get water, but the company said the pump is on company land and we can't get water there anymore. It's too much," she said, breaking down. "How do we live without water?"

"I'm going to get water," I said. "Do you want to come with me?"

"They said they'd throw us in jail if we used that pump."

Out in the alley, Mrs. Rajecich and Mrs. Romau were talking about the situation.

"Let's go to the pump," I said. Each of us took a pail. A pack of little kids trailed behind us.

Deputy Pete Wring was waiting for us. "You're trespassing on company property," he said, blocking our way.

Mrs. Romau, eight months pregnant, kept walking toward the pump. Wring struck her thigh with his club and punched her hard in the stomach. Mrs. Rajecich and I grabbed his arms and we fell in a heap, struggling in the gravel. Other deputies ran to pull us off Wring and drag us down the street to jail, jerking the children along by their arms. Andy screamed behind me.

Mrs. Zbenich and her children were already in the jail.

"Welcome," she smiled. "It's nice to have company. What did you do?"

"We went to get water," I said. "And you?"

"I got into a little argument with a scab on the picket line," she said.

The children didn't like jail one bit. They set up a continuous wail that we couldn't quiet.

"Someone to see you, Mrs. Lahti," the jailer called. Urho had come to bail me out, I thought, but no, it was Mr. Miller and Mr. Jackson, the businessmen.

"We heard the children screaming from the street," Mr. Miller said. "So now the steel trust makes war on children."

"We'll raise money to bail you out," Mr. Jackson said.

"We don't want you to use any money that would go to strikers otherwise," Mrs. Zbenich said. "I don't mind if the county wants to feed me and my children. We can stay here a long time."

"The steel trust is disgracing our city, treating people this way," Mr. Jackson said. "We're getting you out of jail."

My next visitor was not Urho either, but brother Arvo.

"I'm ashamed of you," he said. "I'm so ashamed. What would our family think?"

"Well I'm ashamed of you, because you think that serving God means dressing up on Sunday and dropping a coin in the collection plate. God is here, in this jail."

"You're talking like a crazy woman. We're guests in this country, and you're breaking the law."

"You can afford to judge. You're a single man with no one to support. You can always go home to Finland if things get too rough. What about people who don't have that choice? Don't they have the right to justice?"

Arvo noticed the bruise on my face. "How did you get that black eye? Did the deputies do that to you?" Whatever his feelings about the strike, Arvo felt strongly against men beating women.

"No," I said. "It was Urho. He was angry at me for talking to the businessmen." Arvo turned red and stalked out.

"Arvo," I shouted after him, "It's between me and Urho."

It only took the businessmen a day to raise the money to pay our bail.

Urho said nothing to me when I got home—that is, he wouldn't speak to me at all. I decided that he was most angry because I'd showed that he was wrong—that the world wasn't a black and white place of good and evil that he wanted to believe it was — labor against capital. It wasn't the system, it was what was in men's hearts. Urho couldn't stand the idea that some capitalists might have good hearts, even if they were just small businessmen.

It was more important to Urho to be righteous than to win, if winning meant getting help from the businessmen.

When I realized that, I knew that the strike couldn't succeed. There were too many men like him, men who preferred purity and defeat rather than compromise and success.

We'd lost, at any rate. The prospect of winter did us in. Even before the strike, when the men were working, we couldn't afford to buy fuel so we foraged for firewood. To punish us for striking, the state and the companies got together to forbid us from gathering wood. Our leaders were in jail. We were starving on short rations, hauling water great distances, wearing threadbare clothing, evicted from our homes—and now there was no fuel.

Urho went to one last meeting on a clear September night. We had to move out of our house the next day. But the next morning Urho lay dead on the road with his skull crushed in.

The authorities didn't bother to look for his murderer. Urho was just a Finlander, just a striker. There was no mass funeral show of solidarity, like there had been for John Aller. The strike was over. We had lost. Arvo, Andy and I buried Urho in a plain pine box and took the train to Winton, our belongings packed in the trunks that came with us to the New World. I worked at Laitinen's boarding house while Arvo built a house on a piece of land out of town. I was overwhelmed with regret and guilt. I did the tedious work in the boarding house—washing clothes and ironing them, cooking, washing dishes, scrubbing floors—while my thoughts traveled in circles as endless as the chores. I returned to all the crossroads of my life, willing things to turn out differently. If I hadn't decided to come to America, would Urho be alive today?

What if I'd married Urho's brother Antti instead of Urho? Would it have changed anything if I had obeyed Urho?

No matter how I rearranged history in my mind, I couldn't change the fact that the strike had been lost and that Urho was dead. Was it a punishment from God?

My father preached about an angry God who loved to punish sin, a God who backed up power and authority. You could never be obedient enough to please Him. When I ran away from Finland, I was running from Father's angry God.

Then, in the strike, I'd felt God's presence lift me from anger and fear into love and courage. I'd felt the grace of God when I carried the funeral banner with women who spoke different languages but shared an understanding of the heart, when I spoke to the businessmen, and when I was in the jail with the others, surrounded by our wailing babies.

But now I was in despair. My spirit was dead. God—the God of courage and hope—had forsaken me.

When I got a break from my work in the boardinghouse, I went outdoors. Winter came early that year. I wrapped Andy in blankets for our daily walk, but I let the bitter cold and biting wind cut through my thin coat, piercing into my numbness. The dazzling glare of sun on snow blinded my eyes.

Slowly, my mind began to clear.

Never again would I let a man tell me what to do, I thought. Never again would a man hit me. Never again would a man tell me what to believe.

I was finding my way back to God.

I told Arvo that I would keep house for him only on the condition that he let me be.

"I don't want you to preach to me. Never again," I said. "Tend to your own soul. Let me tend to mine."

Winton was a good place to look for God. In Finland, the state church enforced status, but in Winton there was no rank. There wasn't an established church in the village—just a community church where visiting ministers of different denominations sometimes came, or people gathered to worship with no minister present.

I was free to find my own way. I kept to myself, working hard at Laitinen's, taking care of Andy. I didn't go to the church or the Hall. I spoke very little. People let me be.

Every afternoon Andy and I walked along the railroad tracks or to the top of the hill or down by the river. One dark day when a fierce wind whipped grainy pellets of snow like bits of sand, I thought of staying in, but Andy dragged his blanket to me and tugged at my hand. I bundled him up and we went out into the force of the storm.

70

It was a long winter. April was still gray and cold. Andy and I walked the frozen rutted road to our new land, where Arvo was building the little log house.

"Arvo," I said. "You didn't put any windows on the south. The house will be too dark."

"I like it dark."

"You'll be working outdoors all day. I want windows—big windows—facing south."

We argued. I won.

When the spring peepers trilled their shrill evening song, I heard them with my heart. The first knobby, wobbly calf of the new season staggered to its feet in Gust Johnson's pasture. I saw the delight on Andy's face, and turned to look at the newborn calf as if I'd never seen one before.

We moved into our house in June. Winton had a dance for us at the Hall, to raise money for a cookstove, dishes, pots and pans. I didn't go because my heart was still too fragile to contend with the world.

They understood that I was in mourning.

Was I mourning?

I watched my young son pick strawberries with chubby fingers and squash them into his mouth. I listened to each bird's different voice, calling out in hope another would answer. I worked in the house and field until my body ached, taking pleasure in hard work and deep sleep.

I prayed.

Every day I thought about the strike, how angry Arvo was when it happened, how bitter Urho was when we lost. My strike was different from theirs. I saw women of courage and men of good hearts. I saw people pushed down as far as they could be find power beyond themselves.

I would never find happiness if I had to change the world in order to be happy, but that didn't mean that I had to accept persecution and abuse. I found happiness doing what I knew was right. When I defied the people who abused their power—the steel trust, the clergy, the deputies, my brother, my father, my husband — I had felt God's grace.

"You're smiling," Arvo said to me one day, angrily, reproachfully.

I smiled more broadly.

71

Chapter 8

Ashes: Jussi's Story

Such a strange country. Big fluffy snowflakes drifting down on a warm May morning.

No, not snowflakes. Ash.

I smelled fire. I ran to the barn. Mrs. Järvinen was already there, slapping and cursing the cows, driving them from their stanchions. I helped little Helmi herd them outside.

"Helmi and I can bring them to Isaakson's clearing," Mrs. Järvinen yelled at me. "You stay here."

Mr. Järvinen was climbing the ladder to the roof of the barn. I passed buckets of water up to him, and he threw them on the roof.

Untinen came running up the road.

"We'll try to stop the fire here. Others are coming," he shouted.

I took my place on the ladder, passing buckets of water up to the men who wet down the roof of the barn, dousing sparks that fell on the cedar shingles. Others worked furiously at the edge of the field with shovels and picks, trying to make a trench that the fire wouldn't jump.

Not our puny efforts, but the wind and rain saved the Järvinen farm. The fire took its own course. It burned the sauna that stood beyond the house, but not the barn. It came so close to the yard that the heat ignited the pile of chips under the swing I was making for little Helmi, but the log house still stood.

The fire raged through, heat singeing hair and mustaches, blistering faces. It swept through Birch Lake Township, jumped the lake and burned to the south shore of Fall Lake before the rains stopped it.

Other neighbors didn't do as well. There was no man at the Niemi place, only a woman and her half-grown boys. The boys got their cows out, but when they went home to save something else, the cows followed them back. The cows, house, barn—everything burned except the boys and their mother, and one old rooster, who came out from somewhere after the fire.

My little dog Kauhu blistered the pads of his feet, walking over the smoldering ground. I packed them in a pine tar poultice, and they healed.

Some of the homesteaders who were burned out moved away. The Sutelas left, and the Tuhkanens. I let the Järvinens find another hired man, and went to work in the logging camps on the lakes. I wanted to be near water.

There were over a hundred men in the camp on Hoist Bay. We slept in dark, vermin-infested bunkhouses in long rows, two to a bunk. Two tiny windows let in meager light. We were fed rotten food, mostly beans and tainted salt pork.

I was bitterly sorry I'd ever come to this country, so far from my beautiful wife and my darling little girls in Finland.

"Soon," I had told Irja when I left, "Soon I will send for you."

It was a miracle that she had chosen me for a husband. I couldn't believe my luck. I'm a small man, and not brave. Irja said that she liked my gentle way, but still, it was hard to understand.

After our marriage, my prospects dimmed. My father had co-signed notes for someone who didn't pay up, and we lost the farm. I sent my wife and daughters home to her family, and set out for America to make my fortune.

Every night I dreamed of Irja caressing my face, kissing the lids of my closed eyes, only to awaken to loneliness, tossing about on a lumpy straw mattress next to a foul smelling man.

Often at the camps, talk turned to women. Most of the men had left home as boys so they'd never had a real girlfriend. Now they didn't have much chance of getting one because there weren't enough girls to go around. All they had known were whores.

"What's the matter with you, Jussi," Heikki said, one time up on Hoist Bay. "You never want a woman on payday."

"Don't you like women?" Arne taunted.

I didn't mean to tell them anything, but I couldn't take the jeers.

"I'm faithful to my wife. I'm going to bring her over when I get the money saved for her ticket," I said.

That made their taunts worse.

"And who would marry you? Was she ugly or was she some old hag who couldn't get another man?"

"Irja is young and beautiful," I said.

"Well then, what's the chance that she's faithful to you, runt that you are? There must be lots of big strong men left in Finland who can make a beautiful woman happy."

After that, whenever they came back to the camp, hung-over and broke, after they'd spent all their money in the bars and brothels in Winton, they would make themselves feel better by telling me what a fool I was.

"There you sit, while a man is unbuttoning Irja's dress," Heikki would say.

"Now he's putting his hand on her bare thigh," Arne went on.

Irja stopped coming to me in my dreams. Whenever I closed my eyes I was tormented by visions of her in another man's arms.

I said to myself, she's better off with him than with me. The kindest thing is for me to let her be.

I never talked about Irja anymore, but the men kept on with their mockery, until Antti came to camp.

Antti was a powerful man, over six feet tall, and strong as an ox.

"Which of us was man enough to find a wife?" Antti challenged my tormentors. "Do you think that cutting down a tree makes you a real man? Or gulping a bottle of booze in one swig?"

The others were silent. Not only was Antti a big man, he was strongest on the cross-cut, smoothest with the axe. He could handle a team—four or six horses, it made no difference—and he was a wizard at the forge.

They listened to Antti.

"None of us had what it took to win a woman's love. You're jealous of Jussi because he did. You're just like a mink that pisses on what it can't eat."

That put an end to the teasing, but not an end to my misery. In my heart I knew that the others were right. Irja could never have stayed faithful to a man like me.

When I wasn't at the camps, I lived in Mrs. Rautio's boarding-house in Winton. Saturdays I played my fiddle at the Hall. I learned many things watching the others dance.

I remember the stir Aina Lahti caused the first night she came to the hall. Her little boy hung on her skirt and her brother Arvo walked close behind, but all eyes were on Aina. She fanned flames of hope in every lonely heart. Many men tried to court her, traveling out of their way just to catch a glimpse of Aina working alongside her brother, chopping and grubbing stumps from the field. In the evening she came to the hall as bright and lively as if she'd spent her day crocheting doilies and dining on strawberries.

After every dance, many men asked to walk her down the road and over the stile to her house, but Aina always went home with brother Arvo.

Only Antti seemed immune to Aina's charms. He never danced with her, never talked with her, but I could see him staring when her back was turned.

My fortune changed in the logging camps after Mrs. Rautio taught me to cook. After I learned to bake fragrant bread and flaky pies, thick meaty stews, tender roasts, perfectly mashed potatoes, and rich brown gravy, the bosses came looking for me when they were hiring. The men wanted to know if I was the cook before they signed up.

In the summer of 1929, I cooked for the construction crew that built Maple Isle Resort on Basswood. The owners wanted a grand main lodge made of log. Antti was the master builder. His crew brought great white pine logs to the site, eighty feet long, three feet in diameter. The men worked in teams hoisting up logs to make the walls. When the logs were up, the men portaged long windows, two stories tall, over Four-Mile Portage without breaking a single pane.

For a month they did nothing but gather rocks from the lakeshore, and haul them to the site. The rocks had to be just the right size and shape. While the others varnished logs and planed floors, Eero Maki, artist of rock, lay the massive stone fireplace.

When Maple Isle was finished, it was as grand as the owners' hopes, with two-story windows on one end of the hall and a two-story fireplace on the other, and rooms off the balconies on the second floor.

Women came from Winton on the launch to celebrate, bringing baskets of food. I got out my fiddle and Matti Hekkinen got out his button accordion, and we christened the shiny new floor with a dance. We played no songs of sorrow on that warm summer night. Matti's fingers jumped over the buttons, my bow flew over the strings. Our music lifted the dancers right off the floor. Aina was there as beautiful as ever, though thirteen years had passed since she'd come to Winton. The men had long since given up trying to win her, but waltzing with her still made them feel like they had truly come to the promised land.

Stars shone brightly through the great multi-paned window. Children curled up in blankets and fell asleep. We played on. You should have seen us Finns dancing in a hall that matched the dreams we'd brought to America!

After the dance I was stirred up. I went to sit on a rock by the lake to let the music of the waves ease the music in my head.

I heard someone coming down the path. I knew the voices, though I couldn't quite catch the words. Then Aina said, "only you," and maybe Antti answered, "I'm sorry."

They walked to the edge of the water and stood, silhouettes in the moonlight. Antti reached for Aina's hand. They embraced and I turned my eyes away. I waited until their steps retreated up the hill.

All night I lay awake in our tent. In the early hours before the dawn, I heard Antti—big Antti, powerful Antti—sobbing. And then I cried too, thinking of my Irja, and all I had left behind.

Irja wrote to me for many years, but I never answered.

It was hard to forget my children. I made toys out of wood for Mrs. Rautio's daughters, and gave them nickels to buy candy wondering, how big are my little girls now? Did they call another man father?

Memory dimmed with the passing of time. I'd almost forgotten my long-ago home in Finland when Auvo Pertti came to Winton. I remembered him as a little boy in my village, listening with big ears to stories about the riches America had to offer. He had grown up and come across the ocean to get some of those riches for himself, and to look for me.

Auvo found me in my room at Rautio's boardinghouse. He gave me a letter, crumpled and soiled from travel. After he had gone, I unfolded it carefully.

"Husband," it read.
"I wait for word from you, but no word comes. I fear that you are dead, but I never give up hope that you are well, and will some day send for me. If you are alive, what terrible fate has befallen you, that keeps us apart?
I remain faithfully yours,

Your loving wife.
Irja."

Memories of Finland flooded back. In my mind I followed Irja there alone, the Irja I had not believed in, living through the years on fading hope. What was she doing right now?

76

It was haymaking time. Villagers were joining farmers in the fields, pitching mown grass on stakes to cure. Maybe the haymakers were resting, refreshing themselves with buttermilk and rye bread. Irja would be among them, and the girls. I could see them clearly, a little girl bringing her mother wild berries, the mother caressing her child's hair, bending to kiss her forehead.

I looked around at my bare room. If only the flames that turned Irja's letter to ash could have scorched the shame from my heart.

Chapter 9

Timo's Team: Matt Keskinen's Story

(Published in Jarvenpa. A & M.G. Karni (eds.) *Sampo, The Magic Mill: An Anthology of Finnish American Writing*. New Rivers Press, 1989.)

Early every morning as I walked to the barn, I thanked God. Then I added a short prayer of thanks to Timo Lahti. Everything I had was, in the larger sense, due to the grace of God, but in the smaller sense, inherited from Timo, God rest his soul.

I knew from what he left behind that Timo was a man of great skill and good taste. There was no site in God's creation more beautiful than the little farm he claimed from the forest. His tight, square log buildings with their dove-tailed corners were built to stand for generations. He'd traveled as far as Dakota to find a wife as lovely as Kaija, and Laila, my oldest child, was Timo's own.

For all of that, I never ceased to marvel at Timo's team. They were not poor man's horses. Perfectly matched true blacks, with arched necks and prancing feet, they could have pulled the coaches of royalty.

Timo had trained them himself, and they were a joy to work. Pick up the lines and they leaned into their collars. Cluck and they walked out, matching steps. I'd never driven any like them. Timo got the credit for training them to work as one, because as matched as they were in appearance, they differed in temperament. Kivi was slow and timid. Loistaa was hot-tempered, quick to be alarmed, first to feel a slight. Yet they had learned to pull together, to match steps, to halt in unison.

That team made a pleasure of a day's work. I never tired of watching powerful muscles ripple under sleek coats. We plowed the potato patch, grubbed stumps out of the field, cut the hay and raked it and hauled it to the barn—just me and that team. A man never knew better companions. Ten years we worked side by side, and I expected to be together another ten, fit as they were.

Kaija and I lived like so many others in those days. We milked twelve cows, raised all their hay and some to sell, sold potatoes and a few eggs and chickens. There still wasn't enough money to get by, so in the winter I went off to the logging camps to make a little cash. I hated to leave Kaija and little Ida alone. The older girls stayed in town to go to school. Kaija did not even have a horse to bring her to town. I needed Loistaa and Kivi in the logging camp—a team earned as much in a day as a man.

Besides, I have to admit that I didn't mind the admiration that I got from the other men as the owner of such a team.

The winter of 1928 I was working at Eino Norha's logging camp. I was put to hauling a bobsled from the landing in the woods across the lake to the railroad tracks. The ice was over two feet thick. We'd been working for three weeks in thirty below on that road. In one place the road curved around a stream that flowed into the lake, but the current must have shifted under the ice and made the ice thin under the road.

It was near the end of the day. I was hauling my last load of logs piled ten feet high on the bobsled. I sat on the load, watching my team with pleasure, thinking ahead to the warm barn, of rubbing them down, feeding them their evening oats. The air was getting even colder. Sitting still as I was, arms outstretched holding the lines, I felt the chill work through my heavy wool mackinaw. My hands were nearly frozen inside my choppers.

Ahead of me the ice cracked like the sound of gunfire. Kivi dropped out of sight in the gloom. The sled slid toward a watery hole where Kivi floundered, but Loistaa scrambled to the side, digging caulked shoes into ice. The sled stopped short. My knife was out of its sheath before I landed on the ice. I cut through the hame strap on Loistaa's harness and he lunged free. Kivi thrashed in the water. I freed his tugs from the evener on the bobsled, then lay on the ice to catch hold of his bridle. If I could hold his head out of the water until another sled came, we could haul him out with the other team.

My foot slipped into the hole. The boot filled with water. My arms were soaked. I got hold of the bridle. On the far shore I heard the clink of harness and shoe as the next team came out of the woods and on to the ice road.

My arms grew numb until I couldn't feel the bridle in my hands. Kivi shook himself free with one last plunge, and slipped out of sight under the ice.

Eino Norha brought me to the hospital. The doctor saved my hands but the foot was frozen and he had to cut part of it off. The doctor said I was done with logging. My hands and feet would freeze more easily now. The next time I would lose them altogether.

I didn't have the heart to go back to work in the logging camp, anyway. Never would I know such a team.

They sent me home to Kaija, hands and feet bound, useless for the winter months. I was no help at all, just adding to her work. I went out to the barn to sit with Loistaa. He was mourning. Loistaa, flash of light, had lost his spirit, and so had I. God punishes us for our pride.

I could have gotten another horse to farm with, but unless I went back to the logging camps there never would be enough money.

We stayed on through the summer. Loistaa did the work of two horses, with head bowed and slow step. I limped behind him. Kaija sold some cows.

Late in the summer Kaija came back from town with news.

"Matt, the school janitor left Winton. They asked if you wanted the job."

"How can I take such a job? How do I plow and plant and tend the farm?"

"We'll move to town, Matt."

There was no other way. We sold the rest of the cows. A Yankee family bought our farm. We moved our things to a frame house in Winton.

Kaija and I came back one last time to walk the worn paths from house to barn, the blacksmith shop and sauna. Timo's dream. Our home.

We drove the wagon back as far as the neighbor's house and left Loistaa there with Reino.

Slowly Kaija and I walked to town.

Chapter 10

Jackfish Pete: Pete LaPrairie's Story

I was living in Winton in 1918 when the government agents removed the people on Jackfish Bay, scattering them among reservations in Minnesota and Ontario, as far as Lac La Croix, Grand Portage and White Earth. I didn't know who had died in the flu epidemic and who had been taken away by the agents. I traveled to the three reservations before I found my cousin Mary at Lake Vermilion.

"Your stepmother died," Mary told me. "All your brothers died except Jake. Josie was still alive, too. The agents took them both, I don't know where."

I found my little brother and sister staying with an old woman at Fond Du Lac and brought them back to Winton.

I was working at the Swallow and Hopkins mill planing lumber when the boss came over with a couple of men dressed in silly looking hats and vests with wicker creels slung over their shoulders. "Hey Pete," the boss said. "Take my friends out to a real good fishing hole. Some place where they can pull in one right after the other. Preferably bass. I'll pay your regular wages."

It sounded like a good deal so I took the greenhorns out, cooked for them and showed them where to fish. They caught enough fish to feed a village for a week but they still wanted more—for the sport of fighting the fish, they said.

There's nothing I like better than a meal of fresh fish—but fight fish for sport? If you look at it one way, it's torturing creatures for fun. Look at it another way, you're playing with your food.

Anyhow, those guys were real happy, and they gave me extra money when they left. In a month or two some of their friends from Chicago came up, wanting to catch fish like that too. I was the first real tourist guide out of Winton.

After the mills shut down, I earned enough money from guiding in the summer so I could stay in Winton and keep house for Jake and

81

Josie during the school months. We did okay. I picked up an odd job here and there. Josie sewed most of our clothes, Jake and I hunted, and every year we went over to Nett Lake to make rice. We ate a lot of fish, wild rice, and venison.

I took Sig Olson out on his first trip. That was the year after the government destroyed the village on Jackfish. I told him my name was Pete LaPrairie.

"LaPrairie. That's French. Pete must be short for Pierre," Sig said. "Pierre LaPrairie."

From that time on he called me Pierre.

"Pierre," he said, "You have the blood of romance flowing in your veins. Yours is the legacy of the noble voyageur."

We were paddling across Basswood on a rare calm day, green canvas canoe gliding easily on smooth water.

"Can you sing for me, Pierre? Do you know a *chanson*?"

I sang one of my grandfather's songs.

"*Goutons boire qui le vin est bon, goutons boire, oui, oui, oui ....*"

"That's it, that's it! A *chanson*," Sig cried.

Antti and some of the other lumberjacks had started guiding, but I was Sig's favorite. I took him out many times. He was likable enough, but he was so eager that we couldn't resist having a little harmless fun with him, like the time Antti and some of the guys took him to Laitinen's public sauna.

"Too hot for you in here?" Antti asked. "Well, if you want to cool it down, throw a little cold water on the rocks." Sig did. I've never seen a man so pink move so fast out the door. I don't think he ever went back to the public sauna.

Sig had a knack for asking stupid questions. When I tried to explain he interrupted and told me the answers he wanted to hear. Like how I was a Frenchmen, and what it must have been like to be a hearty voyageur or a simple primitive native. You couldn't take offense at his ignorance. He liked us colorful people.

But when he asked a practical question, none of us could manage a straight answer.

"What's the best firewood to cook with?" he asked.

"Spruce," Antti said.

Next time I was out with him, Sig gathered up armloads of dry spruce branches for the cook fire. The fire roared up, showering sparks into the brush. We built up good appetites stamping out fires around the campsite.

"*Sacre Dieu,*" he cried when I brought him over a portage to a lake he hadn't seen before. "Oh the life of the voyageur! The adventure of exploring new lands is like no other feeling in the world!"

For Sig, an explorer was someone who didn't know where he was going.

He didn't understand the difference between an explorer and a voyageur, either. My grandfather was a voyageur. Voyageurs worked for the big fur companies, men so desperate for work they allowed themselves to be used as pack animals. The company worked them like hell, treated them like shit and expected them to die young. A voyageur got a pension if he got to be thirty years old, and the company didn't spend a lot of money on pensions.

The worst part of working as a voyageur was living without women, Grandfather said. Like a lot of the young men from Quebec, he ran off from the company, married a Chippewa woman, "went native." We were already pretty mixed by then—the trade had been going on for a long time, hundreds of years.

It wasn't blood that made you what you were in this country, it was how you lived. Grandfather was despised in Quebec because his father was poor. Rich people can be very cruel, he said, but the Indians took him as he was, as long as he followed their rules.

The old Chippewa rules made sense to me. When you followed them you didn't own much, but you lived well, but the government wasn't going to let us live like that anymore. Indian agents had come around hassling us for years. It was when the agent came to Jackfish to force me back to boarding school that I ran away and went to work in the lumber mill with Antti.

The mill was noisy and dangerous but it was better than boarding school. Once in awhile I'd go home to Jackfish with presents for everybody, stay up there for a while, and feel all right again. Then the government agents destroyed the village. A few people straggled back, but the real life of the Chippewas was gone from Jackfish Bay. I planned to take Jake and Josie to live on the reservation at Vermilion, but when I visited my cousin Mary and her husband Joe, they talked me out of it.

"The Bureau of Indian Affairs hires agents as firewood inspectors," Mary told me. "All they do is check our woodpiles. If our woodpile is small, they tell us we're lazy. If we have a big woodpile, they accuse us of commercializing in wood."

"We fill out forms and forms about our allotments, but we don't have any control over the land," Joe said. "My allotment was logged off. The government keeps the stumpage fees in an account for us, because they say we can't handle money. But when I wrote to ask how much money was in my account, the government claimed that my allotment hadn't been logged, and there was no money in my account."

"You can't cut and sell your own wood?" I asked.

"No."

"How do they expect you make a living?"

Joe laughed.

"We're supposed to farm. The Indian agent says that farming will make us like white people," he said. "I work in the camps in the winter, do some trapping. Like everybody else."

"It's against the law for us to have guns," Mary said. "I guess they're afraid that we'll go on the warpath." She laughed. The Chippewa had never fought a war with the Americans. They'd preferred negotiation, knowing they'd lose the land either way, but less life if there wasn't an excuse to kill them off.

"How do you hunt?"

"Oh, we have guns. We couldn't survive if we had to obey all their laws. We're even supposed to get a permit whenever we leave the reservation."

The Chippewas had never needed prisons. Now the government put them all in prison. If Sig wanted to think I was French, I'd be French.

"Stay in Winton, Pete," Joe told me. "You know, even Nanaboujou's given up on the Chippewa. When he saw how things were going, he got himself an easy government job working for the BIA."

"Are you going to go ricing at Nett Lake this year?" Mary asked when I left.

"Of course," I said.

Sig and I were up on Kawnipi one time, and he was going on as usual about the glories of living the real man's life out in the wilderness. Usually I didn't pay much attention when he rambled on like that, but all of a sudden I had a vision of my mother kneeling on the rock, dipping water from the lake into her iron pot. My family had often camped on the same site Sig and I were camping on.

"You don't want women here?" I asked.

Sig tipped back his hat and took a puff from his pipe. "Women aren't made for the rigors of the wilderness," he said.

"No children?"

"Boys are okay on short trips."

"No old people?" I thought of my white-haired grandfather playing his fiddle, my father teaching the children to step dance on the cliff.

"The wilderness is a place for men who hunger for action, distance and solitude," Sig said.

Not long ago this country was full of people, a village or a fur post no more than a day's paddle apart. Sig wanted solitude. He could not see the beauty my French grandfather had found in this place, the beauty of people who knew how to get along with each other, who found joy working together, living from creation and protecting each other from its terrors.

"There's more to living up here than paddling and portaging," I said. "It takes skill for a man to provide for others. It's not as simple as paddling through, catching a few fish, maybe shooting some ducks. A man gets his honor by taking care of other people, being generous. That was the Chippewa way."

"What stage of progress did Indians attain? By conquering frontiers, white men created the greatest civilization the world has known," Sig said. He walked to the edge of the cliff and looked out over the lake. "Now we need places like this to reinvigorate ourselves to meet the challenges of civilized life, live like the frontiersman of yesteryear—so we can continue to progress."

I didn't argue. What harm was there in letting a man keep his fantasies?

"Anyway," Sig said, "the Indians couldn't see the beauty here like I can."

One of the first times I guided Sig, we took refuge in a trapping shack during a thunderstorm. There was one like it on every lake, the kind that was thrown together by a couple of guys in a few days, with a little stove and a bed made out of poplar poles and spruce boughs.

"Look," said Sig, "The owner must have left in a hurry. He left his matches and food."

"No," I said. "That's what you do in this country. You leave food and wood for anyone who needs them."

Sig's imagination quickened. "Think of the life this man lived, far from the responsibilities of modern living," he said.

I couldn't tell Sig anything, but I tried to make sure he understood that it was his responsibility to replace the firewood we'd used before we left.

One time Sig wanted me to take him to a lake off the map. I took him up the Maligne River and followed a creek to a little lake.

"Does this lake have a name?" he asked.

"Not on the map," I said.

As Sig stood there, pretending he was an explorer laying eyes on land no white man had seen before, he spotted the cabin.

"This lake's inhabited," he said, with real disappointment.

"Not for a long time," I said.

"Let's go take a look," he said.

"No. Leave it be."

"How come?"

"It's a place of tragedy," I said. "The scene of death."

"Ah, one of your superstitions," Sig said. Since he was in the stern of the canoe, I had little choice when he paddled us over to the cabin.

It wasn't a shack, but a well-made log cabin, though the roof had collapsed and a sapling was growing in the middle. It had been the home of Claude Bouchay.

Claude was married to my mother's sister Nellie. They lived in the cabin during the winter, close to his trapline. My mother worried about them, living by themselves like that.

Claude left Nellie alone with the children while he was checking his traps. Eva was seven, Charlie was five, and Nellie was pregnant with a third child. Something went wrong. The baby came early and Nellie didn't stop bleeding.

Mother said that Grandma could have saved her if she'd been at home in the village.

Eva left Charlie to feed the fire and went to look for her father.

Charlie kept the fire going while his mother died and waited there alone with her body. It was many days before his father came back.

Eva wasn't with him.

They never did find Eva.

Claude brought Charlie back to the village. Claude married again and had other children. All of them died. People said he was being punished. He went to the medicine man, and did what he was told. His next child lived. That was my cousin Mary.

I'd come here often with Charlie and Ira. Charlie said prayers for his mother and sister. Aunt Nellie was a Catholic, so first he prayed for her on her rosary, and then he prayed a Chippewa prayer for the dead.

The door had fallen free of the leather hinges.

86

"Don't go in there," I told Sig, but he didn't listen.

He emerged after a time with a small wooden box and opened it in the sunlight, revealing a tiny pair of soft white rabbit skin moccasins, fur side in, each decorated with three beads.

Nellie had made them for her new baby.

"I'd say that a Frenchman kept a squaw up here," Sig said. "What do you think?"

"I think you should put the moccasins back," I said.

"They'll just rot anyway," he said, putting them in his pocket.

We were paddling home, going around a bend in the Maligne, when I spotted a moose cow with her calf standing near the river bank. I gestured to Sig. He stopped paddling and we drifted by. The cow caught wind of us and lifted her head, a clump of rushes hanging from her mouth. She turned and galloped off into the brush.

"God, there has to be a way to make money off this country," Sig said.

He started an outfitting business in Winton in an old horse barn left over from logging days—Border Lakes Outfitting. Tourists were supplied with grub, packs, canoes, and a guide. That was me or Antti or one of the other guys who'd worked out in the camps.

One day Antti and I took the morning train to Ely to pick up some supplies. We walked past the barber shop.

"I need a haircut," I told Antti, turning back. "You could use one, too."

Antti sat in the chair first. I leafed through a *Field and Stream* magazine while I waited.

"Hey, Antti, there's an article by Sig in this magazine," I said. "About guides. Listen to this. 'As a breed, they are blessed of men, for they live a life more appealing to them than any other occupation on the face of the earth.'"

Antti snorted. "My favorite work," he said. "Wiping the asses of whining tourists."

I read on down the page, "'The longer a man lives away from civilization, the more natural he becomes. Gone is the smooth veneer that makes him acceptable in society, and he is at last an individual with the God-given right to exercise his own free will.'"

"Yah," Antti said. "That's freedom. Go on a camping trip."

"There's more," I said. "'To the true woodsman, the wilderness is always at its best... the motto of the guides in the canoe country is, 'No matter how wet and cold you are, you're always warm and dry.'"

Antti was laughing.

"Jesus, Antti, did you tell him that?"

"It was one miserable trip, rained for days. He started complaining on the second day. So I told him a real woodsman is always warm and dry. I meant a real woodsman knows how to keep himself warm and dry. But you haven't heard him complain about the weather since then, have you?"

Whenever Sig published something after that, the guides passed it around Border Lakes for a laugh. Sig must have thought we couldn't read when he wrote those things—or maybe he didn't care what we thought.

"This is a good one. Listen to this one," Big Art said. "'It was high noon of a breathless day in August when Joe Mafreau, the old half-breed, spotted the magnificent silver black fox and her three pups. In all his years of effort to bring back to the fur trading post a single specimen of the silver black, Joe had been frustrated...' Old half-breed. Must have been talking about you, Pete."

"What were you doing trapping in August, Pete?" Swedstrom asked. Big Art laughed so hard he had to stop reading. Swedstrom took the magazine and read on.

"'He revealed his plans to no one. Jackfish Pete, a renegade Indian, just released from prison, guessed Joe's motives, however.'"

"That sounds more like Pete," Swedstrom said. "Renegade Indian. When were you in prison, Pete?"

I took the magazine.

"'De fines' pup een de worl','" I read. "'Eet ees a shame to put you een a cage wen de woods ees all around. Mebbe who knows, some day you come back to Lac La Croix.'"

"Yup. That's how you talk," Big Art said, and started laughing again.

After Sig put an article in *Field and Stream* about how a person could come up here and find lakes no man had ever seen, we had a new challenge.

"There is one thrill that never grows old," Sig had written. "the thrill of seeing for the first time new land or water. I do not mean water that is new to you only, but new to everyone; a spot of blue that has never been on a fisherman's map, something untried and untouched."

Lots of people read that article, and our customers started demanding to go somewhere no one had been before.

We'd get three or four parties going out at once, each for a week, each wanting to get to a place no one had ever seen.

We consulted each other to make sure that we weren't going to take two parties to enjoy the same primitive view at once. We renamed a few of the lakes.

"I'm going to take these folks up to Unseen Lake," I'd tell Antti. "You better steer your swampies over to Untouched."

Often, when I took a party through Basswood, Old Man Muskrat and his niece Bessie paddled over from the village to give me the news. They enjoyed talking to the tourists.

Sig took me aside after one of those trips.

"I'm getting complaints from customers. They don't like being bothered by Indians."

"It's just Old Man Muskrat and Bessie. We smoke our pipes, talk a little, then they go home. Old Man Muskrat is being hospitable, making visitors feel welcome."

"Well, it annoys the guests. They come a long way to find solitude up here, not be pestered by natives."

I guess you need solitude if you don't know how to be friendly.

Not long after that, government agents came to clear out Old Man Muskrat and the few Indians who were left on Jackfish Bay.

People said Sig was behind it because he was always talking to the government. I asked him, but he wouldn't give me a straight answer.

"It was bound to happen sooner or later," he said. "The Indians are a dying race. They're already corrupted by the white man, and they make people nervous when they hang around. Besides, they net too many fish. They're going to spoil the fishing for sportsmen."

I tried to follow Sig's logic. According to him, Indians were all right if they were stuck in time while everybody else changed, but how could they do that when the land changed, the world changed? If they changed with the times like everyone else, then they were corrupted.

The way Sig had it, Indians were doomed no matter what they did.

It looked like everybody was doomed when the Depression hit. Banks failed, mines closed and lumber camps shut down. Railroad cars rusted on sidings, loaded with logs that rotted away. But there were still plenty of rich people in America who wanted to come up north for a canoe trip. Border Lakes Outfitting did a booming business and Sig built himself a fine house in Ely on Snob Hill, in the darkest days of the Depression. Swedstrom went there once.

"Nice shack," he told us.

By then Jake and Josie were nearly grown, going to school in Ely. They always started school late every fall, after the wild rice harvest, but now that they were in high school I wondered if they would still want to come with me when I went to Nett Lake to make rice.

"You're joking," said Josie. "We wouldn't miss ricing for anything."

We took the train to Tower on a Saturday and waited in front of the movie theater. When the movie was over, out came the Indians.

"Hey, Pete! Josie! Jake! Boujou!" Ira shouted out when he saw us.

"Must be ricing time. Pete shows up," Bessie Waboose teased.

"Good thing, too. We need more pretty girls like Josie over at Nett Lake. You should have come early and seen the show. It was a western," Ben Geshick said.

We walked down to the river where they'd left their canoes pulled up on shore, paddled down to Lake Vermilion and over to the village.

I sat big shot with Ira and Ben in Ben's leaky old birch bark canoe. "We're trying to build a road from the reservation to town, but the government says we can't have one," Ben said. "It's okay to paddle in the summer, and it's not a bad walk over the ice in the winter. But during freeze up and break up, you can't get supplies, can't get to a doctor."

"Why can't you have a road?" I asked.

Ben shrugged. "The government says that isolation protects us."

I laughed. The Indians were always on the go, down to Wisconsin, up into Canada, visiting relatives. Chippewa territory was big country, with cousins all over the place.

Mary and Joe were busy getting their gear together for the trip to Nett Lake. Next day we started out with fifteen canoes. I paddled with Bessie and Old Man Muskrat. Jake and Josie went with the Keewatin kids.

The canoes were packed with babies, old people, teenagers. Dogs raced along the shore. We paddled, shouting and joking across the water, to the place where Chief Wakemup's village used to be on the other end of Vermilion and made the portage to the Little Fork. We followed the Little Fork due west for twenty-five miles and camped overnight before walking the trail to Nett Lake.

Nett Lake was a village of log cabins and tarpaper shacks, like Vermilion. The people who came from Vermilion camped together under the elms and maples.

I stood on the shore, looking out over the vast lake. Across the water, the great bed of wild rice rippled in the breeze, glinting with gold. Maude Waboose and members of the rice committee were out marking ripe patches, sticking tall poles with white flags into the mud. The flags beckoned, fluttering above the gold-green of the rice leaves. From a time beyond history, Chippewa people had made rice here each autumn.

We stayed up late that night, talking around campfires. Little kids sat quietly, drinking in every word of the talk. Jake and Josie laughed with their friends beyond the circle of firelight.

The morning dawned crisp and bright, a perfect day to make rice.

Bessie and I let our canoe drift among the others near the landing, waiting for the dew to dry off the rice, waiting for the signal for the harvest to begin.

I scattered tobacco on the lake. "Migwitch," I said, thanking God for the harvest. Maude waved a scarf. A great roar rose from our throats as we headed out across the lake and into the field of wild rice.

I knocked rice into the canoe while Bessie paddled, thinking of Uncle One-Eye who'd taught me to knock rice. I was careful not to break the stalks, not to shake off the green rice before it ripened, not to knock leaves in with the kernels. I remembered some of his jokes and told them to Bessie, who remembered others. Our spirits were so high we didn't feel our muscles tire.

We paddled back in the early afternoon, to roast the rice we'd harvested. The fragrance of warm, parched rice wafted from the village. Old women stirred the rice in great iron pots. Old men put on new moccasins and danced in the pots, jigging off the husks. Josie worked with Mary and Bessie, tossing rice from birch trays, letting the chaff blow away.

Fires glowed in every yard. We worked steadily through the twilight into the night, murmuring to each other and singing to ourselves while we finished the rice.

Ira came and put his arm around my shoulders.

"It's a good harvest, Pete," he said, and winked. "Looks like we'll be around another year."

Chapter II

My Education: Andy Lahti's First Story

The teacher shouted and shook a ruler at me. I had no idea what she wanted me to do. She looked like she was going to attack if I didn't do it soon. Alma Rautio leaned forward in her seat.

"Repeat the sounds she makes," Alma whispered in Finnish. Alma had learned English at home from her older sisters.

"Ruler," I tried. The teacher nodded and wrote on the blackboard. She held up a book and shouted something else at me.

I wasn't going to cry. I refused to cry. When she let us out at recess, I took off for the river and hid in Antti's boathouse.

Antti found me sobbing under his overturned skiff.

"What's this about?" he asked, picking me up and setting me on a crate.

"You know," he said, when I told him what I was crying about, "I have trouble with English myself. I'll tell you what. You learn English words and teach them to me. I'll teach you trapping. We can trade."

I wanted to trap. I let Antti take me back to school.

By Christmas I'd learned English on the playground from Alma and Jake LaPrairie.

Antti took me with him when he checked his trapline on the river. He showed me where the muskrat lived and how to tell the difference between the tracks of fishers and mink and marten. I learned to read the stories that tracks made in mud and snow, showing where a fox chased a rabbit or a wolf pulled down a moose. Little hopping tracks told of a squirrel traveling from its winter nest to its cache of food, crossing the scurrying tracks of a mouse on an errand.

Antti talked about the days when he trapped with Charlie Bouchay.

"Charlie taught me to farm beaver," Antti said. "You set t
the right distance from the bait so you get just the middle-size
Leave the old sows to breed, and leave the young to grow. I
know a beaver never stops growing?"

We made hoops of birch saplings to stretch the hides. Antti ᴅ.ᴅ ᴀɴ
the skinning at first. If you made one nick in the wrong place, the
hide wasn't worth anything.

Antti ate the beaver meat and wrapped the bones in a little bundle. I asked him why he was so particular about the bones.

"Charlie taught me. If you follow the rules, the game will always
be there."

"Animals know what you do with their bones?" I was skeptical.

Antti looked at the beaver bones he was tying up.

"It's to show respect," said Antti. "That's the first rule. Respect
the life you take."

"The first rule?"

"The first. There are others. Take only what you need to live. Never
waste anything. Be grateful for what you get. Share what you have," he
said.

The rules sounded easy. Practicing them was hard. I had to learn
to understand animals and kill them quickly and cleanly. I had to
check my trapline in howling winds and slushy thaws, never leaving
an animal to suffer. I had to know every hummock and stump of the
territory I trapped. I had to get along with other trappers, because we
depended on each other.

I wanted to quit school and spend all my time in the woods. The
only thing I enjoyed about school was walking there through the
woods, eyes down, reading the ground.

Uncle Arvo and the cows kept me home. I was careful to obey
Uncle Arvo. He had a bad temper and you never knew what he might
do with his dynamite.

He and *Äiti* had planted their first crop around stumps, cultivating
it by hand. After World War I, farmers got dynamite. Boom! Arvo
blasted those stumps right out of the ground. Dynamite was the first
thing he thought of whenever he got riled up.

We had a Model A truck, used to deliver milk to Winton and haul
logs out of the woods. When we weren't going anyplace, Arvo
jacked up the rear wheels and used it as a power take-off for the saw
to make lumber. On Saturday nights, Uncle Arvo, *Äiti* and I crowded
into the front seat and went to the dance at the hall.

One spring when Uncle Arvo and I were making firewood our good frozen winter road started to thaw. As usual, Arvo was pushing it, determined to get into the woods while he could. We were bumping along, low gearing it through the muddy patches, when the truck dropped through the slush up to its axles. Uncle Arvo cursed and rocked the vehicle back and forth, miring it deeper and deeper.

"Let me get the horse," I pleaded. "I'll go harness the horse. He can pull the truck out."

"The hell with the horse!" Arvo roared. Furiously he threw logs off the truck, making a corduroy road over the mud.

"You drive," he ordered, "I'll push."

My feet hardly touched the pedals. I got it in gear. The wheels spun deeper into the muck.

"Useless brat!" Uncle Arvo yelled. He jerked me out of the driver's seat and spun the wheels some more himself, sinking the truck up to its frame.

"Jesus Christ, I'm getting the dynamite!"

I took off running.

"*Äiti, Äiti!*" I screamed all the way to the house. She flew out the door, passed me at a run, and headed up the hill after Uncle Arvo who was already on his way back to the truck with a load of dynamite under his arm.

I sat on the porch steps, breathing hard, hands over my ears, waiting for the blast.

Äiti came back down the hill and went to the barn. In a little while she reappeared with the harnessed horse, and pulled the truck out. Uncle Arvo cursed the logs left in the mud. I gave the horse extra oats.

Evenings after chores I went to Rautio's boardinghouse, where Antti lived with Korva and Jussi—when they weren't out in the woods. They were always willing to teach a kid something useful, like how to whittle a smooth birch handle for a *puukko*. Korva showed me how to carve my own skis, and Antti taught me how to make snowshoes. Jussi tried to teach me how to play the fiddle, but I didn't have the knack.

Alma and Dave Rautio were my age. They were wild kids. Dave did whatever he wanted. Alma was a daredevil. When we were six years old she hung from the timbers under the deck of the railroad bridge while a train rolled overhead. Dave and I chickened out before the train reached the trestle. Alma climbed the tallest trees, dove in rocky places, swam through patches of seaweed, caught snapping turtles. When I competed it made her bolder, like the time we were playing stretch in Rautio's backyard. We threw our *puukkos* into the ground and moved one foot to that point, and did it again. The winner was the one who stuck his knife in the ground the most times before he lost his balance. The idea was to stick it as close to your foot as you could. Alma and I were stretched out to the point of doing the splits when Alma stuck her *puukko* in her leg, right to the bone. Blood flowed down her leg, over her foot, onto the grass.

Alma pulled out the knife without losing her balance.

"Did I lose or do I get another throw?" she asked.

"You get another throw," I said.

After she won the game she stuffed some leaves in the wound and wrapped a rag around it. It kept bleeding through the rag. Mrs. Rautio glanced at Alma when she came out to get the clothes off the line.

"Don't track blood in the house," she said.

Alma and Dave and I were hanging out in front of the Finn Hall, shoving each other and laughing, the Saturday night when Laila first walked up the hill with her mother and sisters.

"There's the new girls," Alma said. Laila was blond and fine and smooth, like something I dreamed of carving out of birch.

I followed her into the hall. *Äiti* looked pleased when I asked Laila to dance. She didn't like Alma.

That night I lay awake, dancing the schottische again and again in my mind, feeling the warmth and suppleness of Laila's body.

The next day I worked at the forge with Uncle Arvo, making knife blades from spring steel. I turned the red-hot steel slowly, watching it glow, remembering my arm around Laila's waist.

"Don't play with fire!" Arvo yelled. "Where's your mind?"

Late that summer Dave and I were fishing from the bridge. "Want to come up to Basswood with me and Alma?" Dave asked me, "Jake's coming, and Frank Makinen, and, oh, did I mention? Laila Keskinen." He grinned.

It was the summer before the ninth grade, before we went to school in Ely. *Äiti* talked to Uncle Arvo, and he let me go.

We canoed around Basswood. One day we camped on a long sandy beach, near Basswood Lodge where Antti was guiding. After we swam and sunned all day, we paddled to the Lodge to visit with Antti and the tourists on the dock.

"Jussi's cooking at that logging camp on Jackfish Bay," Antti told us.

Next day we paddled to Jackfish and Jussi fed us dinner in the tarpaper cookhouse. We sat next to Korva on a bench at a long trestle table. No one talked. When I whispered to Dave, Korva's scowl silenced me. Jussi visited with us while his helpers cleaned up.

"They sure like your cooking, Jussi," Dave said.

"Yah." He sent us off with a bag of giant cookies.

We set up our tents on the site of the old Indian village and sat on the cliff watching the sun set, listening to night noises. The moon rose over the smooth, still water. Laila took my hand and put her mouth close to my ear. "Let's go out on the lake," she whispered.

Warmth rose from the water into the chill air as we paddled to the middle of the bay. I followed the sparkling path of the moon's reflection.

"You can't catch the moon," Laila said. When we pulled the canoe back on shore, she put her hands to my cheeks and kissed me.

On winter nights I walked over squeaking snow in frigid darkness to study with Alma and Laila in the Rautios' sitting room. There was a table, benches along the walls, a couple of ragged upholstered chairs and several large spittoons. Korva sat in his green chair and read while Antti and Jussi played cribbage at the table. From time to time one of them rose to stoke the big wood heater in the center of the room. Korva quizzed us about our subjects.

"They're teaching you militarism and capitalism," he said. "They're teaching you to be obedient soldiers, march right up to the cannons. They're teaching you to work for the companies at starvation wages and never complain while the capitalists get rich."

"In America, a man can be his own boss," I said.

Korva spat his chew into the nearest spittoon.

"Learn to think for yourself, boy, if you want to be a man."

Antti told stories about the logging camps.

"There were rough men in those camps," he said. "One night a new man threw down his bag on the bed next to me. He had black hair, dark eyes, and an ugly scar across the side of his head.

"'That's one ugly Turk,' I told Jussi in Finnish. Next morning when the Turk sat across from us at breakfast, I couldn't take my eyes off the scar. He stared back without blinking. 'Pass the sugar,' he said—in Finnish. He was using a wicked looking *puukko* to cut his pancakes. I thought he looked like a man who might hold a grudge.

"I worked the log drive on Basswood Lake that spring. The logs were held in big booms, waiting to be towed down the lake to the railroad. They were jammed together so tight you could walk across them from one side of the lake to the other. I was walking the logs when I stepped on a piece of loose bark and dropped into the icy water. The logs were packed above my head. There was no way up. Then something gouged into my back and dragged me back into the air. That ugly Turk pulled me through that little hole with his cant hook."

Korva didn't look up from his book. "You never said thank you," he said.

Antti laughed.

Dave didn't study with us. He and Jake LaPrairie were usually out in the woods. Sometimes the truant officer tracked them down.

"I trap to support my widowed mother," Dave said, and the truant officer let him go.

I had a hard time keeping my mind on my schoolwork for daydreaming about Laila. I watched for glimpses of her between classes, ate with her at lunchtime, sat with her on the school bus, danced every dance with her at the hall.

When I went out in the woods with Antti that spring I couldn't concentrate on trapping.

"What's got your mind?" Antti asked.

"Did you ever think about a girl so much that you couldn't think about anything else?"

"So that's the problem. Who's the girl?"

I thought he knew.

"Laila. Laila Keskinen."

Antti shook his head.

"Antti," he said to me, pronouncing Andy in the Finnish way, "You don't know who you are."

"I know who I am."

"What do you know about your father?"

"He died in the strike in 1916."

"That's right. Did they tell you he had two brothers in America?"

"No."

"I'm one of them," Antti said. "Laila's father was the other. You and Laila are cousins."

The bottom fell out of my stomach. Antti was still talking.

"My brother Timo was killed working in the woods before Laila was born. Matt Keskinen raised her as his own. Maybe Laila thinks that she's Matt's child."

"I want to go home right now," I said.

"After we pull in the traps," Antti said. I didn't utter a word for four miserable days before we got back to Winton.

I raged into the house. *Äiti* was at her loom.

"You witch," I shouted. "Did you think that it was a joke, watching me dance with Laila, my own cousin Laila? Why didn't you tell she was my cousin and that Antti was my uncle?"

Äiti shook her head. "It's true I kept it secret that Antti was your uncle," she said. "But I didn't know that Laila was Timo's girl."

I went back to Rautio's boardinghouse. Antti was in the backyard, boiling traps in a kettle over an open fire.

"Why didn't you tell me you were my uncle?" I shouted.

He poked at the traps with a stick. "There was trouble between your father and me," he said.

He sat down on the chopping block.

"I was out in the woods when your mother and Uncle Arvo moved to Winton. The first time I saw you was at the hall, a fat-cheeked little boy. When Mrs. Rautio introduced me to Aina, Aina pretended we had never met. I felt bad because you were my brother's son, but your mother wanted me to be a stranger. Then I found that scared little boy sobbing under my boat. I couldn't walk away."

He should have walked away. Then there wouldn't have been anyone to tell me I could never have Laila.

I went to Laila's house. We walked to the river. Leaning against the rail of the bridge, hunching our shoulders against the icy wind, I told her what I had learned.

There was no expression in her face, smooth as carved birch. She touched my cheek with her mitten.

"That's nice. We can always be family to each other."

Everyone had betrayed me. I lay awake at night fantasizing about Uncle Arvo's dynamite. I skipped school and went into the moonshine business with Jake, Dave and Frank. We set up a still back of the Cloquet Line and drank our own raw whiskey until we passed out.

One evening in early June, Alma and I walked along the river. Frogs croaked in the marsh grass, and a big leopard frog hopped toward the water. I picked up a rock and threw it at the frog to see its guts explode.

"Hey! Quit that," Alma said. "Just because you're mad at the world you don't have to take it out on innocent bystanders."

"Let's go on a trip," I said.

"Want to go to Kashahpiwi?"

"Sure," I said, "Let's see how fast we can get there."

Paddling and portaging like hell didn't take the edge off my anger.

Alma pitched the tent on an island in the middle of long, skinny Kashahpiwi. I used a poplar tree for target practice with my axe.

"Andy!" Alma screamed at me. She stood with her knuckles on her hips. "You've got to quit this!"

I pulled my axe out of the tree and backed up for another throw.

"Look, life goes on," Alma said. "We've been tiptoeing around you, treating you with kid gloves. You're driving everybody crazy, especially Laila, Christ's sake. I'm the only one who can stand to be around you anymore."

"Why?" I said. "Why do you want to be around me?"

"Because," she said.

"Because what."

"Just because."

It was still daylight when we crawled into our sleeping bags.

"Goodnight, Alma," I said.

"I'd do anything for you, if it would make you feel better," she said softly.

Who did she think she was, messing with my rage?

"You'd do anything?"

Alma had never turned down a dare.

"Anything," she said, wary.

"Do you want to heal my wounds?" I whispered. She didn't answer. I unzipped my sleeping bag and unzipped hers.

"Take off your shirt," I said softly.

Alma slowly unbuttoned her shirt, never taking her eyes off mine.

"Take off your pants," I said. She wriggled out of them.

"Panties, too." She took off her panties with the same impassive expression.

I studied her compact, muscular body.

"You're acting like a slut," I said. "Get your clothes on." I rolled over in my sleeping bag and slept.

A squirrel woke me with its chattering. I crawled out of the tent and blinked in the bright sunlight. The food pack and the canoe were gone. All Alma had left behind was my knife, matches and fishing gear.

She'll be back, I thought. There's no way she's going to get that heavy canvas canoe over the portages by herself. She'll get to the first portage and have to come back for me.

I peered down the narrows for a glint of paddle in the sun.

By noon I knew she wasn't coming back. Another party will come through soon, I thought.

Late in the afternoon I started fishing. For six days I roasted fish for breakfast, lunch and dinner. After the second day I gagged on the saltless flesh. My heartbreak and anger paled against the fear that no one would find me.

All day I cast from shore, watching the narrows for the first glimpse of a canoe. From time to time I made myself walk around the island or whittled to pass the time, but I kept coming back to stare down the lake. I ached from the tension. My eyes began to play tricks on me.

I thought I saw a canoe. I thought of the men who went mad from being alone in the woods. The canoe was heading straight for me. As it grew larger I made out two laughing faces—Jake and Dave.

"What made Alma so mad?" Jake asked. I didn't answer.

Alma acted normal when I saw her again, like nothing had happened. We kept hanging around with Jake, Dave, Frank and Laila, going on canoe trips and snowshoe trips. I never told anyone what had happened.

In school, the teachers talked about a great America beyond the woods and lakes, beyond men in ragged overalls who worked on rock farms and in lumber camps, beyond women who spoke Finnish and danced to accordion music on Saturday nights. America, the land of opportunity, was somewhere else.

I went to the university in Minneapolis to find that America. I was in my first year of graduate school when the Japanese bombed Pearl Harbor. I left to work in a defense plant in Seattle.

In the summer of 1942 some of the old Winton gang drove out to see me—Alma, Jake, Laila and her sister Ida. Jake's canoe was on top of the car. They'd launched it in every pothole across the country.

"Nice canoe trip," Jake said, "That portage over the Rockies was rough. Did you hear Dave got drafted? Bet he spends the war in the brig."

We partied for a week, dancing in every place in Seattle, and had a good time in spite of Laila, who insisted on acting like our chaperon.

One night Alma and I, happy and drunk, danced a polka in a bar full of sailors.

"Marry me," I shouted over the noise of the accordion. The next night I won a ring at an amusement park, knocking down wooden bottles with a baseball. I gave it to Alma.

"My engagement ring," she said.

Alma had never backed down from a dare.

We never talked about Kashahpiwi.

Chapter 12

Going Fishing: Ida Keskinen's Story

J ake LaPrairie had that cocky grin, that jaunty walk. He smelled like spruce pitch and pipe tobacco and I wanted him. Jake was eighteen. I was twelve.

Jake ran with my sister Laila's crowd. I was down with his sister Josie.

I figured that I had to be at least fifteen before he'd notice me as anything besides Laila Keskinen's kid sister. All I could do for three years was tag along with Laila whenever I could. Jake was independent as a puma. He quit school when he was sixteen and built himself a cabin on Fall Lake, across the bay from Antti's place. He made his living by outlawing furs, with a little bootlegging on the side, which was the only work that was paying in Winton in the '30s. The men laughed about it.

"Last year trappers were good citizens, then they passed a law, now we're outlaws, doing the same thing we always did."

Prohibition was supposed to save men's souls. It didn't stop anybody from drinking, but it made money for the men who broke the law. Some big-time gangsters from Chicago came through Winton on fishing trips, real dandies with fancy black cars. The operation that Jake ran with Andy Lahti and Frank Makinen was just a small, local business.

The fur laws were supposed to save the beaver, but anybody who went out in the woods knew that there were more beaver than ever, feasting away on the young popple sprouting up where the woods had been cut over. Deer were plentiful too, which was a good thing when there wasn't paying work.

Laws against trapping were good for the trappers because the price of beaver pelts went sky high. Jake never got caught. He was a good trapper, and lawmen weren't as smart as fur-bearing animals.

My father, righteous and God-fearing as he was, didn't expect people to obey bad game laws, but he strongly disapproved of bootlegging. Father was temperance all the way, and thought alcohol was a tool of the devil. But Laila was so pure and virtuous that Father never thought twice when she went off in the woods with her crowd, bootleggers or not, and he thought I was all right if I was with Laila.

On the first long trip I took with Laila's gang, we camped on Jackfish Bay, picking blueberries. The girls picked while the guys hauled full crates to Ely or to the resorts around the lakes. I earned enough money to buy myself a good pair of high-topped, rubber bottomed, lace-up boots. Jake squinted at them with approval the first time I wore them to his cabin.

"Now you're all set to go out on the trapline," he said. "Do you know how to take care of those boots?"

I did, but I let him show me how to rub warm mink oil into the leather.

"Take care of them right, and they'll last forever," Jake said, lecturing like Father.

I was still thirteen. I didn't expect to get his serious attention for two years. At least my feet had stopped growing.

The summer I was fourteen I fished a lot. Antti was on Basswood guiding, so he let me use his wooden skiff. He'd built it himself, Finnish style, narrow at the stern. I rowed from the boathouses in Winton down the river, along the shore past the sandbar, letting my line trail after the boat. I caught lots of fish so no one noticed that my favorite fishing hole was four miles down the lake, in front of Jake's cabin.

When Jake's canoe was gone, which was most of the time, I landed on his shore. Sometimes I went up to his cabin and sat at his table, or lay on his bed, imagining what it would be like if Jake were lying there, too.

I rowed out in early morning through rose-tinted mist when the river was alive with birdsong. The muskrats got so used to my coming and going that they didn't bother to dive when I passed, and the otter mother ceased her scolding.

One day a big wind picked up when I was way down the lake past Jake's place. I turned back to drift with the wind, but then waves washed over the stern of the skiff. I took in my line and started to row the roller coaster waves when Jake's green canvas canoe came around the point, skimming along so fast that he'd soon overtake me.

Inspired, I pulled one of Antti's long, hand-carved oars out of the oarlock and threw it into the lake.

As the canoe drew close I saw my mistake. It wasn't Jake in the stern of the canoe, but Antti, with old one-eared Korva in the bow.

"How'd you lose your oar?" Antti shouted over the wind.

"Big wave," I yelled.

The white-caps rapidly drove me toward the rocky shore.

Antti and Korva came alongside and grabbed my gunwale, but the water was too rough for them to hold the canoe and skiff together. Korva tried to leap into the skiff. As he jumped, a wave caught the canoe, flipping Antti and the packs in the lake. Korva missed the skiff and landed in the lake himself. Antti grabbed a pack with one hand and the gunwale of the overturned canoe with the other. Korva clung to the back of the skiff, and together we drifted to the rocky shore. I could already hear Antti telling the tale on himself—how he got swamped a quarter-mile from his cabin.

We dashed up on sharp rocks lurking below the water. While the men fought to right the canoe, I made my way up the shore to pick up the paddles as they drifted in. When I turned back, Antti was grinning in triumph, waving the lost oar.

"Got a little rip in the canoe and lost a pack. Could have been worse," he said. "I'll never forget the sight of you leaping into the drink," he said to Korva. They sat down on a big rock and laughed until they were out of breath.

Late in August the young people from Winton had a huge bonfire on Mile Island. Both my sisters were there, three of the Rautio kids, Andy and Frank, Josie and Jake, and a dozen others. The hot, dry summer never cooled. We swam in warm velvety darkness after the sun set and sang around the bonfire until the sun came up.

Jake left the bonfire with Helena Rautio. I watched them walk along the water's edge. Jake stopped and pointed to the stars. Helena looked up, tilting her head toward him to catch his words.

Helena was only two years older than I was.

Dave Rautio was sitting next to me, leaning back with his arms around his knees, twig between his teeth. I stood up and pulled at his hand.

"Take a walk with me, Dave," I said. He smiled a friendly, sleepy smile and got up, brushing sand from his pants. We walked up the beach so that Jake and Helena would pass us on their way back.

"What are you going to do when you get out of school?" I asked Dave, making conversation. He shrugged. It was a dumb question. Dave didn't spend that much time in school anyway.

When Jake and Helena passed us, Jake was so absorbed by what Helena was saying he didn't look our way.

Getting Antti and Korva swamped didn't cure me of my fantasies. Somehow I needed to get myself in trouble, preferably during a winter storm, preferably unconscious, so Jake would have to take me to his cabin and nurse me back to health. Unfortunately, Jake knew that I was very capable.

I turned fifteen that winter. Josie and I snowshoed to Jake's cabin early in the morning on New Year's Eve. Jake was out on his trapline. After we got a fire roaring in the stove, we decided to give the cabin a good housecleaning. We hung the bedding out to air, heated up water and washed every dish and pot. I got carried away and scrubbed the floor. We went to bed tired and satisfied.

In the middle of the night Jake burst in, staggered and fell. I jumped out of bed to slam the door against the frigid air that rushed in. I thought he was drunk.

"He's frozen," Josie said, "Help me get his wet clothes off."

We dressed him in dry long johns, sat him by the stove and wrapped him in blankets. He was shaking so badly he couldn't talk, and shook the hot tea we gave him out of the cup. When he thawed a little, the three of us squashed ourselves together on the narrow bed under all the blankets, Josie and I making a warm sandwich around Jake's shivering body.

When I was positive that Jake was asleep, I took his still cold hand and pressed it against my heart.

"I was damn stupid," was all Jake would say when we asked him what happened. "If you guys hadn't had a fire going, I wouldn't have made it." Last year Jake and Andy had found Matti Hekkinen frozen in his bed.

The next day we saw smoke coming from Antti's sauna on the opposite shore. The three of us snowshoed across the bay for a visit.

Josie and I took our sauna first, undressing quickly in the chilly dressing room, our breath fogging the window. We hopped over the frozen floor to the steam room.

The sauna was hot. We sat on the top bench, letting the heat ease into our bodies.

"You like Jake, don't you?" Josie said.

"Can everybody tell?"

"I don't think so."

"Can Jake?"

"I don't think so."

"He won't take me seriously until I'm older."

"You better hurry up and get older then. He's going out with Mary Peterson."

That was bad news. Mary lived above her father's saloon in Winton, open again now that Prohibition had ended. Mary was a party girl with big breasts.

I looked down at my little ones. It looked like the odds were against me.

There was still money to be made in bootleg booze, but that spring Jake branched out his entrepreneurial activities to minnows. He set up minnow traps around Fall Lake, and put in holding tanks at his cabin to catch cold spring water where it ran out of the hill. I saw him in Winton, green canoe on the racks of his beat-up old truck, tanks of water sloshing in the truck bed—peddling his minnows to outfitters and resorts. Sometimes Mary Peterson was in the cab with him. She waved and gave me a cheery smile. Jake grinned his cocky grin.

Laila went to the university in Minneapolis that fall, which meant an end to my winter trips to Basswood with her gang and Jake.

There was no snow that winter. We skated on the river wherever we wanted, avoiding the open rapids.

"Let's skate to Jake's," Josie said one time, and a pack of us did. We traveled four miles up the lake, stopping only to tighten the screws of our clamp-on skates.

Jake thought we were funny. He cooked us coffee and pancakes, and then we skated over to Antti's. Antti had his kick sled out. It was like a chair on long runners. For traction to kick it, Antti had punched holes in a flattened tin can, and bent it so that he could strap it around his boot, pointy spikes down. He stood behind the sled holding on to the back of the chair, one foot on a runner, kicking with the other. We took turns sitting in the chair while Antti pushed us around the bay before we skated home.

"I haven't seen Mary with Jake lately," I said to Josie, when we stopped to tighten our skates on the way back.

"She's going out with some old guy who buys her things," Josie said. "Jake isn't real broken up about it."

That spring Dave Rautio invited me to his senior prom. Everyone was amazed that Dave was graduating from high school. It astonished me that he was going to the prom.

I told Dave I couldn't go because I didn't have the money for a dress, but his sister Alma was home on spring break from the university and she came over to my house to talk me into it.

"What kind of a dress do you want?" she asked. "Come over to my house and we'll fix something up."

She took me upstairs in the boardinghouse, to a room filled with boxes of old clothes and a treadle sewing machine. She pulled out some dresses of silk and satin. I tried to hide my embarrassment at the old-lady dresses.

"Come here," Alma said. She held dresses up to my face. "Royal blue," I think. "Simple and elegant. You aren't the ruffly type. Let me get your measurements."

I didn't know how I was going to get out of the humiliating fate of going to the prom in an old lady's make-over, but when Alma came to see me a few days later, she carefully unfolded a lovely royal blue gown.

"Try it on," she said.

I went into the bedroom to change. The dress had sleek lines and one bare shoulder.

My father looked up startled when I came back into the front room. He turned to my mother.

"Is Ida old enough to wear that sort of dress, Kaija?"

Mother walked over to check the seams.

"You do nice sewing, Alma," she said.

"I want to see what it looks like," I said. Alma got the mirror down from where it hung over the basin in the kitchen, and held it at different levels so I could see myself, one section at a time. The dress was beautiful. It fit perfectly.

"Can I tell Dave you're going?" Alma asked.

"I'm going," I said.

My sister Clara came in.

"Wow," she said. "You'll knock them dead." Clara was going to wear Laila's old prom dress, a frothy pink thing. It suited her.

Prom night was unseasonably warm. Dave borrowed Jake's truck, complete with several dozen minnows swimming around in tanks in back.

"Jake just got off the lake," Dave said when he picked me up. "He's going to deliver these minnows tomorrow."

"I don't mind," I said. I wished I was with Jake in the truck, going someplace more interesting than the prom.

107

The school gym was decorated with streamers and paper lanterns. Dave looked nice in his borrowed suit. He pinned a corsage on my one strap.

"You're pretty," he said. People turned to look at us, whispering to each other. "Look," Dave said, "Everybody is noticing you."

"They're looking at Alma's dress," I said, blushing.

We walked over to Clara and her date, but before we got there, Bernie Stovic asked me to dance. Then George Mattila. Then Tony Marcuse.

"Hey," said Dave between songs, "How about a dance with the guy you came with?"

I danced several with Dave, not letting the other guys cut in.

After the prom we went to a party, and I had some wine. When Dave drove me home, he kissed me before I jumped out of the truck.

First prom, first wine, first kiss. It was a big night, thanks to Alma's dress.

The next Saturday, Bernie Stovic asked me out to a cabin party. Kids were drinking and having a good time, and I got a little tipsy. I made Bernie take me home when he started kissing me.

Next I dated George Mattila, who had his own car. George was a great dancer. Saturday nights we crisscrossed the Range with another couple, dancing at every hall.

When he wasn't dancing, George was dull. He was school-smart, but he couldn't fix a motor, tie a fish net, shoot a rifle, or build so much as a doghouse. He was the least practical boy I'd ever met.

"What are you going to study when you get to the university?" I asked George.

"Engineering," he said.

After George, I went with Tony Marcuse, Elmer Thompson, Eino Paavola, and Henry Lassi.

"You're getting yourself quite a reputation, sister," Laila said. "I'm talking to Father about it."

Father restricted me to one date a month.

I climbed out the upstairs window, slid down the porch roof and went out anyway. Mother caught me coming in at two o'clock one morning.

"You're worrying your father and me to death," she screamed.

"I guess you were never young," I said. "Probably those fanatical people who raised you didn't allow people to be young, like they didn't allow anything else. Deep down in your heart you still think dancing is a sin."

She shut up and I went to bed.

I was looking for a guy who would make me feel like Jake made me feel. I wasn't finding him.

After I graduated from high school, I went to work in Lindy's store. I joked with Jake when he came in for supplies, and I'd tell him what Laila had written in her latest letter from New York. One cold fall day he turned back as he was leaving the store.

"Do you know how to can fish?" he asked.

"Sure," I said. I didn't say that I hated it.

"Want to go whitefishing with me?"

"Isn't Dave..." I began. "Yes," I said. "Yes, I would."

I ran home after work.

"Can I use your pressure cooker, Mother?" I shouted when I ran in the door.

Mother looked bewildered.

"It's for Jake. He wants me to go whitefishing with him and help can the fish."

"Well, for Jake. Of course. You'll need lots of jars, too." She went down in the cellar to gather up empty jars.

My heart jumped when Jake pulled up in front of the house in his battered truck with the canoe on top. We packed the pressure cooker and canning jars into packsacks, and drove to the boathouses. The dark, cloudy day was getting darker but I warmed as we paddled fast down the river, matching strokes, making the canoe surge through the water.

We fed nets into the lake near the shore of Birch Island, and paddled across the lake to Jake's place in darkness. He started a fire and I made supper, feeling as comfortable as if we did this together every night.

"I could get spoiled," Jake said, taking his third helping of *mojakka* and biscuits.

We talked until midnight. Jake unrolled his sleeping bag on the floor and crawled in, and I lay down on his bed, like I always did when Josie and I came to visit. I couldn't sleep, listening to Jake's every breath, close on the floor beside me.

It was still dark when Jake got up to light the lamp and feed the fire.

"Is it morning?" I asked.

"Stay in bed while the cabin warms up," Jake said. I got up and went out on the porch to fill the coffee pot with water. Jake watched while I fried bacon and made pancakes.

"You make good coffee," he said.

"That's because I washed the pot last night," I told him.

There was a skin of ice on Fall Lake. Jake gracefully flipped the canoe into the lake, and we paddled through the crackling ice to the nets.

I paddled in the stern, holding the canoe steady while Jake pulled in nets heavy with whitefish and tulippes. We paddled back following our own trail through the ice.

Jake built a fire on the shore where we warmed ourselves from time to time as we worked to free the fish from the nets. There were at least a hundred.

"What are you going to do with all the fish?" I asked.

"Smoke them and can them," Jake said.

"Can you eat all of them yourself?"

Jake laughed. "I'll send half of them home with you and I'll give most of the rest to Pete and Josie and the neighbors."

I started cleaning fish with my own knife. Jake stopped work to watch with appreciation.

"I've never seen anyone clean fish so fast," he said. I smiled. I had practice the summer I fished in front of his cabin.

"I do have a knack for it," I said.

Jake made a smokehouse from green poles and roofing tins. He lay fish on a rack of chicken wire in the middle, where it slowly cured in the smoke from the alder fire.

"I've always smoked or dried the fish," he said, "but I wanted to try canning them."

"We've canned fish for a couple of years. The extension agent showed us how."

I split the fish and soaked them in brine, drained them, and put them in the pressure cooker. The cooker held five jars at a time, and it took an hour and forty minutes to process a batch.

"It's going to take a lot of time," Jake said.

"It is," I said happily. "Good thing it's cold. The fish will keep until we get them in the canner."

At home canning was an ordeal, but Jake cheerfully told stories and made jokes while we worked so the day went fast. After a supper of sausage and boiled potatoes, I lay down on the bed for a minute to rest before I washed the dishes.

I woke to the sound of Jake shaking down the ashes and opened my eyes to the beautiful sight of a table covered with jars of canned fish.

"The last batch all sealed," Jake said. "You were asleep the minute you hit the bed last night."

"Thanks for covering me up. How are we doing?"

"We're about half way through."

That day we worked together even more easily than the first.

"It's too late to paddle back," Jake said, taking the last batch out of the canner that evening. "I hope you don't mind staying another night."

I didn't. I lay awake a long time, listening to Jake's even breathing, thinking of the time I lay beside him and pressed his hand to my heart.

The next morning we fell into our routine. I started breakfast, and went out for water. When I came back, Jake took the coffee pot out of my hands and set it on the stove. He grasped me by the shoulders, pulling me to his chest.

My cheek pressed into the rough wool shirt. I smelled spruce and woodsmoke, heard the thumping of Jake's heart.

"Do you have to go home today?" he asked.

"No," I said. I was home.

Chapter 13

Dark Water: Helena Rautio's Story

I sat on the dock near the wash houses. The river swirled around the pilings. Cold and black, it whispered, "Slip in, just slip in, slip in." How easily I could slide off the dock. One cold shock—then numbness, then nothingness.

How does such misery come from such joy? How does such sin come from love?

I fell in love with Bill the first time I saw him step off the launch. He had come from Chicago with his family to stay at Maple Isle on Basswood where I was a cabin girl.

It was a wonderful summer. When we weren't working we Maple Isle kids would get together with the kids from other resorts—guests and help alike. We had swimming parties and canoe races. We picked blueberries on Jackfish Bay. Every night we had a bonfire somewhere on Basswood and sang. After the parties Bill and I paddled home to Maple Isle in the still nights, when the sky and lake became a huge starry bowl.

Just before he went home to Chicago, Bill asked me to marry him. He said we would wait until I finished college. I said yes.

I said yes. When he slipped his warm hand under my jersey top I only thought of how much I loved him, how I would miss him when he went back to Chicago, how long it would be before we could marry. When he pressed himself against me, I said yes, again.

When I wrote to tell him that I was in trouble and that we had to get married soon—now, Bill said no.

It was just a summer thing, he wrote. He'd met someone else. He wouldn't be back to Basswood.

The dark water swirled under the dock, inviting me in.

There was nothing my mother feared more than scandal—a widowed woman with four daughters, running a boardinghouse for bachelors. It was better to die than bring shame to my house.

"Just slip in," the river whispered.

There was one other choice. Frank. I almost laughed. Frank adored me. Sometimes I went to dances with him because I felt sorry for him, but his awkwardness embarrassed me. Did he love me like I had loved Bill? Had I made him suffer like Bill made me suffer?

Would Frank still want me, as I was?

The cold October wind cut through my coat. The water beckoned, but I turned my back on the river and walked up the alley past the public sauna.

Just that morning, Prof Eller had praised my essay in English class. He asked if I would go on to the university after junior college. I told him I'd planned to.

"I hope you'll be an English major, Helena. You have a real gift with language." He must have wondered why I ran away in tears.

No one has ever been as wretched as I, I thought, walking up the hill past Kivipelto's house, where the curtains were always kept tightly drawn. Were they closed to shut out the troubles of the world, or to keep others from spying on the troubles within? Both Mr. Kivipelto and Mrs. Kivipelto drank. Mrs. Kivipelto stayed in bed under the covers. Scared, thin little Eila was trying to raise her two brothers. Her father beat her whether he was drunk or sober.

I turned my head away from the Kivipeltos'. Across the street I saw Mrs. Maki's shadow on the upstairs curtain as she bent over the crib. She was tucking in her baby, the baby who would never grow up, who would never even call her Mama. I could see Mr. Maki though the downstairs window. He was smoking his pipe, rocking by the oil heater. Mr. Maki gave peppermints and nickels to the village children—the ones who could run and play and speak.

There was Ida's house. What would she have said if I told her my trouble? I couldn't even tell her. They had their own troubles in that house. Her father's frostbitten feet had healed badly. He limped along, always in pain, and now he had a bad heart, besides. Her mother was thin and tired from working too hard, taking in wash and mending for the old bachelors who lived in the boardinghouses.

I passed our big boardinghouse, weathered gray, where Mother raised five children by herself and looked after the boarders. Timid Jussi would never see his daughters again. Antti would never find a wife. Korva was always looking over his shoulder, never at peace.

Ultrikka lived up the street. She came from Finland with a husband and three sons. Now she lived alone, sewing for strangers, thinking of the people she loved who were far away.

Were all Finnish people cursed? Wasn't there a house without trouble along that street?

I walked past the houses of the others, the people of the other tongue. The Petersons. Mrs. Peterson had lovers call when Mr. Peterson worked night shifts at the mine.

What of the Ordstroms? Mrs. Ordstrom's only baby was born dead, over fifteen years before. She kept a tidy house, went nowhere, and wept for her dead baby every day.

Mr. Whitehead couldn't work, and his children were getting thin. The Holmquists hadn't spoken to each other in anyone's memory. When they drove to church, Mrs. Holmquist rode in the back seat.

Lydia Markon, the spinster, lived with her parents. She was engaged once, but her fiancé drowned. She buried him on their wedding day.

Mrs. Orloff went insane and her husband raised eight children alone. Henry Thompson was sent to prison for killing a man and his parents lived with grief and shame. Jenny Brown, young mother of three, was dying of cancer.

I had never looked at Winton this way before. There was the LaPrairie house. Pete had raised his brother and sister after the rest of the family died.

I had joined the suffering brotherhood. Only mercy could save me. Mercy and love.

Would Frank have mercy? Could he love me as I was?

When he saw me there, standing at his door, he beamed with pleasure.

I prayed. Please God, let Frank have mercy.

Chapter 14

The Big Wedding: Clara Keskinen's Story

Published in Jarvenpa, A. & M.G.Karni (eds.) *Sampo, The Magic Mill: An Anthology of Finnish American Writing*, New Rivers Press. 1989.

Jussi and Korva were patching the roof of Rautio's boarding-house. Jussi began to slide and bumped into Korva. Korva grabbed him around the middle, and in a great bear hug the two men rolled off the roof, knocked over the ladder, crashed through the scaffolding, fell three stories and landed in a pile of sawdust. They lay still for a minute, then slowly rose. Korva knocked the sawdust from his pants.

"Jesus Christ, Jussi," he said. They set up the ladder and climbed back on the roof.

I saw it all from the railroad tracks. I'm not going to marry a Finn, I thought.

Mama often said to Papa, "Matt, you're a rare man." That was probably true, and he was certainly a rare Finn.

What were the others like?

Einard Saari was the most timid man in the world. If he went up the lake for the weekend and the weather was splendid Friday night, he decided to start right back home because there might be a storm on Sunday.

There was Eino Wirtala. If you said to him that it was a beautiful day, or look! the bluebirds are back, or the Sippola's have a new baby, he said, "Yah, yah."

If Aina Lahti walked to town pulling a wagon with four full milk cans and her brother Arvo drove by in his new Chevy coupe, he wouldn't stop to give her a lift. Wouldn't even slow down for the dust.

Then there were the drinkers. Finns are never happy drinkers like Slovenians and Italians. They sit and drink in silence until they are drunk, and then they weep or start a fight. One or two in town didn't dare fight a man so he went home and beat up his wife. Then the other men beat him up.

Mrs. Tuurila shored up her front porch with big timbers. Mr. Tuurila stood by and watched. "Hurry up, dinner will be late," he said.

Legend has it that a Finnish man once loved his wife so much that he almost told her.

Why should I marry any of those men who put salt in their coffee?

Rose Stepanovich invited me to her house for Christmas Eve. Rose and I were friends in junior college.

"Christmas Eve?" I asked her. Christmas Eve was a quiet time at our house. We ate lutefisk and lit the candles on the tree. There's a little more life at Rautio's boardinghouse where the boarders go out drinking. Usually they bring home some stray drunk who sleeps it off in front of the stove on Christmas morning.

I never heard of anyone giving a party on Christmas Eve. Mama was disappointed because Laila had come home and thought we should all be together, but I went to Rose's house anyway.

It was an odd party, kind of an open house. The six Stepanoviches were out visiting everyone they knew, and everyone they knew was visiting the Stepanoviches. Rose and I went down the street for a glass of wine and baked treats, and when we checked back at the Stepanoviches' house, it was full of guests but no hosts. No one cared. Everyone was having a good time. Rose's brother Sam broke off from a bunch of guys and started hanging out with Rose and me. We caroled all the houses in McKinley Location. Sam and Rose drove me home after midnight mass.

Mama was waiting up. She looked worried when I said good night and stumbled up the stairs.

Sam came over the day after Christmas. I introduced him to Mama and we sat in the kitchen, talking about our teachers at the college and drinking coffee. Sam kept looking at me and grinning for no reason at all.

"Do you want to go out with me on New Year's Eve?" he asked.

"Go where?"

"To the dance at the Community Center."

I stopped to consider, but just for a minute. I had planned to snowshoe up to Basswood with Laila and her gang.

"I'd love to go to the dance with you, Sam."

That's how it started. We were still seeing each other when Laila came home for Easter. She was alarmed.

"Clara, are you getting serious about Sam?"

"He's more fun than anyone else I've gone out with."

"What does his family think?"

"His folks are nice enough."

"They probably hope it's just a passing fancy. Mama is worried, you know."

"What should Mama worry about? It's not like I'm behaving like Ida."

Laila let my reference to our younger sister pass.

"Clara, the Stepanoviches are Catholic."

Of course I knew. I said nothing.

"How serious are you, Clara?"

"I'm serious."

"Will Sam leave his church?"

"No."

"Will you convert?"

"I don't know."

"You'd better know. Can you go to Latin Mass, give up meat on Fridays, raise your kids Catholic, never use birth control?"

"I've been thinking about it."

"You'd still be an outcast in both churches."

"Laila, I've been thinking about it."

I thought about it. And then, for Sam, I decided yes. Mama and Papa took it well. Better than Laila had thought.

We told Sam's folks that we wanted to get married. We explained that I would become a Catholic. His mother tried to talk us out of it. She said that kind of mixing wouldn't work. We argued, and finally one day she threw up her hands and said, "Well, then you be my new daughter." She walked across the kitchen, grabbed me by the shoulders and kissed both my cheeks.

Father Petrovich was more skeptical.

"You convert to Catholicism not from the heart but for the boyfriend," he said.

"It is my heart's deepest desire to please God and to please my husband."

Father Pete taught me the catechism and converted me.

The hard part came next.

Sam and I got his folks together and explained that we would have a quiet, private ceremony.

"That's not a real wedding," said Mother S.

"Sam is our first child to marry. We've looked forward to his wedding since he was born," added Pa S.

"Clara's folks can't afford a wedding," said Sam.

"How not afford a wedding! Once in a lifetime!" said Pa.

"I really can't ask them. They have troubles now," I said.

"I've heard about you Finns. You think a big wedding celebration is drinking black coffee in a green church basement. No. My son and my daughter will have a first-class wedding."

Laila was my maid of honor. I had five other bridesmaids. I wore a beautiful gown of lace and satin with a full train. The whole town drank and danced for three days.

We'll be paying off the loan for years to come.

It was worth every penny.

Chapter 15

Army Scout: Dave Rautio's Story

T he game wardens were on the lookout for me and Jake La-Prairie, so in early spring we cached our winter's supply of beaver pelts on Basswood. Late in the summer, we took a canoe trip just like other folks, fishing for bass in dark pools under deadfalls along the shore, trolling for northern across the mouths of bays. In the evening we camped on the point where we'd stashed the pelts, fried some fish and turned in for the night.

Jake roused me from sleep.

"Listen," he whispered.

At first I only heard the wind in the pines and an owl's cry, but when I strained my ears I heard a paddle dipping in water, little waves slapping against the hull of a canoe, the canoe scraping against rock.

We crawled from our sleeping bags and unzipped the tent door one notch at a time. In starlight we crept along the cliff until we saw the wardens unrolling their sleeping bags in darkness. We watched them lay the bags across the path that led to our cache. We stood there motionless until the wardens lay still in sleep before we returned to our camp. Silently, we struck the tent and packed our gear. I put the canoe in the water, planning to take off and abandon the pelts, when Jake signaled to me to follow him down the path. We stepped over the sleeping wardens. In darkness we found our cache, took two heavy packs of beaver pelts apiece and walked back over the wardens. By the time they woke up we were safe on Fall Lake.

Old Antti Lahti had taught me the patience and skill that he'd learned trapping with Charlie Bouchay. After there were wardens and limits Antti kept trapping Charlie's way and paid the fines when he got caught. Jake and I made sport of teasing the wardens. Being a good poacher took as much patience and skill as being a good trapper.

The government put a lot of effort in protecting those rodents from me and Jake but we never got caught with a single beaver pelt. The only time the government kept me from trapping was when it drafted me to go overseas to kill men. Men were not as valuable as beavers.

Jake predicted I'd spend the duration of World War II in the brig, and he would have been right if the army hadn't made me a scout. Scouts didn't have to follow orders or regulations.

When I got to boot camp, they gave me a questionnaire about how much experience I had in the woods, which led to an interview, after which I ended up in a special training camp with eighty other guys. General Timberlake locked all of us up in a bunker overnight, with orders to find ourselves a partner by morning.

"No questionnaire can tell me how to pair you up with the man your life depends on. You'll have to find him yourself," Timberlake said.

We milled around for a while before we separated into clumps. One group would be talking loudly, making big gestures; another huddled together talking in whispers. I kind of liked one man, last name of Anthony, who was a state wolf trapper from Idaho. When I turned around to look for him in the crowd, he was following me. We were together two and a half years but I never learned his first name. I called him Tony.

When we got to Germany, our job was to scout ahead of the lines and figure out where they could move the big guns. There were four big guns—90 millimeter anti-aircraft guns, with a command post that we were to keep moving forward. Then there were worthless 40 millimeter guns that were too small to shoot down airplanes and too big to aim at soldiers. They just kept the sky orange at night. The 50 caliber guns were the outposts that were set up in front of the big guns to keep them from being taken out by German troops. Altogether there were five companies that we scouted for.

The general himself couldn't say move forward until Tony and I said okay. That choked some of the officers and they'd go out of their way to make trouble for the scouts. Smart officers made the most of a guy's talents. One guy in our outfit liked to sneak out at night and take out pillboxes by himself. Instead of court-martialing him for going AWOL, his commander made it official. Same with the guy that liked to sneak up on a double patrol and just kill one German to make them nervous.

Where I was in Germany looked like northern Minnesota. There were deer in the woods like Minnesota deer.

It didn't take long for Tony and me to figure out that there was a difference between a German in an SS uniform and the peasants in the villages with their gardens, geese and cows. They knew there was a war going on, but I don't think they knew what it was about. One time Tony and I were pinned down near a village that the Americans were strafing. An old man motioned to us to come into the root cellar with his family. It was a hard choice, but we went. We sat there for a couple of hours looking at the Germans and them looking at us until the American planes were gone, and then we left.

Our enemies were the elements, the German army, and the American army. I made it through the war without getting clobbered because of the practice I had ducking the game wardens back home.

The first animal I shot over there was a wild boar. This old German woman came running up, crying, begging me to follow her. We'd been warned that the Germans would try to entice us with women and kill us when we got in the house, but I didn't think they'd send an old woman to entice a soldier, so I followed her. There was a huge boar rooting up her garden.

When I shot it she gave a big yell and her neighbors ran out of their houses with butcher knives. In a couple of minutes all that was left was hair.

I made good friends with one German family. Otto Dietrich had been teaching school in England when the war broke out, so we could talk. Domestic meat was scarce for the peasants because everything was taken for the army. The woods were full of deer and those wild pigs but German peasants were not allowed to hunt and had no guns. The upper class, who hunted, were all officers in the army, away making war. Wild boars were becoming a menace.

Otto was so law abiding that if his children were starving to death, there was a boar tearing up his garden, and he had a gun in his hand, he wouldn't have shot the boar. Tony and I were happy to hunt for Otto and his neighbors. The Depression had taught us that you had to break the law if you wanted to survive.

We hunted fresh meat for the army, too. An officer ordered us to deliver fresh meat only to commissioned officers. When we ignored him and brought in pork and venison for the enlisted men, Lieutenant Brown took away our ammunition. We got more, kept it stashed in the woods, and brought the men their meat. You can't stop an out-law in a just cause.

One time when Tony and I came back to camp with some venison, everybody was dead. That was the Battle of the Bulge. The Germans had cut off the bulge in the American line of advance and mowed everyone down. Tony and I had to get back to the U.S. Army. We were crossing a fresh battlefield covered with dead Americans when a company of Germans came through the woods, so I crawled under a corpse and flung his arm over my head. The German soldiers walked around, picking things off bodies. One flopped the corpse I was under over and kicked him, stepped over me and moved on. The Germans made camp at the edge of the fresh battlefield. Tony and I didn't dare move. At night the wild boars came out and ate dead soldiers, rooting and grunting, ripping up the carcasses. They pawed and nosed me before they moved on. That's where I got my terror of pigs.

Tony and I knew how to wait. I lay in that battlefield through the night, imagining that I was at home in the woods, waiting for the dawn and the deer. At the first hint of dawn we started walking west. We didn't dare travel at night because we were afraid we'd walk into a German camp. We walked along major roads in broad daylight, about 300 yards away, out of rifle range. The whole German army was on the move, tanks and men rumbling along.

One night Tony and I took shelter in the cellar of a bombed out house. Germans came and camped above us.

Thump thump.

We listened to their boots for two days, and waited another day before we dared come out. You would think we'd learned our lesson about cellars, but one miserable, sleeting night we took shelter in another one.

We heard it again. That thump thump.

We waited three days before we came out to give ourselves up. All we found was dead apples, fallen on the ground. We watched them drop out of the tree. Thump thump.

We walked from December 18 to January 1. We shot and ate fresh venison on Christmas day.

We were nearing the American lines when we were captured by Americans who thought we were German spies. When we were inter-rogated, neither Tony nor I could answer questions about U.S. sports, or radar. When we finally convinced them that we were Americans, they wanted to court-martial us as deserters. How else could we be alive when the rest of the men in the companies we scouted for were dead?

Tony figured they'd believe us at the court-martial, but I didn't have his faith in army justice. We were standing in line for mess one day. Things were pretty disorganized.

"Come on," I told Tony. "Let's get out of here." We walked away, and walked along American lines like we had walked along the German roads until we came to another command post.

"Okay," I told Tony, "Let's try again." This time the officer we turned ourselves in to believed us, and we were back in business.

After the Battle of the Bulge, some Americans went insane, like the GI who kept shooting dead soldiers after a battle.

Tony and I always scouted ahead of the front lines, so we were the first to find some of the little prison camps. The first one we liberated was for female Polish resistance fighters. We smelled it a day and a half away. Our first sight was skeletons hanging on the electric fence. There were no sewer facilities, no water. The camp guards hated that women would fight. They shot them in the crotch. I couldn't believe that anyone could still be alive, but some were. They looked like corpses but their eyes moved.

Near the end of the war I was guarding a battlefield at night and I saw a figure skulking among the corpses. I called for him to identify himself. When he ran, I shot him. It turned out he was a U.S. soldier, picking gold out of the teeth of the dead GIs. That's when I got court-martialed. Luckily they said not guilty, because the penalty was death. That was the closest I came to getting killed in World War II.

I haven't seen Tony since we got separated from the army in 1945.

In 1946, I had a son. I named him Anthony.

Chapter 16

Getting Trapped: Alma Rautio's Story

F ather swung his bottle at Dave. It glanced off the side of his head, knocking him to the floor. I dragged Dave out the door, screaming at Father to stop. Father staggered after us and threw the bottle, but Dave got on his feet in time to duck. I grabbed his hand and we ran up the hill.

"Hey, hey, what's all this?" Antti said. "What's this crying about?" He and Korva were coming from the tavern. He knelt down to get a good look at the blood on the side of Dave's head.

"Not deep," he said. Dave kept howling. He was three.

"So, you want to come on a trip with me and Korva?" Antti asked him. Dave shut his mouth and opened his eyes.

"Can we really come with you?" I asked.

"What use would a little girl be in the woods?" Korva said.

"The wardens will think that we're taking a nice family canoe trip," Antti said. "It will look like Father and Uncle with the kids."

"As if the wardens don't know us," Korva said.

"Not from a distance. Two little heads in the middle."

It was early summer. Dave and I sat on packs of pelts in the middle of the canoe, skimming along in the northern night. Every star was reflected on the smooth surface of Lake Insula. The only sounds in the great stillness were the tiny splashes of the paddles dipping into the water and the occasional hoot of a far off owl.

After that trip, Mother often asked Antti to take us, and Dave and I tried to learn everything Antti knew about the woods.

One day we nearly stumbled over a new fawn, almost invisible where she lay in the dappled sunshine. Dave kneeled and reached forward to pet it. Antti grabbed his hand.

"You mustn't disturb wild animals," Antti said. "If you do, the mother will abandon her baby." When I was eight and Dave was seven, we thought we knew enough to go out by ourselves.

We were packing for a trip when Sig Olson came by to pick up the little sacks Mother sewed for his outfitting business.

"You let them go alone?" he asked.

"They can take care of themselves," Mother said, her foot keeping rhythm on the treadle of the sewing machine.

We lived in the big boardinghouse next to the railroad tracks. Most of the boarders had moved away so Mother took in wash and sewing. In the summertime she cooked for the resorts and sometimes she took care of a family when the mother was sick, leaving one of my sisters to care for me and Dave and baby Helena. Mother was always tired. We never had any money. There was food on the table because Korva and Antti brought home meat and fish but we wore clothes the neighbors gave us when they were too ragged, even for them. Mother turned the cloth inside out, cut them down and kept us dressed.

Our life got better when Father died.

"Tarmo was a good man," Mother said at the funeral. "He was a good man when he wasn't drinking."

Maybe it was true. I never saw him when he wasn't drinking.

"You have to learn to take care of yourself," Mother often told me. "Never expect anyone to take care of you."

When I was fourteen, I lied about my age and got a job cooking for a boys' camp on Moose Lake.

Dave trapped and made moonshine. Mother didn't make him go to school. I didn't like going to school any better than Dave did, but Mother was strict with me.

"A man can always get work, but a girl needs an education. You have to get a job that pays something when you need to support your children."

My sister Helena loved school. She'd sit with her nose in a book on a bright sunny day. I'd rather haul water from the river to the wash shed out back, split kindling, weed the garden—anything outdoors—than do homework. But I thought of Mother, struggling to raise her kids, Father stealing money from her purse to buy booze. I wanted to take care of myself. I stuck with school until I graduated, and then I went to junior college because it didn't cost anything.

Sig Olson was the first teacher who ever liked me. He taught biology at Ely Junior College. I liked learning the scientific names for things that I saw in the woods. I knew some by Finnish names, and a few by the Chippewa names Antti had taught us, but we had no name at all for many of the plants. It gave me a new feeling about school.

"What do you plan to study at the University?" Sig asked.

"I want to be a wildlife biologist," I said. "I want to work outdoors."

"Well, maybe you could be a biology teacher," he said.

When it was time to go to the university, the ladies in Winton gave me their old clothes. I sewed all summer, making myself pretty dresses with bows and ruffles.

I had never been beyond the Iron Range before. I walked across the university campus, awed by the stately buildings with their Greek columns, and the orderly walks with their canopies of elm.

I realized people were staring at me. At first I felt proud, thinking that they were admiring my pretty dress, but then I saw that the other girls were dressed in woolen skirts, sweaters and saddle shoes, nothing like the fancy dresses I had made.

I should have known better. I should have looked at fashions in magazines, but we didn't have magazines.

My adviser looked at my navy silk.

"Where did you get your dress?" she asked.

"I made it," I said.

"You have a real knack for sewing, don't you? Have you considered a major in home economics?"

"I want to be a wildlife biologist," I said.

"There's a demand for home economists in extension work right now. I don't think there are any jobs for wildlife biologists."

I majored in home ec, with a minor in biology.

Laila Keskinen and I roomed together in a house, sharing a common kitchen with other girls. The landlady was crabby and nosy and kept us to a strict curfew.

We were hicks. Even walking into a department store was an education. It seemed like Laila and I were the only poor girls on campus, and the only Finns we knew. Laila was majoring in elementary education. In my home ec classes, they taught us arts for the home. I learned about taste and design. Furniture had names, like Duncan Phyfe; there was a proper way to arrange flowers; and every home should have a set of good china, silver and crystal.

I worked as a teacher's assistant for my tuition, but it was a year before I could afford a sweater or saddle shoes, which I bought with wages I earned cooking at Maple Isle Resort over the summer.

The other girls in home ec brought their lunches and ate together in the fireplace room. They never invited me to join them until I was a senior, after I showed up in a skirt and sweater. I couldn't afford lunchmeat so I sliced up cold oatmeal and put it between two slices of bread to look like a salmon sandwich, and then I ate with the other girls.

I worked for Miss Weisman. She had been a director for the WPA project in Milwaukee under President Roosevelt, and she was kind to me.

"I was a poor girl when I went to college, too," she said. "It was humiliating. But when you go home, you can teach other girls what you've learned so they'll never have to go through the shock you went through when you came here."

I got a job teaching home economy in Cook, Minnesota, to poor Finnish girls. The WPA project supplied the home ec department with materials so we had beautiful examples of draperies, table linens, china, silverware and crystal. I taught the girls how to put on teas and dinners. I collected nice woolen things for the girls to re-make following the fashions in the latest magazines and we had style shows. I let them borrow my clothes. One time I loaned my best velvet to a girl for the winter frolic. It came back ruined, but the girls had a very, very happy time.

I liked teaching, but the county offered me a better job as a home management supervisor, demonstrating new methods of growing and preserving food in the communities. The government was trying to help people feed themselves through the Depression.

But most of what I taught as a home management supervisor was the home economy I had learned from my mother in the boarding-house, the art of making something from nothing, stretching little to go far. Make the potato peels as thin as possible, or better yet, don't peel the potatoes at all. Use all the animal when you butcher. Make soup from stock, gravy from the juices. Never waste, never throw anything away. Make quilts from scraps, rugs from rags.

I was happy. With my first paycheck I bought a nesting kit and a good sleeping bag. Then I got myself a car and a canoe. I was back in the north and every chance I had, I was back on the water.

When Laila came home on summer vacation, we took a long trip over to Insula, along with her sister Ida and Jake LaPrairie.

We lay on a sandy beach, watching fluffy June clouds form and reform themselves overhead.

"Let's buy Matt Hekkinen's cabin," I said. It was a small log place on the roadless side of Fall Lake.

Laila sat up.

"Our own cabin!" she said. "It's got a real nice beach. What a great idea. It'll be a place where the whole gang can get together when they come home."

We each paid twenty-five dollars and the cabin was ours.

Life was perfect. Then I married Andy.

I thought I knew him. We grew up together in Winton.

"You smell like pines," he whispered in my ear when we danced in Seattle. "Your eyes are as blue as Basswood in October."

Johnny was born in Seattle. Andy was jealous of him, a tiny baby, his own son. I didn't dare leave the baby alone with him.

It's because we're out here, so far from home, I thought. Andy worked long hours at the plant. Things will be all right after the war. But Andy didn't want to go home after the war.

There was a job in Winton, running the Co-op store.

"Why would I want to go back to that dump?" Andy said. "There's no future there."

He got a job in business in Minneapolis and bought a fine brick and stucco house in a good neighborhood. He wanted me to entertain his business associates.

"Put that stuff you learned in college to some use," he said. "Get a return on your investment in education."

In late spring, I took Johnny to Winton on the train. He was delighted when I brought him to the cabin. Everything fascinated him. He watched a furry caterpillar for hours. He compared the different shapes of basswood and poplar leaves, tracing around their edges with a stick in the sand. He learned which berries were good to eat, and found the place where you could dig pure clay out of bank above the shore. He made ingenious little creatures from the clay, and peopled the cabin with them. We pressed designs on birch bark with the sharp end of a can opener, and decorated the cabin with driftwood and princess pine.

In the early morning, we walked silently through the woods, stopping and waiting for the tiny noises of snapping twig and crunching leaf that let us know an animal was near. Johnny laughed out loud at the lumbering porcupine and chattered back at the scolding red squirrel.

"How can you leave your husband?" my mother asked me. "Your job is to take care of your man."

I went back. The brick and stucco house was a prison.

"You call yourself a home ec major?" Andy shouted. "You can't even keep your house clean. You don't even brush your hair in the morning. Have you ironed my shirts?"

He was gone most of the time, taking business trips, working late. I sat in the house, looking at mounds of clothes to iron. I was dying.

In September I ran away, back to the cabin. Johnny and I sat under the great white pines up the hill from the dock looking at the water below, taking comfort from the scent of the needles and the sound of the wind. We were there four days before Andy knew we were gone and came to get us.

I went back to Winton in December. I got Johnny little snowshoes, and we crossed the lake in a snowstorm. We stayed a week before Andy came.

Andy kept close watch on me in the spring because I was pregnant. He wanted a baby girl. He bought frilly baby dresses and lacy nighties. He was so obsessed with the idea of a daughter that I thought he would kill the child if it were another boy.

Just before I was due in July, I took the trolley to the train depot. I didn't go to see Mother when I got to Winton, just went straight to the Co-op for groceries, put them in a pack and went to the boathouses. I borrowed Antti's old green skiff and rowed down the river. Johnny sat quietly with a shining face, looking at cattails and redwing blackbirds, clapping his hands as the great blue heron rose from the reeds.

We had been at the cabin two days when I went into labor. When my body labored for a day and there was no baby, I grew afraid.

"We're going to paddle to town now," I told Johnny, dragging the old canvas canoe down to the water.

"I want to go swimming," he said.

"Get in the canoe right now!"

I set him in the front seat, added weight to the bow and launched us into the bay. Johnny paddled well for a four-year-old. We did fine until we passed the point, when we came out of the lee into whitecaps. Johnny had no strength against the force of the wind and I was exhausted from my contractions. We turned back toward shore.

I'd just made it back to the cabin when Antti came up the path.

"Thought I saw some life on this shore," he said. "How are you doing?"

"I'm in labor."

I'd never seen Antti look anxious before.

"I'll get you to town," he said.

He made me lie in the middle of the canoe and sat Johnny on the bottom in the bow. It was a rough trip across the lake. When I climbed out on the opposite shore we both threw up.

There were roads to the cabins on the south shore of the lake. Antti brought me to a place where the man had just bought himself a new car.

He regarded me with alarm.

"Oh, I don't think that... I mean, my car doesn't..."

Antti gave him a look.

"Yes, yes of course I'll take her to town," he said.

We made it to the hospital. Emily was born in the hallway.

Andy drove up from the city. He was ecstatic to have a daughter. We brought her home to the boardinghouse in a laundry basket. Johnny sat next to the basket in the back seat.

"She's smiling at me," Johnny said. I looked over my shoulder. Johnny's face was close to hers, and Emily clutched his finger.

"Get away from that baby!" Andy slammed on the brakes, whipped around and slapped Johnny on the side of his head.

Andy had to get back to Minneapolis right away. There was a big deal in the works, he said, and real money was at stake.

"You come back as soon as you can travel," he told me. "I'm not supporting you so you can spend your time playing at the lake."

"Your duty is to your husband," my mother said. "Do what he says."

What choice did I have? When I recovered from the delivery, I took the train to Minneapolis to the brick and stucco house where I ironed Andy's shirts and cooked his dinner, when he was home.

But I left Johnny and Emily with Mother in Winton, in the old boardinghouse next to the railroad tracks where I was raised.

Chapter 17

After the Hall: Johnny Lahti's Story

I didn't mean to snoop. I thought Korva was in his room. I stepped through the open doorway and saw the knife lying on his table. I went closer to get a good look. The handle was decorated with an elaborate pattern of inlaid silver. I reached forward— just to touch it with my finger—when I felt Korva's hand on my shoulder.

"That's a murderer's knife," he said.

He put the knife back in its sheath, and wrapped it in a dirty gray cloth. I didn't ask any questions.

Winton was full of secrets.

Emily and I lived in Grandma's boardinghouse. It was a big house with many empty rooms. Four of the bedrooms upstairs were still occupied by boarders. Korva lived in his all the time. Jussi was often gone, working at a resort. Antti usually stayed at his cabin. Another room was filled with packsacks, sleeping bags and nesting kits.

My room had an iron bed, a table, and a flimsy cardboard wardrobe for a closet, just like the men's. I liked to lie on the bed and study the stains on the wallpaper, an interesting world of animals and people with hook noses, long arms and wild hair. Emily came in and lay beside me, and I showed her what I saw. We argued about the shapes.

"That isn't a dragon," Emily said, "See, that part's the hair, and it's really a beautiful princess."

Emily slept downstairs with Grandma.

On rainy days we played in the empty rooms of the boardinghouse. Emily played house with Robin, using the table and benches that Antti had made for them. In another room, Mike and Tony and I hung sheets up for forts. There were transoms over the doors—empty spaces for ventilation—and when we were pirates we climbed over

131

the doors and went through the transoms, dropping down on the shrieking girls.

Then we all went up to the attic, cluttered with ancient trunks filled with musty clothes and boxes of letters. There was a cardboard box of old photographs.

"Look, that's Antti and Korva and Jussi," I said. They were standing in front of a bobsled loaded with huge logs, leaning on their axes.

"They're too young," Emily said.

"See?" I pointed to the photograph.

"Yes, it's Korva," Emily said slowly. "Or somebody else without an ear. Who's the man with the big mustache?"

"That's Antti, silly."

Emily took the picture and looked hard.

I showed her another.

"Here's Grandma and Cecelia and Mrs. Keskinen."

They were wading in the water, lifting long skirts above their knees.

"They were on a picnic," I said.

Emily studied the old picture. I showed her another.

"Look, here's Grandma with Aunt Helena and Uncle Dave and Mother when they were little." They posed stiffly, standing in front of the boardinghouse.

Mike and Tony squeezed in for a look. Emily lifted an old doll with a wooden head out of a trunk. Tony tried on his father's uniform from World War II.

"What does this say?" Mike asked. He was looking at long passages of neat Finnish script written on the wall.

"I don't know," I said. "Korva wrote it."

I lifted Jussi's fiddle out of its case.

"You aren't supposed to touch that," Emily said.

"I won't hurt it." I drew the bow across the strings. Emily put her hands over her ears.

"When Jussi plays, it's beautiful," Emily said. "I heard him once."

"I wonder why he doesn't play anymore?" Tony asked.

"I asked once. He said, 'They took away the Hall'," I said.

"What hall?"

"Who took it away?"

"I don't know," I said. "That's what he told me. Ask Grandma." I lay the fiddle down carefully.

We went down two flights of steep stairs and found Grandma kneading bread in the kitchen.

"Where was the Hall where Jussi played his fiddle?" Mike asked. "What happened to it?"

Grandma kept kneading the dough. "They sold it."

"Who did?"

"It doesn't matter. What's done is done. There's no use talking about things you can't change. Fill the wood box," she said. "Girls, I need water from the pump."

Cousin Laila came into the yard, singing at the top of her lungs.

"I'm going up the lake. Want to come, Robin?" she asked.

"Can I come?" Emily asked.

"Take them," Grandma said, nodding at me and Emily. She put rolls and canned meat into a packsack and gave it to me to carry.

We followed Cousin Laila over the hill to the boathouses.

Only a little light filtered in when the boathouse door was closed. Light danced up from the water, reflecting on the walls. We peered into the river, right to the bottom. Water bugs skated on the surface, minnows darted below. A muskrat propelled himself by. Emily squeezed my hand.

Cousin Laila swung open the big door to the river and light flooded in. I helped Emily and Robin into the boat, guided it out of the boathouse and jumped into the bow.

Sunning turtles dove off rocks as we followed the channel down the river. In the sudden silence when Cousin Laila cut the motor to pull weeds from the propeller, a redwing blackbird called. The blue heron rose up, lazily flapping great wings, then settled back down around the next bend.

"I'm going to stop by Antti's place," Laila shouted over the motor.

Antti's cabin was set back in the trees, gray logs blending with the woods. Antti had scythed a path up from the dock. We followed it to the woodshed, filled with neatly stacked wood. There was a two-man crosscut saw in the shed, a peavey and a cant hook. Traps hung from the rafters. Stored along the walls were a kicksled, snowshoes, and long, beautiful, hand-carved skis. A chopping block, made from a section of a huge birch log, sat in front of the shed.

On the other side of the woodshed, Antti pedaled away at the grindstone sharpening knives.

"*Päivää*," he said, turning away from the lake. "I was just going to have some coffee."

We followed him past the potato garden back to the cabin.

Antti had built his cabin himself. He had carved the smooth handle for the heavy wooden door, and forged the thick iron hinges it hung from. Inside was a table and a cupboard, a cookstove and a bed. A cribbage board lay on the table, with a game of solitaire in progress. We children sat on the bench near the window. Antti set heavy mugs in front of us and poured a little coffee into each, then added condensed milk.

I strained my ears, listening while he talked to Cousin Laila in Finnish.

That's how they kept their secrets. They talked Finnish.

I usually knew what they were talking about, especially when it was one of the old stories. I figured out new words every time Antti told a story over again.

He was telling one of his favorites. His face lit up as he talked.

When he had come home from fishing one hot day, Antti saw that someone had broken into his cabin, ripping up his screen door. He burst into the cabin and found Mr. Bear lying on the cool floor among smashed jars. The bear delicately nosed among them, feasting on blueberry sauce and strawberry jam. He raised his snout to regard Antti as Antti regarded the bear.

Antti grabbed his old muzzle-loading shotgun from the corner and backed out. He went behind the cabin and banged on the wall with every noisy object he could find in the woodshed. The bear didn't leave. Antti heard him inside, breaking more jars. When he had broken all of them and knocked down the cupboard besides, the bear ambled down to the lake for a drink of water. Antti slammed the heavy wooden door shut and ran down the hill after him. By the time Antti reached the shore the bear was swimming leisurely across the bay. Antti suddenly realized that he had loaded the shotgun with a slug to scare off varmints, one he'd made by wadding up lead foil. Angrily, he raised the gun and fired. The foil bullet flew through the air, opened itself up, and settled gracefully on the bear's head like a little peaked hat.

I waited. Now Antti was going to point to the stains on the cabin floor, left by the blueberry sauce. We all laughed.

"Antti," I said, "have you ever seen the strange knife with the silver in the handle that Korva has?"

Cousin Laila squinted her eyes, pursed her lips and shook her head at me. That meant I shouldn't ask questions.

"No," Antti said, "I haven't."

The story was over, the coffee drunk. We left Antti and finished the trip across the bay to our place.

It was the second summer I was working on my own log house in the woods behind the cabin. Antti had helped me cut the logs, peel and scribe them. I'd raised the walls up past my head, and Antti was going to help me when it was time to put on the roof.

I told my father that I was building a cabin back in the woods when he came up the lake early in the summer.

"I built a cabin when I was a boy," my father said. "Now *that* was a solid structure. I believe it's still standing. Ask *Mummu* where it is when you go to see her."

He didn't come to look at mine.

I was working on my cabin when Emily came crying up the path.

"What's the matter?" I asked.

"Robin says this is Cousin Laila's cabin, not our cabin, and that makes it her cabin because Cousin Laila is her aunt."

"This cabin is Mother's too, and Cousin Laila is Dad's cousin, so we have as much right here as anybody."

Emily kept on bawling.

"Go ask Cousin Laila, then."

Cousin Laila was sitting in the screen porch.

"Cousin Laila," I said, "This cabin belongs to Mother, too, doesn't it."

"Yes," Cousin Laila said, "but she'd come here if she cared about it."

"She does care! She does care!" Emily bawled.

"Hush! The owl will hear you," Cousin Laila said.

Emily clamped her lips shut. She had a terror of owls since Cousin Laila had shown her the headless body of a rabbit. "The owl did that," Laila had said. You could make Emily do anything if you threatened her with owls.

We went to bed at sunset, Laila and Robin in the bed, me and Emily on the floor.

"Cousin Laila," I said, as we lay there before sleep. "Teach us some Finnish."

"*Yksi-kaksi-kolme-neljä-viisi-kuusi-seitsemän-kahdeksan-yhdeksän-kymmenen*,"Cousin Laila said, fast as she could.

"I know how to count," I said. "I need other words."

"Some other time, Johnny," Cousin Laila said.

I didn't ask her what had happened to the Hall.

Emily and I were staying at Dad's old farm with *Mummu* and Uncle Arvo. I lay under Uncle Arvo's bed, waiting for him to come in and undress. Soon I saw formless slippers shuffle through the door. The feet kicked them off, one at a time. He lowered the suspenders from his shoulders, unbuttoned the wool shirt he wore summer and winter. His pants dropped down and he shook them free, leg by leg.

I reached forward and grabbed his skinny blue ankles.

Uncle Arvo roared. He whipped around to peer under the bed as I scrambled out the other side. He ran around the foot to grab me, but I jumped over and got out the door.

Uncle Arvo shouted and cursed, chasing me into the front room.

"Arvo!" *Mummu* said sharply. "You're in your underwear."

Uncle Arvo looked down and retreated, rear flap dangling from one side.

"I'm going to have to replace that button," *Mummu* said. "Don't tease an old man, Johnny. His heart could stop."

Emily backed out from behind the armchair.

"*Mummu*, tell us about the Hall," I said. I got more curious, the more people wouldn't talk about it.

"We used to go there for dances and plays."

"Jussi played the fiddle," Emily said.

"Yes. And Matt Hekkinen played the accordion. He's the man who built your mother's cabin."

"See," I whispered to Emily. "*Mother's* cabin!"

"When your grandfather Rautio died, Cecelia taught your mother the Orphan Song and she sang it barefoot, dressed in rags. Not a dry eye in the Hall."

"Did Mother have a pretty voice?" Emily asked.

"She has a beautiful voice. Haven't you ever heard her sing?"

"Did Dad dance, too?" Emily asked.

"He was a wonderful dancer. I taught him when he was a little boy. He loved to dance at the Hall."

"Did Antti dance?" Emily asked.

"We all did. We were young, you know."

"Even Korva?"

"No, Korva didn't dance."

"What happened to the Hall?"

"They moved it. It's a resort now, on the other side of Shagawa Lake."

"Why did they move it?"

136

"It's your bedtime," *Mummu* said.

Uncle Arvo was still grumbling and cursing in his room when I carried the kerosene lamp up the narrow stairs. Next day he got me alone in the woodshed.

I was asleep in my room at the boardinghouse when Korva's scream woke me. I ran down the hall to his room and lit the kerosene lamp. He thrashed about, talking deliriously. His eyes had sunken in. Without his teeth and missing the ear, his head looked like a skull. I shook him by the shoulder, and he swung at me before he opened his eyes. He kept ranting in Finnish.

"I'm Johnny," I said. I kept repeating it.

After a while he lay still and his eyes focused on me.

"Go to my trunk," he said hoarsely. "There's a bundle in there, a gray cloth bundle. Get it out."

I brought it to him. He unwrapped the knife and pulled it from its sheath. I thought he meant to plunge it into his heart, but then he wrapped it up and gave it to me.

"Throw it in the River Lena," he said.

"Where's the River Lena?" I asked.

"Throw it in the Lena," Korva said, and passed out.

Korva hadn't wanted a funeral, but Cousin Laila made the arrangements. The minister said that Korva was going to hell, and we should mend our ways.

After the funeral, I took Korva's knife down to the river. I didn't know where the Lena was. The Shagawa River would probably be all right. I sat on the bank, looking at the beautiful knife, tracing the pattern on the handle with my finger. A murderer's knife, Korva had said.

"What do you have there, Johnny?"

Cousin Laila was standing over me.

I didn't say anything. It was between me and Korva.

"That's the knife you asked Antti about, isn't it?" Laila said, trying to sound sweet. "I better take that."

"No!" I said. I threw it as far into the river as I could.

I sat on a stool at the table in the kitchen of the boardinghouse. My parents were shouting.

"I'm not going to Minneapolis," I said. "I'll run away and live with Antti."

"You have to come if we say so. It's the law," Dad said.

"Who's the law and what's the law?"

Dad jerked me off the stool by one arm.

"Get your things and let's go."

"Come on, Emily," I said.

"Emily stays here," Mother said.

Emily hid behind me, hanging to my waist.

"Who's going to take care of her?" I asked.

Mother pulled Emily away and carried her screaming out of the room.

"Emily doesn't make trouble," Dad said.

I started to cry.

"I didn't steal the knife. Korva gave it to me to throw in the river."

Dad hit me.

The vine-covered brick and stucco house in Minneapolis always smelled like garbage and sour milk. In school I got beat up because I was the new kid. At home I got beat up because I was the kid.

On warm days I hid by Minnehaha Creek, in a cave I dug in the creek bank. Otherwise, I stayed in my room, making plans to escape and go home to Winton. One night I asked Dad about the Hall.

"Hall?"

"Finn Hall. In Winton," I said.

"I sold it."

"You? Why?"

"It needed a new roof. Upkeep is expensive. Those old people don't need a hall. It's not practical," he said.

Chapter 18

Just At Twilight: Antti Lahti's Story

That terrible fight between Father and Urho in the barn sent Urho, Timo and me off to America. We ended up at a boardinghouse on the Mesaba range where red ore dust covered everything. Urho complained bitterly and soon Timo took off with a harvest crew for the Dakotas, but I didn't mind the place so much because I liked the Finnish girl who served meals in the boardinghouse. I was too shy to talk to her at first, but I liked to watch Aina bring in the plates and take them away. She was very pretty. One day I got up my courage to ask her to go walking with me on Sunday afternoon, and she said yes. It was a golden afternoon and Aina had the sweetest laugh. Urho saw us come in together.

"Why are you out walking with that meek servant?" Urho said. But after that he started to talk to her and give her compliments. When I saw them walking hand in hand, I headed for the logging camps north of Ely. Later Urho wrote, inviting me to his wedding with Aina. I didn't go, but I went to his funeral four years later. He was killed during the big strike. In my wild imagination I thought I might have another chance with Aina when she moved to a farm near Winton with her brother Arvo, but she had become a different woman, grieving for my brother. Her son was named Antti, after me.

It was just as well. I liked the woods.

I was good with horses. The foreman in my first logging camp made me a teamster. In the winter we shod the teams with caulks and iced the roads so one team could haul a load of logs twenty feet high—if the road was level.

I met Charlie Bouchay in that camp. He didn't look like I expected an Indian to look. I was picking up some English and listened carefully to Charlie when he told me about trapping beaver. In early spring, Charlie asked me if I wanted to run a trapline with him, so I told my bunkmate Jussi goodbye and left the camp. A couple of years later, when I spoke a little Chippewa and Charlie talked a little Finn, I asked why he'd picked me for a partner.

"Because you don't talk much," Charlie said.

I learned a lot about the woods from Charlie Bouchay.

I built myself a cabin on Fall Lake on the cut-over side, opposite the shore that had burned over. I squared the logs on my cabin and dovetailed the corners the Finnish way. Charlie was impressed. My cabin was two portages away from Charlies' village on Jackfish Bay and four miles down the lake from Winton, where they ran the big lumber mills.

I heard that Timo had died when Charlie and I brought our winter's haul of pelts to Winton one spring. He left a pregnant bride, but she was already remarried and expecting another child by the time I heard of Timo's death.

The five years I spent with Charlie were good ones. We traveled the lake country during the summer. In autumn we made wild rice on Mahnomen Lake and did some trapping before heading back to the logging camps.

One time I was picking blueberries with Charlie's sister Mary on the high cliffs of Jackfish Bay when we startled a mother bear. She came after us so Mary and I went right over the side of the cliff. Mary was laughing and I thought, I'm not too old to marry that girl. But then the Spanish Flu killed Charlie along with half the village and the government took Mary and the others and put them on the reservation.

A couple of years after that the mills in Winton shut down, but a man could still find work in the woods in the winter. In the summertime I worked as a guide.

That was work. The guide's the expert, but some of those tourists thought a guide was a servant. One time a man gave me his cup and told me to get him a drink. I dropped his cup in the lake. He shouted curses at me before he looked around and realized that he didn't know how to get home. He was polite to me after that.

After Charlie died, I spent the winters in Mrs. Rautio's boardinghouse with Jussi and Korva. I remember one night when Jussi staggered into my room, drunk and sobbing.

"I'll never see my little girls again," he cried. In the eighteen years I'd known him, he'd never mentioned that he had a family. The next day he bought two dolls and sent them back to Finland. He'd lost track of time. His daughters had to be over twenty years old.

I was saving my money so I could return to Finland, buy a farm and find a girl to marry, but when the Depression hit I lost it all.

It was all right. Winton was a fine place to be. There was a fine Finn Hall, at least five saloons and a public sauna, so it was pretty lively in the winter. Every spring I moved back up the lake.

One time one of my landlady's daughters asked what I would do when I got too old to trap and guide. What the old men did in Finland, I said: live somewhere where I could feed the woodstove in exchange for a warm corner and a little food.

Sometimes I think of that midsummer night when Urho talked me and Timo into coming to America. For opportunity, he said.

We were young and we had no fears. Urho had big dreams but he was impatient. Timo worked hard and would have got what he wanted, if he'd lived. My dreams weren't so grand. Mostly back then I imagined myself bringing a present to a pretty girl who waited in a fine parlor. I didn't know what to expect from the opportunity that Urho talked about so long ago in Finland.

Years ago, Jussi scratched a message on my cabin wall: "November 24. Antti and I netted whitefish. Got 34 whitefish and 2 tulippes. Antti fell in. We got drunk. Had a good time."

Only sometimes, when I sit near the shore at my cabin, watching the waves ebb in the waning light of midsummer sun, does my heart fill with old yearnings.

Chapter 19

Winter Trip: Andy Lahti's Second Story

Published in a slightly different version in Jarvenpa, A. & M.G.Karni (eds.) *Sampo, The Magic Mill: An Anthology of Finnish American Writing*, New Rivers Press, 1989. Republished in *North Writers: A Strong Woods Collection*, University of Minnesota Press. 1991

C ousin Laila's call woke me.

"*Setä Antti on kuollu. Voitteko te tulla?*"

So the old man finally died. I hated to take time off work for a funeral, but I'd do it for Laila's sake.

"I'll leave early tomorrow."

I left the Cities at 4:30 a.m. and got to Ely by ten. I brought Emily along. All the kin he had left in America would be there to send Antti off.

I took the old Winton road out of Ely, to stop by the farm to see *Äiti*. I hadn't seen her for several months, since Uncle Arvo died. The dazzling white world blinded me when I stepped from the car. Clear air, clean snow. It felt warmer than the official ten below reported on the radio. I breathed in the fragrance of wood smoke.

Äiti and the scent of cardamom welcomed us into the warm kitchen. Finnish biscuit baked in the cookstove.

"You look tired," *Äiti* said. "Emily is too thin. That's such a long trip." She set out wild strawberry jam and took the biscuit from the oven.

"How are you managing here by yourself, *Äiti*?" I asked.

"It's all right. Johnny comes to cut wood—and I can always hire someone. The Finnish Stock truck doesn't deliver anymore, but Laila brings groceries and takes me to the doctor. I set up my loom in the parlor. Come and see."

Äiti's parlor was a porch that stuck out of the south side of the old log house, with large windows on three sides. It was bare except for bright rugs and the loom that made them. Sunshine gleamed from the polished wood floor. Tidy piles of rags lay about. On the loom, *Äiti* was finishing a rug of reds and blues.

Emily chattered to her grandmother over biscuit and jam. I finished my coffee.

"We should go to see about Jussi," I said. "We'll be back by supper. Should I bring groceries?"

"No, that's all right. I have peas soaking for soup."

We traveled on to Winton. Laila's ancient pickup truck was parked in front of her house. Emily jumped out and ran up the slippery porch steps, but I sat for a minute, looking at the shabby frame house. Laila had it painted from time to time, but it promptly shed off the new paint down to its ancient weathered clapboards. I'd run up those steps, eager as Emily, when Laila and I were young and every day was a new adventure. Now there was just the creaky old building and Laila, spinster school teacher.

I walked in without knocking. Laila was showing Emily a robin with a twisted foot that she kept in a cage in the kitchen. She gave me a quick hug.

"How good to see you. Can I get you some coffee and some *korppu*?"

"No, thanks. We came from *Äiti's*. When is the funeral?"

"Tomorrow. But Jussi doesn't know yet. He's caretaking up at Cliffrock Lodge. I thought we could drive up to Basswood and get him." I looked out the window at her truck.

"Let's take my car," I said.

Laila laughed. "There's nothing wrong with my truck. Johnny keeps it running," she told me.

"Where is he?"

"He's around. He stays here sometimes."

"Does he go to school?"

"No."

I dropped the subject.

"Let me make a thermos of cocoa and some sandwiches and then we can go." She went into the kitchen. Someone came in the back door.

"Johnny!" Emily ran back to see him. I followed more slowly.

"Hi, Dad," he said. Emily was hanging on his neck. "Thought I'd go up to Basswood with you."

"How are you doing, John?"

Johnny sat down and looked at the floor.

"I'm fine," he said.

"Load up," Laila ordered. "I'm ready." She looked us over. "Is that all you people have to wear?"

She rummaged in the closet and threw out snowpants, hats, scarves and mittens. Emily bundled herself up and I took a scarf for my neck. Johnny stayed bareheaded and barehanded. Laila made another attempt.

"It's only ten below but the wind might be bad on the lake."

Johnny grinned and stuck the tips of his fingers in the pockets of his jeans.

We took my car. The new county boat landing was built on Frank Silvola's old place. Had they burned down his cabin? The road ran right off the landing on to the ice.

"Ice is two feet thick, Andy." Laila said, sensing my hesitation at the shore. The road was much smoother over the ice. Plowed clean, perfectly level.

Emily bounced around on the back seat.

"Driving on the ice!" she said. Laila looked at me. We'd lived our winters on the lake. How could things be so different for Emily?

The road ran down the middle of Fall Lake and disappeared into the woods at Four Mile. At the end of the portage, smoke curled from the little store.

"It's just a winter caretaker, but he'll sell cigarettes to the desperate," Laila said.

"There's a huge locomotive wheel right off the landing there, under the ice," Johnny told Emily.

"Logging train," I said.

The road dropped to the ice again. Antti had taken me on my first trip to Basswood, the first of countless trips. I still knew it as well as anything in this world. The road branched out occasionally to this resort or that.

"This will be the last year for most of them, Andy. I think only Hubachek will be left after '63," Laila told me.

"I know." The government had banned the resorts to make a wilderness area. Some would be moved, others burned. I asked Laila about their fates. Beautiful buildings had already been burned. The waste made me sick.

At Cliffrock, Jussi's little caretaker cabin smelled of fried pancakes, coffee, and damp wool socks steaming dry by the stove. Laila gave Jussi the news.

"Antti dead!" He sat down. We all sat. "Well, he was sick now, for awhile. But dead." Jussi rose and set out heavy chipped mugs, coffee, and a can of condensed milk. "He saved his suit for the funeral. It's at his shack. I know where."

"You knew him a long time," Laila said.

"I was in his first logging camp, just after he came over from Finland. Yah, we partnered off and on for almost fifty years. Logged, trapped together. That's all done now. All done."

"What will you do next year, Jussi?" I asked. Next year Cliffrock Resort would be ashes and pine seedlings.

"Time to hang my teeth on the nail."

"Antti wanted you to have his cabin," Laila said.

"Nah, I'll stay in town." Jussi picked up the mugs and put them in the dishpan. "I gotta fix up some things here, then I'll come with you guys, show you the suit."

"Let me take Emily out driving on the ice," Johnny asked.

"Please, Daddy?"

"Okay," I said, reluctantly.

Laila and I walked up to the little point of rock overlooking the great frozen lake. Five hundred miles around if you paddled next to the shoreline, half of it in Canada.

"Who will see it like this anymore?" I asked Laila. "Remember how we snowshoed from Winton to the Canadian ranger station on Friday night, and went back home on Sunday? Fifteen or twenty miles each way. Why did we do it?"

"For the glory of the frozen world," Laila said.

"What were there, twenty resorts? Twenty-five? Scattered over five hundred miles of shoreline? Why didn't they just ban new buildings and leave these until their owners retired?" I thought of that first scent of smoke and the glimmer of a caretaker's lamp in a far off window when we'd made those long treks from town.

"That isn't the way they do things, Andy."

Far below us on the ice Johnny was whipping Andy's car in circles. The car came to a stop and Emily and Johnny walked around it, switching places. The car started in jerks, then traveled slowly along the ice road. Emily kept carefully to the right.

"Are you ever coming back up here, Andy?" Laila asked.

"It's too late," I said.

Below us, Jussi opened his cabin door and threw pancakes to the Canada jays.

"He always cooks extra for the birds," Laila said.

We started back to the shack. Jussi was putting on his mackinaw.

"I'll show you Antti's suit now," the old man said.

We hailed the children from the dock. Emily drove up sedately, precisely, and stepped from the driver's side grinning. She and Johnny climbed into the back seat with Jussi. Jussi was melancholy.

"Used to be life on this lake," Jussi said. "There were some characters in those logging camps. Yah, there were still Indians when we got here. Antti partnered up with that Charlie Bouchay for years. Used to be three, no four villages on this part of the lake. Used to trade furs with the Canadians right here. Government took all the Indians. Now it takes everybody. Antti's better off, dead."

No one said a word on the rest of the trip to Antti's cabin. On Fall Lake we left the plowed road, making our own track to Antti's bay.

It was colder inside Antti's cabin than it was outside in the sunshine. Jussi went to the bed and pulled a torn cardboard suitcase from underneath. We stood and watched expectantly. Inside was a heavy wool suit, once black, now tinged with green.

"Last time he wore this suit he danced on the boat from Liverpool," Jussi muttered, lifting it from the suitcase.

"Look!" cried Emily. Three little books—bankbooks—dropped from the folds of the suit. She picked them up. Three accounts at the First State Bank of Ely.

"Look at this. Look at all the money he had," she said. I took the bankbooks from her. Frequent and regular deposits were listed through the 1920s in all three books.

"Lots of beaver pelts," said Jussi, looking at the figures. The entries stopped in October 1929. I totaled the figures in my head. Antti had lost more than $3000. It was a lot of money for an immigrant worker in 1929.

"He used to talk about going back to Finland to find a wife," Jussi said. "He almost made it."

"Can't we get out the money, Daddy?"

"No, Emily. The banks failed a long time ago. There is no money."

"What happened to Uncle Antti's money? Who got it?"

"It was the Depression, honey. No one got the money. It was just gone."

Laila took the suit. Johnny pocketed the worthless bankbooks. We looked around at the few dishes and pots, then went up to the wood-

146

shed. A half cord of split wood spilled from its pile, and rusty traps hung on the walls. I set up the kicksled that lay tipped on its side.

"Anything you want, Jussi?" Laila asked.

"Nah."

"You can stay at my house overnight," Laila told him. "I'll take you home after the funeral."

"Nah. Take me back now. Dead is dead. What's a funeral?"

I followed him back into the cabin. Jussi looked around, then picked up a mug from the shelf—an ordinary coffee mug with one line painted near the rim. "I'll take this."

We drove Jussi back to Cliffrock. He got out of the car without looking back. I shut off the motor and watched him climb the hill to his cabin, shoulders stooped under torn mackinaw, coffee mug dangling from bony fingers. He'd never looked so small or lonely.

The trees along the lakeshore were silhouetted against a red-streaked sky as we headed back to Winton. Two trips to Basswood in one day. I marveled over it to Laila.

"Do you remember the time we snowshoed home in the wind, wrapped in blankets from the ranger station? It took us fourteen hours. I've never been so cold."

"I thought we were dead," Laila said. "Can I make you some supper?"

"No, *Äiti's* expecting us. Want to come to the farm for some pea soup, John?"

"No thanks, Dad. You can let me off here."

I dropped him off on the road to Ely.

"Will you be at the funeral, Johnny?" Laila called out her window.

"Sure. One o'clock, right?"

"Right."

He stood, hands in pockets, back hunched against the wind, waiting for a ride to town.

I pulled up behind Laila's battered pickup. I wanted to talk to her, but I didn't know what to say.

"I'll see you at the funeral, then," Laila said, hauling out the shabby suitcase with its ancient suit. She closed the car door, then opened it again.

"Antti had a long life. Don't grieve."

I said nothing. All I felt was grief. Emily spoke.

"He had a good life. The best."

The air had grown bitterly cold. We drove home to *Äiti's* warm kitchen.

147

Chapter 20

Child of the Place: Frank Makinen's Story

Winner of the Lake Superior Writers' Short Fiction Contest, 1999

My parents came from Finland, first in a crowded boat over rough seas, then by railroad, tagged like pieces of baggage. My father went into the mine and my mother struggled with her grief, alone among strangers. The land of opportunity was bitter disappointment, but their children would do better, they said. It was all for the sake of the children.

My six brothers and sisters made my parents proud when they went to college. Some have two and three degrees. I'm the black sheep. My parents are ashamed because I followed my father into the mine.

My parents ask, why don't you leave Winton and go someplace where you could make something of yourself? I can't answer them.

Maybe when I was a child I lingered too long in the soft light of a summer evening, popping wild cucumbers by the garden shed.

Maybe it was the smoky smell of birch heating the sauna stove on a crisp September day, or plunging into the lake when it was the bluest of blue, trimmed with autumn gold.

Should I have left when the whitefish were running? Or when my blood rose with the tang in the November air at hunting time?

I didn't understand how anyone could leave, once they'd snowshoed across Basswood Lake when it glittered in twenty below.

And how could I leave the old people, speaking musical Finnish in the Co-op, in the post office?

My parents say the immigrants were fools who expected to find streets paved with gold. They got hardship and misery. But if you go out walking in the early spring when the marsh marigolds run riot, you will find the woods carpeted with gold.

My dad is crippled with arthritis so my boy Mike and I make firewood for the folks. One May afternoon I was over at their place stacking it, and stayed to have coffee and *pulla* with Mother afterwards. We sat on the porch, looking out over the empty fields on the edge of the village. Bright green leaves of birch and poplar budded out in the woods beyond.

"Your brother Esa bought a new house, Frank," Mother told me in high, scolding Finnish. "He got promoted at his job. It's too late for you to make something of yourself, but Mike is taking after you. You should make him see there's no future up here."

"Let Mike live his own life, Mother," I said. "You got lots of other grandkids who can make you proud." Most of them couldn't be bothered to send her a Christmas card.

"Mike's smart. He takes after his mother. That girl would have been something if you hadn't ruined her life—getting her in the family way, making her drop out of college."

"I know, Mother," I said. "Helena could have been something."

I thought of the dark autumn day she'd come to my door, pregnant. Only Helena and I knew that Mike wasn't my baby, and I would have forgotten long ago if I wasn't reminded, like Mother reminded me now.

"Somebody told me that Mike's making moonshine. He's hanging out with the wrong crowd," Mother said.

I smiled. I'd made moonshine with Jake LaPrairie, Dave Rautio and Andy Lahti. It was serious business back then. Good to see the kids keeping up tradition.

"He'll be fine, Mother," I said. "I gotta go."

I walked home over Finn Hall Hill, past the empty lot where the Hall had been. I turned at the top to look back at the village below. It had changed over the years, but in some ways it hadn't changed at all. To the west, the tracks came out of the woods following the bend of the river. A kid was fishing from an old wooden skiff near Laitinen's public sauna. The sauna was closed now; Cecelia lived alone upstairs in the big blue metal-clad building.

Clapboards on the old false-fronted boardinghouses that lined the street were fading to rusty red and weathered gray. The few old bachelors they still housed had weathered, too. Jussi was sitting on a bench in front of Rautio's boardinghouse, leaning forward, cap tilted against the sun, elbows resting on his knees. A bunch of kids and a couple of dogs played in the street. Heikki was going home from the saloon, not too steadily. Old Mrs. Tanttari was on her way to the post office with a package.

To the east I could see where the river flowed into Fall Lake. In my mind I traveled north with the current, over Pipestone, through Newton, on to Basswood.

I felt good when I looked at Winton from the top of the hill. I sat there for a few minutes before I walked home in the spring evening, fresh with the scent of balm o'gilly.

Mike was in the backyard with Johnny Lahti, taking apart a 36 Chevy coupe. They were fine looking boys in their engineer boots, jeans and white t-shirts. Both wore their hair combed back with a curl falling over their foreheads. I marveled that their hair stayed in place even when they were working under the hood of the car.

"Hey Dad, give us a hand with this block," Mike called. I went over and wrestled with the tri-pod awhile before Helena called us in to eat.

"I got a job driving truck on Four Mile for the summer," Mike said at supper.

"And then you can go to junior college in the fall," his mother said.

"Don't nag, Mom. I'm not going to college," Mike said. "Dad's gonna get me a job in the mine."

Helena glared at me. The girls looked scared, expecting a fight. Helena walked around the table, throwing scoops of mashed potatoes down, plate by plate.

"When does the job start, Mike?" I asked.

"Day after graduation."

"We won't have time to go on a fishing trip then."

"I'll skip a couple of days of school. Grades are in already, anyhow."

Helena slapped down slices of meat loaf. Then she stood back, hands on hips.

"What's the matter with you, Mike?" she said. "Do you really want to end up like him?" She jerked her head in my direction.

"Yeah, Mom. That would be fine," Mike said evenly.

Her face got ugly and contorted. She stared at Mike for a moment and then stormed out of the room.

"I'm going to college," Cindy whispered to Penny.

We finished supper in silence. Helena came back downstairs to make my lunch. I was on the graveyard shift, eleven to seven. We changed shifts every week. Even though I'd been at the Pioneer Mine for sixteen years, I never got used to switching shifts. I was always tired when I worked graveyard.

150

Helena was still tight with anger. I would have tried to comfort her, but I was what was making her hurt.

She packed meatloaf sandwiches in the lunch box with an apple and some date bars. Cindy and Penny cleared the table and washed dishes, trying to be invisible and good at the same time.

Helena turned to me, anger gone. She sounded tired.

"I'm sorry, Frank," she said. "You've been good to me. I just wanted more for Mike."

I shook my head. There was nothing I could say. The painful thing was that I loved Helena like I always had, helpless to defend myself. If there was more that Mike could have from this life than I had, it would be loving a woman who loved him back.

I went up to get a few hours rest before my shift.

I was proud to be a miner. I went down the mine at the beginning of World War Two as a general underground worker. Next I was a timber trammer. It took six years to work up to contract miner.

The Allies couldn't have won World War II without the ore from the Iron Range, and the U.S. wouldn't be the greatest country in the world if we hadn't won the war.

I was too upset to sleep, but I lay there until it was time to go to work. Then I walked around to the Old Winton Road and waited for my ride. It was a soft, clear spring night, with pockets of chill in the low places.

Bernie waited for me outside the minehead. We'd been partners since 1948. You never called your partner by name, just Partner. I saw more of him than I did of Helena and we got along better, too, but then, we were clear about our job and how to get it done. Our lives depended on it.

The whistle blew at eleven sharp. We got in the cage and dropped 1300 feet in a minute and a half. I popped my ears without thinking about it.

The way it worked, there were six guys on a contract—two guys on each shift. The company gave you the contract and set the rate. If it was easy going you got paid less, hard work you got more, so it evened out. We got paid by the ton, and the six men on the contract divided the pay for the contract equally. That meant we couldn't afford to tolerate anybody slacking off.

We met our partners coming off swing shift in the tunnel.

"What's in the place?" I asked.

"It's ready to drill: you have to get the bits," one of our partners said. You could see he was proud of the fact they'd done a hard day's work.

We had good partners. One time Bernie and I were in a contract with a couple of guys who put a sloppy set. You can't be off a sixteenth of an inch when you set timber, or you're going to get somebody killed. Bernie didn't hesitate to let them know.

"Ever do that again and you'll wind up with an axe in your head," he told them. They shaped up.

We did cave mining in Pioneer, taking out ore six feet at a time. Set timber, drill, blast a cut and six feet would cave down. Hang a block on the last set of timber and work the scraper, scraping up all the loose ore out of the drift, and start again.

The conditions were always different. Maybe it was wet, and you had to wear rubber suits, which was miserable. Maybe when you blasted a piece of ore would fly down the drift like a cannon shot and hit one of the sprags—braces—on a set five back from the end of the tunnel, making five sets of timber come down. A mess. If it was real good going you could make a round in a shift, but in hard ground it might take more than one shift just to drill the holes.

We were drilling hard ground that night. Drilling is like being in an eight-foot square room with two fifty-caliber machine guns running steady for eight hours. When we had to communicate, my partner and I signaled each other with our headlamps. After the shift I couldn't hear myself speak when we met our partners coming on shift in the tunnel and told them what was in the place.

All of us contract miners get hard of hearing after awhile. I felt real bad when I realized that I couldn't hear spring peepers trill or birds sing.

I never could sleep in the daytime. The thing to do on a fine spring morning was to go fishing.

Helena gave me a meek smile when I came in the back door. She was making breakfast for me, like always. She did her job in the marriage. I did my job. That's how most marriages worked. Why did I feel so bad about it?

"Want to go fishing?" I asked.

She looked out the window at the fresh green world, and glanced back around the kitchen.

"Sure," she said. "I'll pack a lunch."

One of the things I loved about Helena was that she was always willing to go to the lake.

We drove up the Fernberg Road to our cabin. A week before we'd done spring clean up and put the boat in the lake—a seventeen-foot Grumman with a three-horse Johnson motor. I carried the gas can down to the dock, Helena brought poles and bait and we bailed out the boat with a coffee can and a sponge.

We motored along the shore, Helena looking for signs of life at neighboring cabins. I looked out for deadheads. Back in the logging days, when inboard launches towed booms of logs across Fall Lake to the lumber mills in Winton, some of the logs sank. Now, fifty years later, they popped back up, darkly waiting to break the shear pin on my motor.

Several boats of fishermen bobbed at the edge of the churning waters at the bottom of the dam. Names of resorts were stenciled on most of the bows. It was a good spot to fish, especially if you hadn't gotten out to a quiet bay at dawn.

I cut the motor and Helena baited a hook for me. She liked to fish. It was something we still enjoyed together.

Helena had her own reasons for wanting Mike to go on to college. She wasn't like my folks who wanted their children to achieve to make them look good. I hadn't realized how bad it hurt her to drop out of school when she got pregnant. She thought Mike would suffer the loss she had if he didn't go. She'd never been so angry about anything before.

Mike was a good student so she assumed he'd go on to college. The duck's ass haircut should have tipped her off. I could tell when Mike and his classmates decided whether they were going to leave or stay in the north way back in grade school. It didn't have anything to do with being smart, or getting good grades. It was something else. They started to dress differently from each other, talk different, make different kinds of jokes. Same when I was a boy.

Helena had loved school and I had loved the joy in her. I would never have taken it away.

While she fished, watching clouds pile up in magnificent thunderheads, I glimpsed the Helena I loved. I didn't want to break the mood, but later, after we'd caught our limit and were sitting on the bench by our dock eating lunch, I tried to talk to her.

"It's okay if Mike turns out like me," I said, " because I like my life. What you don't want, is for him to turn out full of regret, like you." I'd worked to figure that out and it cost me to say it, but it came out wrong.

153

Helena stuffed the lunch mess in the bag and stomped up the hill to the cabin. I finished my sandwich, watching gulls bob out in the lake.

Mike and I got in a quick trip to Basswood. We took the Grumman over Four Mile into Back Bay. Walleyes were biting.

Mike's a good partner—quiet, patient, good sense of humor. He's got a real generous nature. When he was a little kid, he started fishing by himself off the White Bridge in Winton. He'd fish from the bridge all day if we let him. When Helena told him we couldn't eat so much fish, he brought fish to his grandma and her boarders and to the other widows in town. He knocked at their doors with one hand, holding his other arm straight up to keep the stringer up off the ground.

We sat on a ledge, listening to loons, having a smoke. I was thinking about Helena when she was young.

"You know any poems?" I asked Mike.

"Has Miss Gjervik let anyone get through Ely High School without memorizing poetry?" he asked. I laughed. I'd had her, too.

I recited some Chaucer.

Mike countered with "Sumer Is Icumen In," while the sun sank through mountains of clouds, changing from brilliant red to deep purple. If the sunset made music, it would have sounded like a pipe organ.

"Maybe those English poets got it right about their place," Mike said, "but this sure isn't England. Robert Service knew the north."

We recited Robert Service poems.

"I liked one Spenser poem," I told Mike. "How did it go? 'My love is like to ice, and I to fire...'"

"'How comes it then that this her cold so great/ Is not dissolved through my so hot desire/ But harder grows the more I her entreat?'" Mike responded. "You must have been in unrequited love, too." He grinned a crooked grin.

Mike was in love with Kathy Chelik, but he was from the wrong family, went to the wrong church.

"So," he asked, "How long did it take you to get over it?"

They always say, oh, you're young, you'll get over it. Or, you're young, it's not serious. Bullshit.

"I didn't," I said.

"Oh," said Mike, light dawning. "You married her."

I thought I could prove my love, when Helena came to my door asking if I still wanted her. I thought my love would fix everything.

154

I almost told Mike why I married his mother, that it wasn't my fault she ruined her life—and it wasn't his either, no matter what he did with himself. But as long as Mike thought he was my son, he was my son. I never wanted him to find out otherwise.

He was going to be sticking around, up on Four Mile this summer, down in the mine come fall. There'd be lots more fishing trips.

At the beginning of every summer, my brothers and sisters wrote to announce which week they planned to come up and stay at our cabin. Helena, normally sociable, was getting annoyed. It was fun when the cousins played together in the lake, roasting hotdogs and marshmallows on the beach in the evening. But now the kids stayed home, and the adults came for solitude. They treated us like the maid and handyman at their own private resort.

Brother Esa—the one who had a big promotion and a new house—wrote that his wife wasn't coming this year, either. He was going to bring his boss up for some fishing.

"Third week in July. The nicest week of the summer," Helena said. "I bet he expects us to supply the food, too."

She was right. They arrived at the cabin in Esa's brand new Chrysler, equipped with nothing more than fishing tackle and beer.

"Frank, Helena. This is Bill Stevens." Esa introduced us to a man expensively dressed in woodsy clothes. Stevens extended his hand with a politician's smile.

"Pleased to make your acquaintance. Good of you to have me," he said.

"Come on up to the cabin," I said.

We sat in the wide screen porch I'd added to the original log structure, on comfortable wooden furniture Mike had built in shop. Esa passed out beer. I accepted. Helena declined.

Stevens settled himself down with a satisfied sigh.

"God's country," he said, looking through the birch trees down to the lake. It was, as Helena had predicted, the height of summer glory.

"I used to come up here summers with my family when I was a boy," Stevens said. "Haven't been up for quite awhile. Too long."

"Well, you've traveled all over. You can't be everywhere," Esa said.

"That's true. I found a nice little fishing lake way up in Canada. Have the whole lake to myself. Fly in at least once a summer. We like to go to Colorado in the winters. One thing about Minnesota, whole place is flat as a swamp. Earlier this year I was in the Andes.

That was something else. Climbed peaks no one had ever climbed. You can't imagine," Stevens said, turning to me, "what it's like. Stepping where no man has stepped before."

"I can," I said. "It's not a big deal."

Esa glowered at me. Stevens turned red.

"I hardly imagine that you could have any idea what it's like," he said. "If you ever did it, you'd know that there's no feeling like it in the world."

"I've done it," I said.

"You? When did you ever step where no man stepped before?" he challenged, looking around our modest cabin with contempt.

"Every day. After I blast out a chunk of rock 1300 feet underground and go in to set timber, I *know* I'm stepping where no man has stepped before."

"Frank!" Helena sounded like she was choking. Her face was twisted with distress. "I have to go home."

I rose and shook hands with Stevens, who radiated hostility.

"See you, Frank," Esa said curtly.

We drove in silence until just before the Garden Lake Bridge. Then Helena broke down in horrible sobs.

I'd never seen her cry before. I'd really done it this time.

"I'm sorry, Helena," I said.

She twisted around and lay her face on my leg. I put my hand on her hair.

"That was him," she said through the sobs.

"Who?"

"Stevens. He's Mike's father."

My hand froze where it was, there on her head. I concentrated on driving with the other hand. When we got to the boathouses I needed both hands to shift and make the turn to Winton.

I parked in the alley. Helena walked past the girls in the kitchen and straight upstairs.

"What happened to Mom?" Penny asked.

I sat down at the table. Cindy was sewing herself a dress, and Penny was making a doll from the scraps.

"The man Esa brought to the cabin hurt her feelings."

"Jeez," Cindy said.

"Yeah," I said. "I guess I'll go talk to her." I felt low as dog crap.

I went up and sat on the edge of the bed. Helena had rolled herself up in a blanket cocoon, still sobbing.

156

I couldn't tell where my hurting left off and hers began. Her sobs tapered off.

"He didn't even recognize me," she whispered after awhile. "I'm glad he didn't, but doesn't he remember? I know I've changed a lot, but Helena isn't that common a name. Wouldn't it jog his memory? God, he never thought about me or Mike at all. Just came up here, enjoyed himself. On to Canada, Colorado, the Andes. Yeah," she said bitterly, "he likes to go where no man has been before. Penetrate virgin territory." The sobs returned.

"I'll tell you what hurts worst, Frank," she said, struggling to get herself under control. "I thought I was in love with him. I wanted to marry him. How could I have been in love with that prick?"

She pulled the covers off her face and looked at me with red puffy eyes.

"I never saw you cry before," I said. Or heard her use bad language. It scared me.

"I haven't cried since I found out I was pregnant with Mike," she said. She started sobbing again. "How could I have loved that terrible man?"

I lay down next to her and fumbled around in the blankets for her hand.

"That was the summer after our first year at junior college," I said. "I was working for the Forest Service. You were working at Maple Isle." I let myself go back in time.

"There never was a more beautiful summer," I said. "The long drought had broken, but it only rained at night. Every morning the world was fresh and clear. Every day was sunny, with just a gentle breeze. Basswood smelled of sun on pine and lichen. The cliffs were full of berries. The lake was warm, with miles of sandy beaches."

"We got together with kids from other resorts for bonfires on the beaches," Helena said.

I remembered Helena's easy, transparent joy.

"You loved the whole world, Helena. Bill was part of the world you were in love with. Mike was conceived from that golden Basswood summer."

Helena sat up. She looked at me in amazement.

"That's right, isn't it," she said slowly.

"You've been too hard on yourself, Helena. You keep punishing yourself on account of one mistake."

"You never held it against me," she said.

"Why would I? Mike's a great kid."

"I don't want him to wreck his life like I did."

"Yeah. If you hadn't gotten pregnant you could have stayed single and taught English poetry to hoods with DA haircuts. Or maybe made a lot of money and gone mountain climbing in the Andes."

I thought I'd made her cry again, but no. She was laughing.

"God, is he a jerk," she said.

I rolled her over onto my chest, wrapped up in her blanket cocoon. She let me hold her there and rock her while her laughter changed back to sobs.

Chapter 21

Clearances: Emily Lahti's First Story

When I was fourteen, my father left without saying good-bye. My sister Janie was seven. Johnny was eighteen, but he didn't live with us anymore. Mother was already half nuts. When Daddy left, she went over the edge, waking us in the night with her screams and ranting, sometimes turning on me in a frenzy of rage. I packed some things for Janie and took the bus up north. We stayed with *Mummu* at the farm and went to school in Ely. Janie sat still most of the time, gazing into space. If you called her name she turned vacant eyes toward you but she didn't hear what you were saying. She never cried. Mother appeared on a dark winter day, took us out of school, and brought us to a big drafty house near the university in Minneapolis. The furniture hadn't come, the stove wasn't hooked up and there was no telephone. There wasn't a book or a toy for Janie.

Mother alternated between screaming and stony silence. She wanted me to say that Daddy was a bastard. She told me things his girlfriend had told her, dirty sexual things. I ran out of the house to get away. When I came back, she took my coat away and burned it. In the middle of the night I opened my eyes and saw her arm raised above my head. I curled up like they'd taught us in civil defense and let her beat me until she was exhausted.

Early in the morning I woke Janie. Silently, we ate cold cereal. I put on my mother's black coat, walked Janie to the school up the hill and asked the principal to put her in the second grade. I told where we had come from, school before Ely. The principal looked at the thin, pale child with dead eyes and led her away by the hand. I asked the secretary where the high school was. She told me how to get there and loaned me twenty-five cents for the bus, round-trip.

I found the office and asked to register. The coat was way too big, much too long. I wouldn't tell them anything except my name and the school I had come from. The counselor and the principal consulted, looked at my coat, and put me in a class next to a girl with five livid razor scars across her face.

The day school let out for the summer, I hitched home to Winton. Johnny was living alone in the old boardinghouse. I dragged Antti's thin cotton mattress up the narrow attic stairs and lay it next to Jussi's trunk. I slept through the days. The night was mine. I wandered the house, rummaging for scraps of food in Johnny's dirty kitchen. Outdoors I walked in safe darkness along the river or up to the top of the hill. I could look down and see by the light in the old shed across the alley that Johnny was working.

Johnny was using Cousin Laila's washshed as a studio. He made sculptures, refashioning pieces of metal into creatures with beaks and wings. He worked when he wanted, dropped off to sleep next to his torches. Friends dropped by, day and night. I watched from the attic window. Johnny worried about me.

"You have to stop this, Emily," Johnny said. He was sitting on Korva's dusty trunk. "You can't go on living like this."

"What do you want me to do?"

"Go out in the daylight, at least."

"Why?"

"See some friends. Robin's working in her Dad's bait shop. Go see her."

"Why?"

"Jesus, Emily."

He went to look down from the window at the backyard, then gazed for a moment at a blank spot on the wall over Korva's writing. He took a pencil from his pocket started to draw. Over his shoulder I watched a perfect caricature of Daddy emerge. He labeled it, "Dad." Behind Dad, almost entirely obscured by his pipe, he outlined the top of a head. Above it he wrote "Me."

"Let's go to Basswood," I said.

Johnny smiled. "Maybe Robin can get away from the bait shop for a few days," he said.

We paddled steadily, eyes on the far horizon. Johnny was in the stern of the Grumman canoe. Robin LaPrairie and Paul Keewatin followed in a green canvas Old Town. I shielded my eyes from the sun and scanned the shoreline, looking for the site where Cliffrock resort had been. Johnny smoothly turned the canoe toward a cliff that rose sharply at the mouth of the bay.

160

"That's where Jussi's caretaker cabin was," Johnny said, pointing to a clearing. He steered to a little beach inside the bay. I climbed out and held the canoe steady while Johnny scrambled over the packs.

We climbed the cliff for a closer look. Except for a clump of daylilies, there was nothing to mark that the cabin had ever been there.

The clearing was planted in pine seedlings. Robin and Paul pulled their canoe up on shore and went to look for the dump. I followed and found them rooting through a pile of broken dishes and dented pots. Robin retrieved a speckled enamel coffeepot and a washbasin. Johnny raised his eyebrows.

"Don't worry, I'll portage them," Robin said. "Look at this waste."

Johnny nudged the rubble with his foot.

"Waste," he said.

We were heading to Jackfish Bay to look at the place Paul's grandmother came from when it started to drizzle. Then the heavens opened with thunder and lightening and torrents of water.

"Go to Maple Isle," Johnny shouted to Paul.

We hunched down, paddling fiercely against the headwinds, exhausted and soaked when we reached the lee of the shore.

"Does somebody live here?" Robin shouted over the storm.

"It's condemned," Johnny answered.

We hauled canoes on the shore, flipped them over, grabbed the grub pack and the sleeping bags, and made for the lodge. The door hung open.

We stepped into a monumental log building. On one end stood a massive stone fireplace. On the other, two story multi-paned windows looked out to a stand of white pine. Running along each side were balconies.

"Whew," said Robin. "This is class."

"We're trespassing," I said.

"What's the difference?" Johnny said. "The government took it. They're going to burn it down this winter."

"Couldn't they salvage something like this?" Paul said.

"They moved the smaller guest cabins out last winter. This was too big."

"Was this the place that the Forest Service put all that stuff out on the ice so it sank in the spring?" Robin asked.

"One of them," Johnny said. "Mike really wanted that Model A they sank."

161

"Hey, look," I said. "Books." Robin came over to look through the summer reading that filled the bookcase built in next to the fireplace.

Paul and Johnny found dry wood and got a fire going. We spread our sleeping bags near the fire and read old mysteries while the storm whipped against the tall windows. I lay close to Paul. When the light dimmed I put down my book and studied his profile. He set down his book and smiled at me.

"Why did you switch to Ely High School for your senior year?" I asked.

"The school in Tower never graduated anyone from the reservation."

"Never?"

"Never."

"He did just fine in Ely," Robin said.

"What are you going to do now?" I asked him.

"I'm going into the army in the fall."

"No kidding?"

"No kidding."

"Isn't that dumb?" Robin said. "Dad wants him to stay here. Said he'd make him a partner in the bait shop."

"Your dad would pass on the business to some shirttail relative and leave you out in the cold?" Johnny asked.

"I have higher ambitions than being the leech queen of Winton," Robin said. "Paul can have the bait shop."

"Well, somebody has to defend our shores and make the world safe for democracy," I said. I was sorry Paul was going away. Many times that night I wakened to the storm and drifted back to sleep listening to Paul breathing near me in the big empty room.

We were the last guests at Maple Isle.

I started hanging out in Johnny's studio, smoking filterless Camels and drinking moonshine that Johnny and Mike Makinen made in the copper boiler Grandma had used to heat wash water in. When friends dropped by I argued with them about Nietzsche, Sartre and Ayn Rand. One night Peter Johnson came with somebody from Ely. We were in the middle of an argument over whether the only way to prove free will was to commit suicide.

"That's crap," Peter said, and walked out. I followed him.

"Do you need a ride?" I asked.

"I'll walk."

"It's four miles to Ely."

Peter nodded.

"Wait for me," I said. I went back in. "Can you pick me up in town later?" I asked Johnny.

"Sure. Be in the park at one."

"We can take the old road, the highway, or the railroad tracks," I told Peter. He didn't seem displeased with my company.

"Railroad tracks," said Peter.

The ties were set too close for a comfortable step, and the gravel banks were rough and unstable. We switched back and forth from ties to banks. The Milky Way lit the river below.

"I don't remember seeing you before," I told Peter. "Do you go to school in Ely?"

"I graduated last year. I'm a sophomore at the University."

"I'm going back to Minneapolis this fall. Mother bought a house near the U. I'll be a senior."

"Someone said you were only fifteen."

"I am."

"A real prodigy," Peter said, sarcastically.

"What does your dad do?" I asked.

"He's a miner. A hard rock miner."

"Is he proud of you, going to college?"

"He doesn't care. Just so I get a real job someday."

"What do you want to do?"

"Teach college."

"Is your mother proud of you?"

"She's dead."

Peter took long strides to double step the railroad ties, while I scrambled along on the gravel bank.

"What do you like to read?" I asked.

"Everything," said Peter.

"What are you reading now?"

Peter thought for a while and then began to talk. The tracks led into the pines. I heard the river tumbling nearby. We came out of the dark woods into a moonlit poplar grove. Peter talked on, like no one had ever listened before.

The woods opened up and we looked through a chain link fence over a vast hole. The lights of Ely were on the other side.

"Let's cut across," I said.

"That's the open pit," Peter said. "It's honeycombed with tunnels underneath the ground. The company stopped pumping water when they abandoned the mine and the whole thing collapsed, full of bogs and fissures. It's not much farther up the tracks. Look, we're nearly to the mine."

He pointed to the silhouette of the great metal frame. A lighted box ran up. When it reached the top, a bell rang.

"That's the ore. They send it up and it dumps down a chute to the ore cars." The cars clanked as the next one moved under the chute.

"My dad's down there right now," Peter said.

A gravel road intersected the railroad tracks, and we turned off on a quiet location street.

"White picket fences and little green lawns," Peter said. "They don't want anything more out of life than that." He nodded at a picture window, glowing blue from the television inside.

"What do you want?" I asked.

"To get out of here," Peter said.

We walked across town to the park. Peter strained to see his watch under the streetlight.

"It's nearly one o'clock. I'll wait with you."

"You don't have to."

"I'll wait."

Peter sat on the grass. I lay a short distance away and looked up at the sky.

"Do you think about infinity?" I asked.

"About what?"

"Infinity."

"I never think about infinity," Peter said.

I heard Johnny's thirty-six Chevy coupe coming up the back street.

I jumped up. "Goodnight!"

"Hey," called Peter. "Come to Maid-Rite. Tomorrow. Eight o'clock."

"Okay," I yelled over the roar of the coupe. Johnny slowed down and I jumped on the running board and tumbled into the open rumble seat.

I went back to high school in Minneapolis in the fall. Peter was at the university. Neither of us had money so we spent our time together walking. Peter walked me home through the campus down the tree-lined mall in autumn twilight, carillon bells chiming. Sometimes we went past fraternity row, where loud and boisterous parties spilled out on to the lawn, but the route along the Mississippi was prettier and longer.

Saturdays we took a bus to another part of town. We walked around Lake Calhoun and Lake of the Isles and then back downtown, across the swath wrecking balls cut through the center of the city, four blocks wide, demolishing buildings to make way for the freeway.

Peter and I stood in a small crowd to watch a three story brick and stucco Tudor come down. The swinging ball crashed through a leaded window on the staircase, splintering the polished banister within. The ball smashed through heavy oak doors with crystal doorknobs, through a chandelier in the dining room.

"Someday I want a house like that," Peter said.

"Let's go, Peter," I said.

Peter and I walked through the winter, warming up over cups of hot chocolate, looking for sheltered places for furtive kisses, stamping frozen feet waiting for busses that kept no schedules.

"They're shutting down Pioneer mine," Peter told me one night.

"Did the ore run out?" I asked.

"No. The taconite process is cheaper. Less skilled and more mechanized."

"What's your dad going to do?"

"Drink himself to death."

"I mean really."

"Really. He's too young for full pension. They won't hire him at the taconite plant because they'd have to pay him too much with his seniority. What's he going to do at fifty-three? He doesn't have enough pension to live on. It's enough to drink on, though."

"Will you have to leave school?"

"I'll get a bigger loan. I'll get a job."

One spring afternoon I was called to the office from biology class.

"Family emergency. Your brother is here to take you home," the secretary said. Johnny was there, grinning. He'd gone out to California when they tore down the boardinghouse last fall.

"Hey!" I said, outside. I gave him a big hug. He opened the door of his roadster convertible for me.

"Nice car," I said. "How's art? How's San Francisco?"

"Things are happening. You have to come out and see it."

"Janie will be ecstatic to see you. Have you been home yet?"

"Not yet. I came right to the school."

We drove across Nicollet Island. Old men leaned against the bridge rail, warming themselves in the spring sunshine. Johnny looked at them as we went by.

"They're dying off," he said.

"The bums?"

"Jesus, Emily. They're just old guys, like Korva and Antti. Immigrant labor who never had families."

"Then if Antti had been down here, he'd have been a bum."

"Don't say bum."

"That's what they're called. Look around you," I said.

We were driving through an area that looked like it had been bombed.

"God," Johnny said, "What happened? This was the historic part of town."

"It's called urban renewal. They're getting rid of the old men, the bums, to make it nice."

"Where are the old men going to go?"

I shrugged.

We drove around for hours. Johnny told me about San Francisco. When we got home, Mother was in one of her rages. Janie sat blankly at the table. Mother screamed at Johnny until he left. When he came back she called the police on him. She'd found marijuana in his coat pocket. Janie cried when the police took Johnnie away.

I visited Johnny in jail. I was used to it. Mother had put Johnny away before.

"When you get out of here, stay away from Mother," I said. "She's getting worse."

"I try to stay away," Johnny said. "Then I start thinking that I should work things out, you know?"

"She doesn't want to work things out. She wants power. Dad and she would have killed each other if he hadn't ditched."

"Where is Dad?"

"I don't know."

When they let Johnny out he headed home to Winton.

I didn't go to my senior prom. My mother would have made me wear one of her made-over dresses, Peter couldn't afford to rent a tux, and neither of us knew how to dance. Instead we walked along empty sidewalks on the swath where demolition work had been completed for the freeway. In lilac-scented twilight, we rested on a low wall that protected a garden where tulips and daffodils bloomed.

"They don't know no one lives here anymore," I said, looking at the flowers. "They bloom to please themselves."

"Next year they'll be under concrete," Peter said.

"There were day lilies blooming at the old Cliffrock site when I was on Basswood last summer. I wonder if some Forest Service crew lost points."

"Lost points?"

"The crews compete for awards in wilderness restoration."

I got off the wall, walked up the front walk that ended in a pile of rubble and picked a tulip. I peered into its dark center.

"On Basswood they say they're restoring the past and here they're supposed to be clearing for the future," I said, "but its looks the same. Making wilderness—places where man passes through and does not remain'."

Peter didn't answer. He was already moving on.

Chapter 22

Doing It Right: Paul Keewatin's First Story

I stood statue still in the frozen woods. Twenty feet from me a doe and her fawn browsed on poplar twigs. They hadn't seen or smelled me yet, and they were coming nearer. It was a game to see how close I could get to a deer, and this was the closest yet. I could see the doe's bottom lip moving as she chewed. I could see the brown and black and white hairs mixed together in her coat. Abruptly she jerked up her head and stared straight at me. It must have been my scent because I hadn't moved a muscle. The doe paused a moment, then leapt away, her fawn close behind.

I warmed as I trotted home in the waning light. By the time I burst in through the kitchen door only my face and fingers and toes were numb. Mom was making fry bread in her new deep fryer. In the old house she would have been cooking at the wood stove, and I could have stood by it to warm up. Now I stood over a hot air register and waited for the furnace fan to switch on.

"Do you have homework, Paul?" Mom called.

"No, Ma. Is Ira coming to dinner?" I asked.

"Yes. How did you know?"

"Cause you're cooking extra and looking grumpy."

"He's working with Pa out in the woods. He'll be eating with us for awhile."

"Ira said he was bringing me a twenty-two next time he came."

"So he said."

"Then I can get some squirrels and partridge."

"That'll be nice, Paul. Just as long as you get your homework done."

I sat through supper as patiently as I could. Pa and Ira were arguing about thermal underwear. My sister Dorothy joined in, siding with thermal cotton over woolen union suits.

"The thermal won't shrink like wool, either," she said, backing up our father.

"Cotton is never going to take the place of wool," Ira said obstinately. Ira hated change.

"I got real close to a couple of deer today," I broke in. "From here to there." I nodded at the couch in the living room. Ira was immediately interested.

"What were they?"

"Doe and fawn."

"You'll be a good hunter, Paul. The best hunter gets closest to the game so he won't make a bad shot."

"I could hunt now. I could get squirrels and partridge."

"You so good with a slingshot?" Dorothy asked.

"Seems you'd need a gun all right. Don't you have a gun for the boy, Adrian?" Ira asked my father. I tried to hide my disappointment. Ira had forgotten about the twenty-two.

"I don't know if he's ready for a gun. Paul's only eight years old."

"Big as you when I started taking you out."

"Yeah, well I'm too busy working in the woods. I don't have time to take Paul out."

I couldn't understand why my father and uncle and sister were all laughing at this conversation.

"You've teased enough," Ma said, looking straight at Ira. Ira stepped to the back entry and brought out an ancient rifle.

"Still in perfect condition, Adrian."

I had to wait and watch Dad heft the gun and peer down its sites. "This was a good old rifle," he said fondly. Finally he handed it me.

"It's not a toy, Paul. Don't ever, *ever* point it at something unless you want to kill it."

"It's not even loaded," Dorothy said.

"Always treat every gun like it's loaded," Ira said. "Brenda killed her mother with a gun she thought wasn't loaded." Brenda was a girl in Dorothy's class, forever forlorn.

None of this talk checked my spirits. I stroked the barrel of the twenty-two.

"Hey, don't handle the barrel. The salt on your hands makes it rust. Here let me show you how to clean it," Ira said. He went back to the entry and brought out a pouch with rod and pads and gun oil in. Dorothy helped Mom clear away the dishes and Dad laid papers down on the floor where he started working mink oil into his work boots. I poured oil on the little pads Ira gave me. There was nothing nicer than the smell of gun oil.

On Saturday Ira came over and set up targets. I wanted to go in the woods right away.

"Most important thing you'll ever learn is patience," Ira told me. "It also helps to know how to aim."

It wasn't as easy as I thought it would be. The first time I squeezed the trigger, I squeezed my eyes shut, too. It took another three shots before I could force my eyes to stay open. After I went through a box of cartridges I could hit a target at thirty feet, but not always the bulls-eye.

"When can I go out in the woods?" I asked Ira at lunch.

"When you hit the bulls-eye every time. That target isn't even moving. You want to be a good shot. You don't want to go out wounding things."

I knew that. I would never shoot badly.

Every day after school I practiced on my own, until I hit the bulls-eye every time. I knew I was a good shot. I couldn't wait for Ira to take me out on Saturday. One afternoon I took the rifle like I was going out to shoot targets and just slipped off into the woods. It was already dusk. I wanted to find a partridge or a squirrel, but the light was fading fast. There was a blue jay scolding from a low pine branch. He sat there boldly while I took aim. It was a good clean shot.

I ran home and burst into the kitchen with my prize. Pa and Ira were already there.

"Got your first game, son," Dad said mildly. "Well, let's go clean it."

"But it's a blue jay. You don't eat blue jays."

"If you kill it, you eat it. You don't waste," Ira said.

"I think it'll make a meal in a soup with a little wild rice," Ma said.

I felt ashamed. Even Dorothy looked sorry for me.

I kicked at a broken paddle in Ira's yard. We were supposed to be out hunting, but Ira was arguing with some white guys. They'd come with a wrecker and a winch. When Ira started hollering, I got interested in the argument.

"That's not junk. That's my spare parts," Ira said, pointing to a '52 Chevy, two-tone aqua and white. "Over there," he gestured to a '48 Ford pickup, "that just needs a new transmission."

"What are you going to say about this wreck?" the bald man challenged. He was staring at the Model A truck without wheels.

170

"Wreck?" shouted Ira. "Wreck? That's my power take-off. That's what I run the saw rig with, and the rice roaster."

"We have the authority to remove all this junk," the scrawny guy said, "before we begin constructing the new house."

"I don't want a new house. Just get out of here!"

The bald man ignored Ira and calmly gestured to the wrecker. They'd driven all the way out from Cook, and I didn't recognize the men. They calmly attached the cable to the Chevy. For a minute I thought that Ira was going to attack them, but instead he turned and stalked into his house.

Ira's house was full of interesting things. Old baskets, and traps of every size, and rice poles, moccasins and a fully beaded powwow costume that his dead wife Nellie had made for him. On the porch mink and muskrat pelts were drying on stretcher boards.

Ira sat at his table with his head in his hands. I didn't dare say anything. Finally Ira spoke.

"Scavengers!" he said. He got up and picked up his gun. "Let's go hunting, boy."

It was my first deer hunt. I had Dad's thirty-thirty. I'd shot targets with it, gotten use to the heft of the gun, its violent kickback. I knew the deer trails. I knew how to wait for the deer. I didn't think there was anything else to learn.

Ira thought differently.

"You'll get buck fever. It's different when you see a deer when there's a gun in your hand than when you're just standing in the woods watching. Your heart's going to race, and your hands will start trembling. *Never* take a shot when you have buck fever. You aren't in your right mind. You might be shooting a man. Or you'll shoot badly, maim the deer. When you get buck fever, stop. Take deep breaths."

"What if the deer gets away?"

"Let it go. Don't shoot unless you're in condition to take good steady aim."

We found fresh tracks in the light snow. Ira was right. It was harder to stand and wait for the deer when you were hunting them.

"What does a hunter need first?" Ira asked.

"Patience," I answered obediently. Then we didn't talk any more. We sat on stumps in a clump of poplar and waited. It was more than an hour before a deer approached. Ira nodded at me and I raised the gun. I sighted carefully down the barrel. My heart began to race and

171

my hand shook. I took a deep breath and calmed. Just as I fired the buck turned. It leapt away.

"Did I miss?"

"No. Shot in the lungs, I think," Ira said. He sat back down on his stump and took out his pipe.

"Aren't we going after it?"

"If you chase him he'll panic, then he can go for miles, even days. He'll panic the other deer. A run deer tastes sour. Fear ruins the meat. Wait, and he'll just go off a little and lie down. He'll stiffen up. You can finish him off."

"How long do we wait?"

"About as long as it takes to smoke this pipe."

Ira was right. We followed the blood trail about seventy yards, and found the deer lying there. He lifted his head but didn't rise. I felt bad. I loved to see deer spring and leap. I had dreamed of taking one with a quick kill. I hadn't thought of this. I shot again and the buck was gone.

"That's a fine two point, Paul," Ira said. He deftly cut under the deer's jaw and stood back while he bled. "Watch now," he said, as he slit down the belly. He took butcher wrap from the back pocket of his mackinaw and lay the liver, heart and kidneys there. I unwrapped the rope I had around my middle and fixed it to the little antlers. I carried the bundle of organ meats under my arm and together with Ira I pulled the deer out of the woods. I thought of bringing the deer to Mom. There in the fresh fall snow, with Ira and my first buck, I felt a fine sense of exhilaration.

Mom cooked the liver for supper. Ira stayed to eat. He was ranting about the men who had been at his house that morning.

"The BIA is going to tear down my house. They're going to bulldoze it down."

"But you'll get a new house, Ira," Mom said.

Ira looked around at the all-modern kitchen with contempt. "I don't want a new house. I built that house myself."

"The BIA is going to clean the village up. Your place is just a shack, Ira."

Ira jumped up from his chair and stomped across the kitchen. He turned back with his hand on the doorknob.

"Well, I don't call this a reservation," he growled, and slammed out.

I was sitting in the corner of the kitchen, cleaning my new thirty-ought-six. My doe was hanging in the tree out in the yard. I'd waited for hours in the cold, and hauled the deer for miles. I wanted to settle back and let the weariness mix with contentment, but my sister Dorothy and Ira and Mom and Dad and Dorothy's husband Fish were beginning to shout in one of their interminable arguments about the changes that were coming to the reservation.

"There isn't anybody without a decent house now," said my mother. "Are you going to tell me that's wrong?" Mom had been educated at boarding school, and she was always on the side of progress.

"Well," said Dorothy, rocking her sleeping baby, "They gave out new houses to the worst bums, and put them next to people who were working, and so what's the point of working? And look at how those people treat those houses."

"They built them in the wrong places," said Fish. "People got along in the village because the Cadotte faction was all on one side and the Gejik people were all on the other. The BIA stuck anyone anyplace, now they're fighting all the time."

"Well, it never would have gotten out of hand if the DNR hadn't come out when we were making rules for the rice harvest and said we had no authority to make those rules. That's when it got out of hand."

Everyone sat silent for a few minutes. Charlie Gejik was dead and Billy Cadotte was in jail.

"The Cadottes and Gejiks have been at it for two hundred years," said Ira. "But nobody ever fought about the rice before. They always obeyed the committee."

"I'm talking houses and programs," Mom said. "That rice war was something different. But these programs, they're going to make jobs on the reservation."

"What I see," said Fish, "is white guys coming up from Minneapolis telling us how to run things. That's the jobs I see on the reservation. Hand us out commodities, send us to detox. I don't see jobs for Indians on the reservation."

"Indians don't want to work anymore anyway," said Dad sadly. Once he had ten guys working for his logging company. Now he had Fish, and Ira if he wasn't trapping or hunting.

"Who needs to work?" asked Ira. "They just sit home and pick up the commodities."

"Hey, they'd work if there were opportunities," said Fish.

"That's what these new programs are going to bring in, opportunity," Mom persisted. "Paul could go to college and come back and make a decent living right here on the reservation." Everyone turned to look at me.

"You planning to go to college, Paul?" Fish asked.

"He's got the grades," said Mom. "He could go."

"Yeah, Pete LaFreniere went to college, and he wasn't as smart," Dorothy said.

"You know why Pete went? He went to get out of the draft," said Fish. "First he tried to say he was some kind of conscientious objector because he was apprentice in Grand Medicine, and traditional Chippewa religion was pacifist."

"Tell that one to the Sioux," Ira snorted. "I'll tell you one thing, whatever else, us Indians made good soldiers."

"Yes we did," said Dad.

"I don't know why you're so proud of fighting for the U.S. government when they're the ones that took your house, Ira," Dorothy said.

"That's something different altogether," Ira said hotly. "That's BIA politics. I fought for this country."

"Indians had most volunteers in World War II, had the most decorations and took the most casualties," said Dad.

"And I don't understand why," said Dorothy.

"They wanted to prove they were good citizens," said Mom.

Ira snorted again. "Prove nothing. It's our treaty obligations, and it's our duty. Indians never shirked from a fight."

"So, are you planning to go to college, Paul?"

"I don't know," I said. I thought it might be worth it if it could get me a job on the reservation, like Mom said. I didn't plan to sit around and pick up commodities. But I sure didn't want to leave home, either.

I cradled my M16 in the crook of my arm. If I wasn't in uniform, and carrying a gun, I could have just disappeared into the crowds of Da Nang. Maybe I was a little taller than most of them, but even in my uniform I felt like I stuck out less than when I went to school in Ely. In basic they talked about gooks. We ran at dummies with bayonets and screamed when we stuck them. Now that we were here, you couldn't tell who was a good gook and who was a bad gook.

I thought the Vietnamese were beautiful, especially the girls with their long black hair. I didn't understand what the war was about. I

174

knew that when I was on patrol I had to kill them or they'd kill me. I thought that they wouldn't be likely to do that if I was back at home on the reservation, but the only way I could go home now was to go home with honor.

We'd sat in the jungle for more than a day. Some of the guys were getting jumpy. I knew how to wait. Then we saw them, coming through the thick brush. "Cong!" one of the men hissed. I wasn't sure. They could be peasants, ARVN. I waited until I thought I was sure. I sighted in on one. Through the sights I saw a young man with an uncanny resemblance to my brother-in-law, Fish. My heart began to race and my hands started to tremble. I took deep breaths. My hand steadied. I shot when I knew my aim was sure. It was a clean hit.

Chapter 23

Tamarack Autumn: Aina Lahti's Second Story

Winner of *The Finnish American Reporter's* 1994 Grand Prize in Fiction.

It was a lovely, warm Indian summer day. I sat on my porch, waiting and rocking. Emily was coming. The grandchild, the golden child.

My yard was tidy, ready for winter snow. I had dug up the dahlias and mulched the tulips. The roses were covered too. I'd raked the fallen leaves from the grass.

Beyond the yard the fields were no longer tidy. Fields that Arvo and I had cleared and tended were being reclaimed by the woods. Tamarack and alder had moved in; now the tamarack was flaming gold. It brought its own light to the low places.

A car turned into the driveway, and then Emily was bounding up the porch steps. I started to rise but Emily threw her arms around me as I sat in my rocking chair.

"Oh *Mummu*, how good to be home!"

Emily's serious young man was standing uncomfortably behind her. He reminded me of the young Lenin. He must have worked hard at the likeness, with his high collar and the little wire-rimmed glasses. He extended his hand formally.

"How are you, Peter?" I asked.

"Pekka," he said.

"Yes, *Mummu*. Peter is studying Finnish at the university. He changed his name to Pekka."

"My major field is American history, of course. My specialties are immigration and labor," Peter-Pekka told me.

"*Mummu*, Pekka wants to interview you on the tape recorder. About Grandpa and the 1916 strike. He's writing his dissertation about the strike."

176

The old terror stirred in me. I'd thought that when Urho died I buried the tragedy with him, but here was this humorless young man looking for his history, bringing back the dread of 53 years as fresh as if a policeman were here on my porch, come to take me away.

Emily sat with her head leaning against my knee, just as she had as a child. I stroked her hair. Peter-Pekka had already turned on his recording machine.

"Aina Lahti; subject Mesaba Strike of 1916: date of interview, September 19, 1969: Pekka Johnson, Interviewer," he said tonelessly into the microphone. He began to ask questions in a strange, stilted Finnish that I couldn't understand.

"I'm sorry," I said. "I know my English isn't good, but too many Finnish words have changed. My Finnish is so different from yours."

Peter-Pekka looked disappointed but he switched to English without comment. I couldn't think of how to stop him. I could only tell him what he wanted to hear. He asked where I was born in Finland and how I came to this country. I explained that I came with my older brother Arvo.

"Why?"

"It seems silly now. We wanted adventure. We were young. American streets were supposed to be paved with gold."

"Do you remember Ellis Island?"

"What I remember better is crossing the North Sea to Liverpool. I didn't believe anyone could be so sick and live. "And then Ellis Island, yes, and then the train trip to the Mesaba. Others from our village had gone before. They found us a place in a boardinghouse. I worked there in the kitchen as a maid. Arvo went to work in the mine. The streets were dirty with the red dust of the iron ore, not paved with gold.

"How did you meet your husband, Urho Lahti, hero and martyr of the Strike of 1916?"

For a moment I permitted myself to remember Urho as he was when I first saw him. He lived in the boardinghouse. He was very handsome, but there was something else about him—a kind of fire from within. I mistook his fervor for love. How easily I married him. After we were married I learned that his passion was of himself and that it quickly found new objects. Not women. Ideas. I didn't tell this to Peter-Pekka. Only how we met in the boardinghouse.

Peter-Pekka wanted to know about the conditions that gave rise to the strike. Yes, the work was dirty. Yes, the conditions were bad.

177

Yes, pay was low. Peter-Pekka warmed to his sense of injustice and the glory of the protest. Urho would have liked this boy. They could have fed each other's anger, talked injustice for hours on end. They might have been striking comrades.

"Can you tell me anything about the way Urho died?"

There it was. Slowly I shook my head.

"He was killed by company goons and left in a ditch by the side of the road, isn't that true?" Peter-Pekka demanded.

"Yes, he was found dead by the road. It wasn't determined who had killed him."

"Wasn't it reasonable to assume that it was the company goons, considering his leadership position in the strike?"

"That's what was assumed."

Peter-Pekka was disappointed because I gave him no more, but he had had me say on his tape machine what he wanted to hear. After a few more questions, he shut it off and stood to stretch his legs. He looked about him, seeing the old farm for the first time. His eyes settled on the tamaracks below.

"What's blighting those fir trees?" he asked Emily.

She smiled at him. "Those are tamaracks. They look like evergreens with their needles, but they aren't. They loose their needles every year, after the other trees have lost their leaves. But for a while right now they really light up the woods. It's one of my favorite trees."

"I'm going to have a look." With a glance Peter-Pekka commanded Emily to accompany him. She started to rise, but I put my hand on Emily's shoulder.

"Sit here a little while with your old *Mummu*," I said. I smiled at Peter-Pekka apologetically. He turned and strode down the porch steps.

"He's very brilliant, *Mummu*," Emily said when he had gone. "I'm glad that he's going to include Grandpa in his history."

"Emily ..." I began. "Emily ..." I tried again.

"*Mummu?*"

"The history in books .... It isn't the history in life."

"I know, *Mummu*. I study history, too, you know. I know how limited we are by the sources, and . . ."

"Emily ... I'll tell you what happened to your grandfather."

Emily became very still.

"They say that the Finnish women knew that their men were doomed when they went off to fight the Russians. The women knew, but the men still went."

178

"But Finland maintains its independence today because all those men were willing to die."

"Yes. And that's how it was with the strike as well."

"You mean you knew it was doomed? Weren't you a socialist, too?"

"I knew we couldn't win the strike."

"But if people hadn't been willing to strike over and over again for an eight-hour day and better conditions, they never would have gotten reform."

"Yes, that's true. That's what Urho wanted to die for."

"Isn't that what he died for? *Mummu?*"

"It's easier to find two sides in history than in life."

"*Mummu?*"

It was hard to begin to speak of things that I had never spoken of, but I didn't have much time. Peter-Pekka was upon the tamaracks and beginning his inspection.

"Andy, your father, was only three. The strike had gone on for months. There was little fuel. We were nearly out of food on very short rations. There was no milk for the baby. We were losing the strike. Urho only knew how to fight, he didn't know how to lose. He became obsessed. He worked day and night, went to endless meetings, tried to keep spirits up against certain defeat. But at home—when he came home—he grew angrier and angrier."

That awful night lived fresh in my memory. I could almost smell the smoky kerosene lamp that burned dimly near the window when Urho burst in the door.

"The night he died," I continued, "he was very angry. He was feeling the despair he never showed outside our house. The baby was crying. He was always hungry and he often cried. Urho came in, walked right over and slapped him. I ran to push Urho away from the baby. Urho turned on me and began to hit me. All the anger over the strike. He hit me and hit me. And then Arvo burst in..."

"Uncle Arvo?"

"Yes, of course. Arvo came in and tried to pull Urho off me. They fought. In the fight Urho's head hit the edge of the cookstove. I didn't see how it happened. But Urho lay still and there was blood on the stove."

"He was dead?"

"Yes."

"Daddy saw Uncle Arvo kill his father?"

"Yes."

"What did you do then?"

"Arvo took his body out in the middle of the night and put him in the ditch. Of course everyone thought that the company had him killed."

"Don't cry, *Mummu*," Emily said quietly. She put her arms around me. Peter-Pekka was returning from his inspection, nearing the porch. He didn't notice my tears.

"Kind of a shabby tree, really," he said. "Mrs. Lahti, it occurred to me to ask you a few questions about life after the strike."

He flicked on his machine again.

"When did you move away from the Mesaba and up to Winton with your brother?" he asked. I was ready to answer.

"Just after Urho died. Arvo wasn't really with the strike, you know, but they blacklisted all Finns just alike. There was no work. Arvo liked farming better than mining anyway."

"Did they try to deport you as Mongols under the Oriental Exclusion act?"

"Oh no. Not us. We got our papers without trouble. Maybe others had trouble."

"They tried to classify Finns as Mongols, who were seen as dirty yellow dogs." Peter-Pekka burned with anger at the history of oppression.

"How did you manage then, after the strike?" he persisted.

"Well, in Finnish they say, 'When a cat has to climb a tree, it finds its claws.' We just lived. Milked cows. Planted potatoes. Arvo worked in the lumber camps in the winter. We got active in the Co-op."

Peter-Pekka lost interest in my story, and flicked off the recording machine. I was thinking of spring mornings scented of lilac and the long shadows of the midsummer evenings. I'd like to see another spring, I thought. Peter-Pekka looked from his watch to Emily. Emily got up slowly.

"I'll come again soon, *Mummu*." She leaned down to lay her cheek against mine, and I felt its wetness.

"I won't tell, *Mummu*," she whispered.

"Don't cry, Emily," I told her, and then they were gone, and I sat alone in the fading afternoon, alight with the golden glow of the tamaracks.

Chapter 24

Winter Silence: Robin LaPrairie's Story

I was a party girl in junior college. I went to college because it was close to home, it was cheap, and my friends were going. We had our parties at my cabin, or rather, my folks' cabin. It was on the roadless side of Fall Lake, but one of the guys plowed a road over the ice with his dad's truck so we drove right up to the shore.

The cabin was made out of logs, one large room with a bare floor, plus a porch kitchen. Cindy and I would go out on Saturday afternoon to warm it up and heat the sauna. In the evening carloads of kids started arriving with food and beer. We ate, drank, took saunas, sang, laughed, talked, and then staked out a piece of floor when it was time to go to sleep. In the early dawn I got up to feed the fire, stepping over bodies in sleeping bags as they began to writhe.

I liked college.

There was a bitter cold spell in early January, thirty to forty below for two weeks. It broke on a Friday. On Saturday people started coming out to the cabin in the early afternoon, right after Cindy and I had gotten there. They built snow forts and had a snowball fight. People kept coming all afternoon. By night there were too many people in the cabin and the air was thick and hot. A drunken guest sat at the stove poking at the fire, complaining loudly of claustrophobia. I had to get out of there.

"I'm going skiing," I said to no one, walking out the door. I pulled a pair of skis out of the snowbank and slipped my boots into the leather toe loops. The door opened behind me.

"I'll go with you."

I turned around. "Johnny!" I said. "You're supposed to be in California!"

"I was," he said.

"How long have you been here? I mean, at the party?"

"I came out with Mike."

He strapped on the other pair of skis and we skied down to the moonlit lake. My dog Skipper raced ahead of us and bounded back with spaniel joy. We skied to the middle of the lake and stopped. The frozen silence filled with the sound of my heartbeat and the ringing in my ears.

"How long are you staying?" I asked Johnny.

"A day. Maybe a week." We skied on. "I'm on my way to Canada. I have a friend who has a cabin in Ontario. He's going to let me live there."

"I thought people went to California for the winter, and came here for the summer."

"It's winter I miss."

Most of the guests had crashed by the time we returned to the cabin. We nudged some over to make a space on the floor.

"Where's your sleeping bag?" I asked Johnny.

"I don't have one."

I crawled under my quilts and lifted a corner for him to join me.

"What are you going to live on, in your cabin way up in Canada?" I asked.

"Squirrels are good food. Potatoes grow in the north."

"Seriously."

"I'll live like Antti."

"You'll be a trapper?"

"I'll be self-sufficient. I don't need much. I can do odd jobs and sell a sculpture from time to time, for a little cash. Earn enough to get by."

"Antti wasn't a hermit," I said.

"I won't be a hermit. I'll go to town to buy salt," Johnny said.

"Salt," I said. Johnny lay still for a long time. I thought he'd fallen asleep. Then he leaned over and put his mouth close to my ear.

"Ammunition," he whispered.

"Ammunition," I whispered.

"Pots and pans."

"Pots and pans. A plate and a cup."

He didn't say anything more and again I thought he'd fallen asleep. Then he rolled toward me and rested his hand on my stomach. I covered his hand with mine and we slept.

Cindy's eyes were open when I stepped over her the next morning to start the fire. I knelt beside her.

"Cindy?"

"Yes?"

"Did you know Johnny was home?"

"Yeah, he's staying with Mike." Cindy rolled over and pulled her sleeping bag over her head.

I was busy making breakfast for everybody and cleaning up, and I didn't notice Johnny leave.

Wednesday night the temperatures dropped far below zero again. Cindy and I were studying for a biology test at my folks' house in Winton.

Someone knocked on the door. I opened it to a gust of bitter wind. Johnny was standing there.

"Come in," I said.

"No. I just wanted to look at you."

"I didn't hear your car."

"I walked."

"From Ely?" It's four miles, for God's sake. Well, come on in."

"No, thanks." He turned and disappeared into the darkness.

"Cindy," I said, "Johnny is nuts."

"But boy, what a way to make a point," Cindy said.

"What's the point?"

"He wants you."

"He's known me since I played outside in my diapers."

"He just noticed that you grew up."

Johnny came to the college on Thursday. His eyes followed me in the library and cafeteria. He wasn't there on Friday. Saturday I waited for him to come to the party at the cabin, but he didn't show up. I was asleep on the floor when someone touched my cheek.

"Want to go skiing?" Johnny whispered in my ear. I followed him outside, and again we skied out on the lake, making shadows in the moonlight. A pack of wolves called, deep in the bay.

"Let's ski over there," I said. We skied toward the dark shadow of the shore, into the circle of the wolves howling around us. The sounds that break the silence of the north are haunting sounds—the crying of the wolves, the loons, the wind.

That night we lay together again under my quilts, in the corner of the cabin.

"Antti took me trapping the winter before he died," Johnny said. "I could be a trapper."

"Remember the stories about the guys who trapped alone, who went mad from loneliness?"

"Yeah," Johnny said. "You go crazy from being alone."

I held his hand against my cheek.

"You don't have to be alone," I said.

Afterwards I only remembered images from that time—images in silhouette, Johnny and me against glittering snow on frozen lakes. We skied to the falls and watched otters play. We snow-shoed to the cliffs and climbed high enough to see the lakes beyond. We ate cheese and bread with numb fingers and drank wine under the pines. Later I remembered how we looked at each other, losing ourselves in each other's eyes, warming ourselves with kisses.

One night we lay together in the dark, looking through the window at the cold starry sky.

"Salt. Ammunition," Johnny whispered. "Pots and pans. A wife." He pulled me into his arms and moaned like the pines in the wind.

Johnny didn't show up the next day, or the next. I went over to Mike's house, but Mike hadn't seen him. I called off the Saturday night party and sat at the cabin with Skipper, hoping for a knock at the door, knowing it wouldn't come. My hands and stomach were numb with fear.

Monday Johnny was at the college, but he refused to talk to me. He wouldn't look at me.

"Did you fight?" Cindy asked.

"No," I said.

"I don't understand it," she said. "I never saw anybody in love like you guys."

I tried to be brave. I was not going to make a fool of myself by betraying my feelings. I went to classes, took notes, went home.

Johnny was there on Tuesday, sitting with Cindy in the cafeteria. I sat down on the far side of the room. When Cindy saw me she came back to my table. Others turned and saw us there, and one by one my classmates came to sit around me—every one of them—leaving Johnny alone in the corner. They were my party friends, and they meant to stand by me. I'd never felt so alone.

"Please," I whispered to Cindy. "Don't do this to Johnny." I picked up my books and went home. Johnny never spoke to me again. I sent him a note at Mike's house: "Please. What happened? What did I do?" He'd gone back to California.

I quit giving parties, quit going to them. Kept to my books, became a serious student.

"You know, Robin," Cindy said one time, "I still wonder what happened with you and Johnny. Did you ever hear from him?"

"No. Somebody saw him in San Francisco."

"I don't understand what happened."

"Love opened his wounds."

"What do you mean?"

"Johnny gets by as long as he's tough," I said. "When he starts to feel, all the pain comes in."

"Love is supposed to heal the pain."

"There's more pain there than love can heal."

It was the last time Johnny came home.

Chapter 25

Trip to Duluth: Mary Bouchay Keewatin's Second Story

P aul wouldn't come home. He'd come half way around the world and gotten as far as Duluth but he couldn't make the last leg back to the reservation.

"Give him time," Adrian said. "It takes a while to leave a war behind."

"They pamper these boys," Ira said. "One year of Vietnam and then it's R and R in Hawaii. We were in our war for the duration. We had to win it if we ever wanted to come home." Ira was launched on his favorite topic. I went out to find my other grandson, Joe.

"Where did you see Paul?" I asked him.

"Oh, Grandma, you don't want to know," Joe said.

"Take me to him."

Joe thought about it.

"Okay," he said, finally. Ira was still railing at Adrian about the virtues of World War II soldiers when I went in the house to take the money out of my mattress and put it in my handbag. They didn't see me leave with Joe in his Chevrolet.

Joe took me to a filthy building in Duluth. There was a stench in the dark hall. I followed him up three flights of stairs. At the landing at the top, Joe knocked once on a door and walked in. A man who wasn't Paul sat hunched over at the table. He didn't look up.

Paul was asleep on the couch, surrounded by empty beer bottles. Joe stayed by the door. I looked around and found a dirty towel in the bathroom. I soaked it in cold water and then coiled it around Paul's face.

He swung out at me, knocking me off my chair. I lay on the floor looking up at his wild eyes. It was a long time before he knew who he was looking at.

"Grandma," he said. He sat on the couch, face in his hands, not offering to help me up. I got back on my chair and looked at Paul. His hair was long and greasy, tied with a red bandanna headband. He was all slumped down, looking like a man who lost a war.

"Go home, Grandma," Paul said.

"Come with me."

"I can't."

"Then I'll stay."

"You don't understand, Grandma. Go home."

"Paul!" I spoke in a tone I'd needed only once before with the boy. "Get your things and come with me."

I didn't expect him to obey, but he did. Slowly he rose, stuffed some dirty clothes in a duffel bag and left without saying good-bye to his companion. Joe followed us down the stairs.

Out on the street, Paul balked.

"I can't," he said, looking at Joe's Chevy.

"Bring us to a nice hotel, Joe," I said. Paul got in the car.

We checked into a clean building near downtown.

"I'll call you, Joe," I said. "Thanks."

Paul slept for three days. He woke and raged from time to time. He wanted more booze but I talked him out of it. He wasn't the Paul I remembered.

"Listen, Paul," I said. He was lying awake, staring at the ceiling. "I know about demons."

I told him how it was when Ira and I were taken from Basswood, leaving Father and Aunt without spirit houses, leaving Charlie unburied, taking nothing with us but Charlie's Winchester.

I had never talked about that time before.

Paul rose and stood over me.

"This time, Grandma, I was the man with the gun who drove people away from their homes."

"It wasn't your idea."

"I could have disobeyed orders."

"And come home dishonorable? That wasn't a real choice." I was thinking about how his father and Ira would have acted if Paul had dishonored them. "We both lost our choice to do what was right."

Paul didn't believe me. I'd said the wrong thing. Maybe we had lost Paul, like Joe thought.

We went on long walks around the city. We ate at nearby restaurants, took a bus down Park Point and walked in silence along the beach. One day we went to the zoo. People stared at us, me old and little and prim in my white spring coat, walking with dirty, long-haired Paul in his army jacket. You would think they had never seen Indians before.

One afternoon we wandered into a museum. There was a display of old Indian artifacts—arrowheads, moccasins and the like—covered with dust behind a dirty glass window.

"Grandma, what's wrong?" Paul was looking at me in alarm.

I'd blanked out for a minute, and there I was, sitting on the floor again.

"That's...it's Charlie's powwow outfit," I said. I'd watched Aunt sew it, bead by bead. In that moment Charlie was as alive to me as the night at the powwow when he danced in splendor, the night Antti had watched me in the circle of dancers, following me with his pale eyes.

"Come on Grandma," Paul said, pulling me up. "Let's go home."

Chapter 26

Silver Thaw: Emily Lahti's Second Story

A black cloud blotted out the sun. Large drops of rain struck the windshield and a clap of thunder startled me out of my reverie. I was driving back from Diana's place on Lake Vermilion. Diana and I had dropped out of graduate school at the same time, but she went to law school and made money. She used to come up to see me at the cabin every year, until she decided to buy a "little lake place" as an investment. Her little place loomed over Vermilion. It had three bedrooms, two baths, and a big screen TV.

The storm hit in full fury as I passed through the reservation. My wipers couldn't keep up with the sheets of rain and I had to pull over. I turned on Ely radio. "… surprise ice storm," it was saying. "Travel is not advised." The announcer listed canceled events.

It was late. I had to get back to Winton to pick up Molly. When the rain let up a little, I put the car in gear and eased onto the pavement. There was a sheen on the road. I tested the brakes and went into a skid.

I crept along at fifteen miles an hour. The wipers iced up and the road blurred in front of me. My wheels bumped off the pavement, hit gravel, and then I was sliding down the steep bank into the ditch. The car came to rest on its side.

"Shit," I said out loud.

I pulled myself up through the driver's door and clawed my way up the icy bank.

There was a dirt road up ahead. I clutched my jacket around me, bowed my head into the sleet and walked on the icy shoulder, hoping I'd find a year round home instead of a summer place. My light wool jacket was already soaked and my teeth were chattering. Tire tracks on the driveway gave me hope.

189

A quarter of a mile in from the road I saw the weathered-shingled shack. In front sat a battered red pickup with a cracked windshield, next to a logger's boom truck.

There was no answer to my knock. I knocked again.

A middle-aged Indian man opened the door and regarded me.

"Come in," he said.

I stepped into the warm kitchen.

"I went in the ditch," I said, "Could I use your... Paul? Paul Keewatin? I'm Emily. Emily Lahti."

When he smiled I knew for sure it was Paul.

"So you are," he said.

"I haven't seen you since high school. Since you went into the army. How long has it been?"

"Twelve years," Paul said.

"My God," I said, "that long." I stood there staring at him. He looked older than he was.

"You have to get those clothes off," Paul said. I was shaking violently.

"My car's in the ditch and I'm supposed to pick up my daughter. Do you have a phone?"

"No," said Paul. "Where's your daughter?"

"In Winton. Robin's taking care of her."

"She'll be okay, then," Paul said.

"Robin will think I had an accident."

"You did." Paul looked out the window. "Robin won't get exited until she knows there's something to get exited about. I'll get you some dry clothes."

He brought me a worn flannel shirt and a pair of faded jeans. I changed in Paul's small bedroom. My hands were shaking so badly that I could hardly manage the zippers.

"I'm making you some tea," Paul said, when I came back, holding up the jeans with one hand and carrying the bundle of wet clothes in the other. Paul hung them on the clothesline that ran across the kitchen and pulled a chair up next to the wood cookstove.

"Sit down," he said, wrapping a threadbare Hudson's Bay Blanket around my shoulders. "You've got hypothermia."

I looked around the cabin. The kitchen was marked off from the living area by the faded linoleum on the floor. Besides the cookstove, it had a table with two chairs, an old round-topped refrigerator, a cupboard, and a sink with a hand pump.

190

Paul added wood to the heater on the side of the room with the shabby couch, overstuffed chair and a shelf of books. A hide stretched on a hoop lay on the bare floor.

The kettle whistled. Paul came back to make the tea.

"Where did you go in the ditch?" he asked.

"Not far back, before your driveway. A real steep place."

"When the storm lets up I'll pull you out with my boom truck," Paul said. "Is your car smashed up?"

"I slid down real slow, but it tipped on its side."

"Nothing we can do now, in the dark, in the storm. I'll look it over in the morning."

"I'm lucky you live here," I said.

"Yeah," he said. "You are. Drink your tea and warm up."

He lit a kerosene lamp.

"Don't you have electricity?" I asked.

"No," Paul said. "It costs."

"REA doesn't cost that much."

"It isn't the money. Depending on it is expensive."

"I like lamplight," I said.

"Do you like venison?" Paul said. "Or you want some fish?"

"Either."

He fried venison steaks, boiled potatoes and opened a can of peas. We ate in silence. Gradually I stopped shivering.

"I was really hungry," I said. "Thanks."

Paul sat back in his chair.

"I heard you married Peter Johnson," he said.

"We're divorced. I live in Duluth. Just came up for Thanksgiving. What about you? Aren't you married?"

"Divorced."

"I'm sorry. Do you have children?"

"Two. They live in Milwaukee with their mother. I never see them."

"That's too bad."

"Yeah," he said. "It is."

Paul didn't say anything for a while, then he said quietly, "Things seldom turn out the way we expect them to." He got up to wash the dishes. I watched the fire flash through cracks in the cookstove. The sky was black and sleet whipped at the windows. Paul carefully wiped the dishes and put them back in the cupboard. He returned to the table. In dim lamplight, Paul looked younger. It was something in his manner, deliberation or resignation, that made him seem old.

191

"You have just the one child?" he asked.

"Yes. Molly. She's two."

"Last I heard you were heading for a brilliant academic career."

"Things don't always turn out the way we expect them to," I said.
We lapsed back into silence.

"Remember the last time we sat out a storm together?" I asked.

"Maple Isle. Finest accommodations I ever had. What do you hear
from Johnny?"

"I haven't heard from him for a couple of years. He was out in
California."

"It isn't like Johnny to stay away from Winton."

"No. I went out to look for him last year. I reported him missing
to the San Francisco police. They gave me a fat book full of pictures
of unidentified dead hippies. I couldn't look at it very long."

"He used to talk about going to Mexico. Maybe he's down there."

"Maybe."

"Let's sit in the living room." Paul said.

I shuffled over to the couch, wrapped in the blanket. Paul opened
the front door of the wood heater and set up the fire screen so we
could watch the flames. He sat down in the chair.

"What do you usually do in the evening?" I asked.

"Grease my boots, sharpen my chainsaw. Read a little. I go to bed
pretty early."

"Did your wife want a fancier life?"

"She wanted a sober husband," Paul said. "I was a drunk."

"Oh," I said.

"What brought you back to northern Minnesota?" Paul asked.

"Why are you back on the reservation?" I countered.

Paul snorted. "I'm an Indian."

"You were heading out into the world when I knew you."

"I was heading for Vietnam."

We didn't talk for a while. It was a strained silence. I wanted to
be friendly again.

"I needed to come home," I said, answering his question. "but
things changed so much I feel like my planet was blown up. Now
I'm drifting through the universe."

"Yes," said Paul, "that's what it feels like."

"Even on the reservation?"

"Especially here. Indians don't remember their culture. They
make it up and sell it to white people."

192

"You mean art, crafts?"

"No. Like fake spirituality. Like cures for social problems. Like grant proposals to 'restore the Ojibwe heritage.' My grandmother was a Chippewa, but the academics and politicos say she should have called herself Ojibwe. They know who she was better than she did, right? You know what I liked about the culture? Tolerance, frugality, humor, generosity. How do you restore that with funding? Those are the things money destroys. Windigo's moved onto the reservation."

"Windigo?"

"The greed monster. He's so greedy that he eats away his own lips."

"Yech."

"He's the most terrible of the Chippewa monsters. Grandma always warned us about him. Well, he's on the loose, eating the hearts out of people. Do you know what a give-away is?"

"I've heard of it. I don't understand it."

"Chippewas used to get status and honor from generosity. When somebody accumulated a lot of wealth—more things than he needed—he'd have a big party and give things away."

"It sounds strange."

"It had a lot of great consequences. The wealth got distributed, people felt good sharing with each other, and you didn't have to exploit more resources than you needed to impress anybody."

"It sounds too ideal."

"My point. It sounds ideal to you because you can't even comprehend how good it feels to be that generous. Giving was more satisfying to people than hoarding. It used to be an old European value, too, but it got lost, somehow."

"Almost lost, anyway."

"We don't have give-aways anymore, except when somebody dies, and then we distribute their stuff around the village. People started coming up from the Cities, people whose families haven't been on the reservation for three generations, for give-aways at the funerals of people they didn't even know. They smirk and take the loot, thinking we're stupid backwoods chumps who don't know the value of a rifle or a canoe."

"When someone thinks you're stupid because you're being generous it makes you feel bad," I said. "Taken advantage of."

"Yes. But they're the stupid ones. They're cutting themselves off from the whole world of generosity. Worse, they're destroying it. That's Windigo at work. Greed got them. It's contagious."

193

"Adam Smith said competition would check greed."

"My experience is that competition teaches people to fight dirty and sabotage good work."

"It isn't a friendly world when everyone is a competitor. My father even saw Johnny as competition. His own son," I said. Paul didn't answer.

"There's some community feeling left in Winton," I said after a while. "When my car breaks down somebody pulls over and looks under my hood or changes my tire for me and I'm on my way. One time I didn't have a jack, and four guys held up the car while the fifth changed the tire. It was just a little Volkswagen."

Paul laughed.

"Yeah, that's the tradition. It isn't all gone here, either," he said. "It's how people get along. I saw it in the villages in Vietnam. North Vietnam and the U.S. were competing to destroy it. That's what the war was really about."

"Why? Why is power compelled to destroy that kind of cooperation?"

Paul shrugged. "You're the historian," he said.

"I don't understand power. That's why I left graduate school. I was a good student. Tops. But the history they taught was all about power, and the academic politics they practiced were all about power. I wasn't man enough to take it. But by the time I left graduate school, I wasn't what a woman should be, either." I rewrapped my blanket and went into the kitchen to check my clothes. I put them back on in the bedroom. When I returned, Paul was staring into the fire. I had the impulse to touch him when I passed his chair.

"Do people treat you differently when they find out you're a Vietnam vet?" I asked when I'd settled back on the couch.

"Yes."

"Did you go through terrible things?" I asked.

"I did terrible things," he said.

There was nothing I could say.

"My Dad and my cousin Ira promised me that an Indian gets to be a real American by joining the army," he said. "But my war was different from theirs."

"Do they understand that?"

"No." Paul was quiet, thinking. "The two lowest things in America are Indians and Vietnam vets. I'm both."

I wanted to say, no, you're wrong. But he wasn't.

"It isn't my memories from the war that are hardest to live with, it's having to pretend it didn't happen," he said. "To protect good citizens from being contaminated by their war."

I knew how it was to experience horrors that you couldn't talk about, that put you beyond human sympathy. I wanted to tell Paul about Johnny, what they had done to him when he was little, but I didn't want to insult him. It wasn't like Vietnam.

Paul looked up at me. His eyes were bottomless, with no defense to love or pain. Only the sleet against the windows and the crackling of the fire broke the silence.

"Would you like coffee?" he asked. "Or more tea?"

"Tea would be nice. Let me make it."

"No, I'm the host." He went to fix the tea. "Sugar?" he asked.

"No, thank you. Straight."

I needed to go to the bathroom, and went to the door. It was forbidding outside.

"I'm going out," I told Paul.

"Be careful," he said. "Here, put my coat over your head. Take the flashlight."

It was an ordeal making my way over the treacherous ground to the outhouse and back. I splashed water from a dipper onto my hands over the sink and went back to the warmth of the fire. Paul had tea waiting for me. "Out west they call an ice storm a 'silver thaw'," I told him.

The portable radio was on. Bob Dylan was singing "North Country Blues."

> "...Then the shaft was soon shut
> And more work was cut,
> And the fire in the air, it felt frozen.
> 'Til a man come to speak
> And he said in one week,
> That number eleven was closin'.
> They complained in the East,
> They are paying too high.
> They say that your ore ain't worth digging.
> That it's much cheaper down
> In the South American towns
> Where the miners work almost for nothing.
> So the mining gates locked
> And the red iron rotted
> And the room smelled heavy from drinking..."

195

"Here's a funny story," I said. "I was going to high school next to the University, and one day my friend said, 'Hey, there's a kid from Hibbing singing at the Ten O'Clock Scholar, I bet you want to hear him.' I was always telling her about how different things were up North. So we went and there was Bob Dylan, rasping out a song. I said he sang funny and he'd never make it."

Paul laughed.

"Remember when we hung around Johnny's washshed, talking about how nobody could ever explain what it was really like, coming from the north?" he said.

"Dylan tried."

I sat in the middle of the couch and drank my tea, then wrapped myself in the blanket and slowly drifted to sleep watching the flames. I awakened to the rattle of grates. Paul was adding wood to the fire. "I'm sorry I woke you," he said.

My neck was stiff and cramped. I got up to look out the window. The storm hadn't slackened. I went back to the couch. Paul sat in his chair, watching me.

"I was thinking about Johnny," Paul said, "People used to talk about him like he was a bad boy, but that isn't what I remember. I remember that he had an aura of love about him. He made me feel like he could draw me into that circle."

"Thank you," I said. "That's what I remember, too. But he got pretty screwed up there at the end, with the drugs and everything."

Paul's sympathy had caught me off guard. I tried to hold back the tears, tried to brush them away without Paul noticing.

"I'm sorry," I said. "I miss Johnny so badly, and I don't even know if I should be mourning."

"He might have gotten himself out of it, Emily," Paul said. "People do. I did."

I put my face in my hands and sobbed.

Paul sat next to me and put my head against his shoulder. I cried with the wind howling in the eaves and the sleet whipping against the windows.

"Silver thaw," he murmured.

"North Country Blues," Bob Dylan, *Writings and Drawings*, Alfred A. Knopf, Inc., N.Y. 1973.

Chapter 27

Veteran's Peace: Paul Keewatin's Second Story

Y ou have to promise me something," my cousin Ira had told me. "I want to be buried on Jackfish Bay in the old cemetery, near my mother. I want a spirit house. And don't forget, I have to have my moccasins."

"You'll be around a long time yet," I said.

"What year is it?"

"1978."

"Then I'm over seventy years old. I could go any time. You promise me."

"All right. I promise."

It was March, and we were in the woods. I had a skidder and a couple of guys working for me, cutting pulp. Ira worked whenever he felt like it. He wasn't as fast as the young men, but it was surprising what his steady work produced, and he was careful. He'd never had an accident, or caused one. He never was sick, either, but when he had a hangover, I kept my distance.

On July 16, Ira and I were coming out of the woods with a load of pulp wood. When we hit the main road, I stopped the truck to adjust the load. There was an unearthly crackling noise when I raised the boom. Ira stepped out of the cab to see what the noise was. When he put his foot on the ground 7200 volts of electricity hit him. I saw Ira's body land in the ditch and then I looked up. The boom had hit the power line. I leaped clear of the truck, ran to Ira and pressed my ear to his chest. There wasn't a heartbeat, and Ira wasn't breathing. I put my mouth to Ira's to breathe the life back. I breathed and breathed, but Ira didn't come back.

I tried to flag down a car. Little foreign cars with canoes on top zipped by on the highway. I didn't expect them to stop for a big Indian in torn jeans. Then a battered jeep slowed. The old lady who was driving smiled at me pleasantly and opened the door.

"My uncle's been electrocuted," I told her. "The boom hit the wire. Can you get to a phone and call an ambulance? And have the electric company cut the power? Can you describe the location?"

"Oh, my god, I'm so sorry. Yes. County 404 west and 169."

She sped off. I sat in the ditch and looked at the boom crackling on the wire. I put my face in my hands so I wouldn't have to look at Ira's body, but then I saw the faces of other men I'd killed with no more malice than I'd killed Ira.

I sat in my mother's kitchen. My parents were discussing funeral arrangements. "We need to tell the Legion. They'll do a ceremony," my dad said.

"Ira told me he wanted to be buried on Jackfish Bay in the old cemetery, with his moccasins, and a spirit house," I said.

"Of course we'll bury him in his moccasins," my mother said. "But nobody has a spirit house anymore. And how are you going to get permission to bury him on Jackfish Bay?"

"I promised Ira," I said. "I have to keep my promise."

I went home and changed into my newest shirt and cleanest jeans. I hated to go into Ely in the summertime and I hated dealing with the Forest Service any time. Not so long ago loggers were considered good citizens and the Forest Service worked with us but things had changed. Ely was on the front line in a war against loggers that was going on across the whole country. Every week there was an article in Time magazine about saving the trees. Only two years before, during the oil crisis, a student at the college stuck a bumper sticker on my truck that read, "Trees: America's RENEWABLE resource." But attitudes changed fast and the tanned, blond tourists who strode the streets of Ely now regarded me with contempt.

Max Swenstrom, the old district ranger, had been a friend. Max had lived in Ely for thirty years. He was a forester, left over from the old Forest Service that supervised timber production, kept the portages in good repair, and hired kids in the summertime. Then the Forest Service shipped Max out to Arizona, replacing him with a slick young fellow who enjoyed staring people down. Loggers began to have a lot of problems with the paper work on our bids, and when we went in to straighten things out, the new ranger acted like he didn't understand the first thing about logging, and less about the regulations. I spent hours in his office while he read through the fine print on maps and manuals. The books on Max's shelves had run to Conifer Production in Acidic Soils, and Hardwoods in the Pulp Process. Now I was looking at Strategies for Conflict Management and The Human Element in Change.

One time I asked the new man what he had studied in college. "Public administration and human relations," he said.

The Forest Service offices were housed in the Post Office, built by the WPA in the 30s. Faded murals in the lobby depicted miners and lumberjacks with honest faces and massive biceps toiling heroically to build America.

"Mr. Bertrecht is in a meeting. He has a very full schedule. Can I make an appointment for you for Thursday?" his secretary asked me.

"I need to make arrangements for a burial," I said. "Thursday is too late."

"A burial? I'm sure you have the wrong office."

"A burial in the Boundary Waters Canoe Area."

The secretary looked at me as though she didn't know what to ask next, and then went into the office behind her. Bertrecht followed her back out.

"A burial in the Boundary Waters Canoe Area?" he asked.

"In the old Indian cemetery on Jackfish Bay."

"I know of no such cemetery."

"It's old."

"No one is permitted to live there now. You know that."

"I know. My uncle is dead."

"There is no authorized cemetery. Of course, I could appeal up the line, and perhaps we could make special arrangements," the ranger said helpfully.

"My uncle won't keep."

Bertrecht smiled.

"Thanks anyway," I said. I turned and walked out.

I was disgusted at myself for trying to get authorization. I'd known better, but I thought I'd try because I didn't want to be hauled back to town when the woods police found a corpse in my canoe. I had to find another way.

I walked down the hill on main street, passed Dee's Bar, and doubled back to see who was in there, talking about the latest developments with the new wilderness bill. Things changed from day to day, so I didn't know whether I'd be in business next year or not.

Dee's was cool and dark, but crowded for mid-afternoon. Men and women sat in small groups talking intently, gesturing wildly, shouting occasionally. I got a beer at the bar and headed for the small knot of loggers.

"Heard about your uncle, Paul," Jim Krupka said. "I'm real sorry." Jim was just a little younger than Ira. He'd been logging since the mine closed.

"Thank you," I said. "What's the word on the bill?"

"We're all goners," Mike Makinen said. "Wiped out. Pack your belongings and head south."

"I don't know," said Jim. "They're talking compromise."

Jim moved deeper into the booth to let me sit down. I drank my beer and listened.

"The '64 legislation was supposed to be the final compromise." Mike said.

"We just started to recover from that one."

"In '64 the government was promoting selective cutting as the best way to maintain healthy forests."

"I don't get this wilderness fantasy. Those people use wood and paper. We're practicing sustainable harvest. Would they rather get their resources from South America?"

"Sure. Someplace far away so they won't have to look at the consequences of their lifestyles."

"Even in the compromise, logging is done for. All they're arguing about now is a few motor and snowmobile routes. How far to push back the line. Which cabins and resorts will go."

"If the bill passes."

"It's going to pass."

"None of that woods where we were allowed to cut was anywhere near the lakes and canoe routes. We practiced sustainable yield. I don't understand why they're banning cutting in there."

"They draw the lines in Washington. They don't know what they're doing."

"I heard the craziest thing. There's supposed to be a provision in the bill to let lightning fires go. Burn up the whole goddamned BWCA."

"That's just a sick rumor. Who'd want that? Why would they ban logging outside the canoe routes, and then burn up the canoe routes? Logging doesn't destroy the soil like fires do. Why waste the timber?"

"What I want to know is, what do those tree lovers wipe their asses with? Don't they know where paper comes from? They must have killed a million acres of trees putting out the propaganda on the BWCA alone."

"One of their pamphlets had a picture of the Little Sioux Burn, with a caption: 'Ravaged by loggers.'"

"Shit."

"Hey, that was a Forest Service project. One of their 'controlled burns'."

"Burned a couple of thousand acres before they got it under control."

I finished my beer and got up to leave. Sandy Tyman separated himself from another group and came over to put his hand on my shoulder.

"Real sorry about Ira, Paul," Sandy said. I bowled with Sandy Thursday nights.

"Thanks." I said.

"Did you know Emily got back from Washington?"

"No," I said.

"I saw her in the Alliance Office this morning," Sandy said. "This whole thing has been one heck of a civics lesson, I'll tell you. The government still hasn't paid us for Maple Isle. That was sixteen years ago. We won three jury trials on that settlement, and we haven't seen a penny yet."

I smiled. "The Bois Fort band is still waiting for the money for its land. That treaty was signed in 1854, I think."

"My dad told me to get out of the resort business when they drove us off Basswood, but I never thought they'd stretch the line to Snowbank."

"Are they going to get you out?" I asked.

"Looks like it." Sandy smiled. "We're all Indians now."

I walked over to Chapman Street. A paper sign taped in the window of an abandoned store read "Boundary Waters Conservation Alliance." Emily was intent on her typing and didn't hear me come in. I kissed her neck.

"Hey!" she jumped, looked up and smiled. She stood to give me a hug. "I heard about Ira. I'm really sorry."

"Thanks. I see you made it back alive."

"Barely," she said.

"Ira used to tell stories about Indians who were sent back dead when they went to Washington to protest treaty violations."

"Then I'll consider myself lucky," she said.

"But not successful."

"Oh, I impressed them. I went there and said, hey look, the border lakes have been under federal management since 1909. I explained that we aren't big developers, that we want to keep it like it is. We just want to be able to make a living and go fishing sometimes, and the law will wreck our lives. Oh yes, I really impressed them," she said ruefully, "up against slick lawyers in three piece suits who call themselves environmentalists. Who lie," she said. "We can't be heard. We're still peasants."

I laughed. "Sandy just said now we're all Indians."

"Same difference. Easy to kick off the land. People in power always know a better use for land than the people who live from it."

"When they took Grandma off Jackfish, they told her she should farm."

"Right. Like my grandmother did. God, she worked to clear those fields. Farmed them for one generation."

Emily leaned forward in her chair, elbows on her knees.

"I was so idealistic that back on Earth Day, I thought, well now that we know there's an environmental crisis we'll become frugal again, like we were in the depression and World War II," she said. "We'll stop consuming like crazy and work toward an equitable distribution of resources. But what did the environmental groups put their energy into? Creating wilderness for recreation so wealthy folks can have all their city luxuries and then enjoy a vacation of solitude. They'd rather have massive bureaucracy and petty law and Nazis patrolling the woods than share them with us grubby people. Solitude means having a million acres of public land to yourself. How greedy can you get?"

"Hey. Do you want to take a little illegal run up to Jackfish Bay with me?"

"Sure," she said happily.

"I'll pick you up Monday morning."

"I'm getting Ira cremated," I told my father.

"What about the wake and the honor ceremony?"

"I'll have him cremated after the honor ceremony."

"That's going to be expensive. Kind of a waste after the funeral home embalms him."

"I'll pay," I said.

"Well, at least we don't have to borrow a shovel from the white man to dig his grave," my mother said. It was a family story from the depression.

At the funeral home, my mother and sister dressed Ira in the dance outfit his wife Nellie had made the old way, thousands tiny beads sewn in elaborate floral patterns on the black cloth. They tied bells around his ankles, and lay the fur headpiece under his arm.

"Give me the moccasins," I said. "I'll take them with the ashes."

We had the give-away in the cafeteria of the Tribal Center. Ira lay in his casket in the middle of the room. On a table nearby were his possessions: a heavy wool blanket, traps, four rifles. My father called out a name, someone stepped forward, and my father made the presentation.

"Paul."

I came out of the crowd. My father lay Ira's thirty-thirty in my hands.

Twenty American Legion members came from Tower and the reservation for the funeral. They stood together, saluted the flag-draped casket, folded the flag, and presented it to me. Ira was forty when he went to his war, I thought. I was eighteen when I went to mine.

Monday morning I parked at the federal landing on Fall Lake, and took my square-stern canoe down from the racks. Emily lugged the three-horse motor down to the lake. I put the canoe in the water and fastened on the motor.

"This is canoe country, buster," one of the tourists screamed from shore as we pushed off.

"I guess they don't like the motor," Emily said.

We didn't meet anyone on first Pipestone portage. I carried the motor and canoe, Emily carried the packs. One light pack contained Uncle Ira and a bundle of small cedar boards.

On the second portage we met the woods police.

"Got a permit?" the ranger asked, nodding at the old Evinrude. I set the motor down and produced the slip from my back pocket.

"Right," the ranger said, and went on.

The water was low in the little river between Pipestone Bay and Jackfish. We talked about going around Wegan's Point, but decided to paddle the river instead. We weren't likely to encounter anybody on the river.

Ira had taken me to the old cemetery many times. He'd been a young man—he reckoned about eighteen—when the Spanish flu hit Basswood. Later he learned that it came with the soldiers from World War I, and that it went over the whole world. At the time, he only knew that it killed half his village.

Before Ira could bury his father, the government came to the village and took the survivors. Even Ira was too weak and grief stricken to resist.

I was bringing Ira home. The sun glinted off the lake and baked the tall cliffs. I nosed the canoe slowly to the shore. Emily pulled it up on some rocks and tied it to a bush. I carried the packs up over the hill to the cemetery.

There were still spirit houses there when I was a boy, with little fences around them. Every so often there would be a fresh grave. Ira always knew who they belonged to. There were things on the graves—cooking pots, axes, a rifle. Once there was a doll. But then one time when we came the things were gone, and there were never any new graves after that.

I set the box of ashes down, and took boards and nails from the pack. I built a spirit house like I remembered them, only it was two feet long. I set Ira's moccasins on the box of ashes, and put the folded flag on top of the moccasins. Carefully I covered them all with the little spirit house. I walked back up the hill to see if anyone would spot it easily, but it was well hidden.

"I don't think anyone will find it," Emily said. "Tourists don't come here looking for souvenirs anymore."

I walked back to the little spirit house. I looked up through the pines and began the keening chant that Ira had taught me, that Ira had sung each time we came to the cemetery. It was the only Chippewa song I knew.

"The Ball Club powwow is Saturday," my mother told me.

"I don't go to powwows," I said. Ira always went to the Ball Club powwow. I missed him badly and I couldn't shake my terrible guilt.

"You better come. We're sponsoring a memorial dance for Ira."

I drove to Ely and found Emily at the Alliance office. She was talking intensely on the telephone.

"I'm going to get myself a business card," she said when she hung up the phone. "It's going to read 'Crusader Mouse: No Cause Too Lost.'"

"Do you and Molly want to go to the Ball Club powwow?" I asked. Molly was four. She'd like it.

The powwow was always held in late July, on a hot, muggy weekend. I stood behind the bleachers holding Molly, looking down the aisle toward the drum pavilion. Emily stood next to me. The MC announced the memorial dance for Ira Bouchay. Everyone hushed and waited. My father stood in front of the drum and spoke into the microphone.

"This is a dance for my cousin Ira, who died earlier this month," he said. "Ira survived the terrible flu that killed most of his family. He was decorated in World War II for his valor and came home in one piece. He worked in the woods, and he could have lost his life many times. One time he went through the ice and almost drowned. Another time a bear attacked him in his camp and he killed it with his axe. He died instantly when he was electrocuted by a power line. He never suffered."

Old man Wawagan pushed his way through the dancers and staggered up to my father. With a sick feeling I realized that he was drunk. I wanted to get Emily and Molly away from there.

"Let me tell you," the old man bellowed, "that Ira Bouchay never sponged off of no one. He worked hard and he shared what he had. He never cheated and he never wasted. He was a real Anishinabe."

I strained to hear the end of the speech. The drum had started. My father and mother linked arms, bowed their heads and slowly began to dance. Others followed: young men in fancy dance outfits, old ladies in jingle dresses. A little boy in an outfit with a tiny feather bustle danced beside a girl in a dress of blue velvet. Solemnly they followed my parents. The stream of people swelled. Five women danced in a row, fringes of their shawls swinging in unison. All the dancers were moving now, and others came down from the bleachers to join them, ragged jean jackets mixing with beads and feathers.

"Can I dance?" Molly asked me.

"Sure." I set her on the ground. She took her mother's hand and Emily followed her into the ring.

The chanting of the drummers rose in pitch. The drumbeat grew stronger.

I felt myself moving forward, drawn into the river of life that flowed around the circle. My feet moved with all the feet, in time to the beat of the drum.

It was the beat of my own heart.

Finnish Words and Names

Finnish words are always accented on the first syllable.

Äiti (ay'eetee): mother
Kor'ppu: baked toast
Kor'va: ear
Mojakka (moy' ah kah): stew or chowder
Mummu: (muum'mu): grandma
Päi'vää: hello
Puuk'ko: a distinctive Finnish knife
Pul'la: cardamom biscuit
"*Setä Antti on kuollu[t]. Voitteko te tulla?*" ("Winter Trip")
"Uncle Antti is dead. Can you come?"

Names:

Aina (eye'nuh)
Antti (un'tee)
Irja (ear'yah)
Jussi (yus'see)
Järvinen (yair' vinen
Kaija (ky'ya)
Keskinen (kes'kinen)
Lahti (lah'ti)
Laila (ly'lah)
Rautio (rau'tee o
Timo (ti'mo)

Bouchay Family

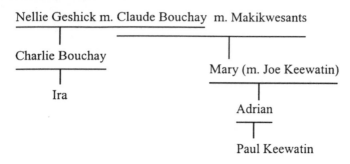

Nellie Geshick m. Claude Bouchay   m. Makikwesants

Charlie Bouchay

Ira

Mary (m. Joe Keewatin)

Adrian

Paul Keewatin

LaPrairie Family

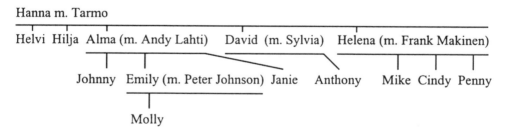

Sarah Geshick m. Henri LaPrairie m. Louise

Pete   Jake (m. Ida Keskinen)   Josie

Robin LaPrairie

Rautio Family

Hanna m. Tarmo

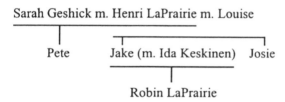

Helvi Hilja Alma (m. Andy Lahti)   David (m. Sylvia)   Helena (m. Frank Makinen)

Johnny Emily (m. Peter Johnson) Janie   Anthony   Mike Cindy Penny

Molly

Rautio Boarders

Jussi
Korva
Antti Lahti

Lahti Brothers

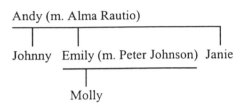

Urho m. Aina Maki   Antti

Andy (m. Alma Rautio)

Johnny   Emily (m. Peter Johnson)   Janie

Molly

Keskinen Family

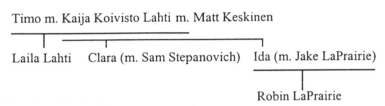

Timo m. Kaija Koivisto Lahti m. Matt Keskinen

Laila Lahti   Clara (m. Sam Stepanovich)   Ida (m. Jake LaPrairie)

Robin LaPrairie

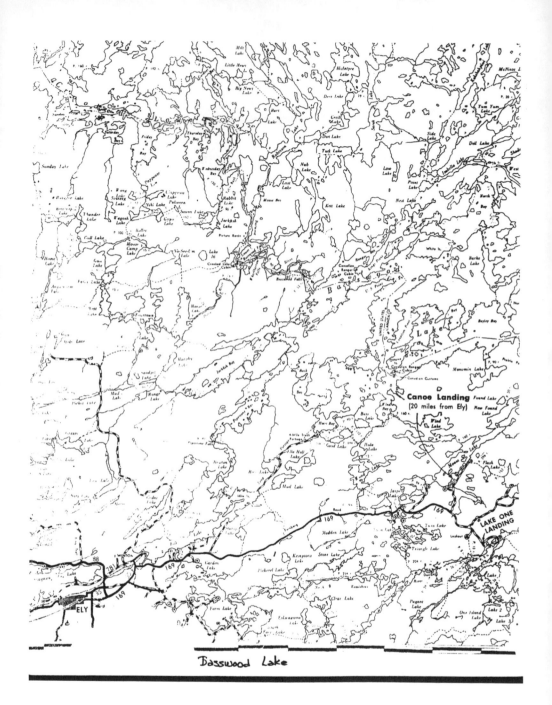

Canoe Landing
(20 miles from Ely)

LAKE ONE
LANDING

ELY

Basswood Lake

A Selected List of Fine Books Available from
Aspasia Books

ISBN 0-9685881-4-X Hietamies, Laila: *Red Moon over White Sea*
US $19.00 CAD $25.00
ISBN 0-9689054-4-7 Laitala, Lynn Maria: *Down from Basswood*
US $16.00 CAD $23.00
ISBN 0-919045-61-8 Lindström, Varpu: *Defiant Sisters*
US $16.00 CAD $23.00
ISBN 0-9685881-3-1 Lindström, Varpu: *From Heroes to Enemies*
US $19.00 CAD $28.00
ISBN 0-9685881-2-3 Lindström & Vähämäki (eds.): *Connecting Souls*
US $16.00 CAD $23.00
ISBN 0-9685881-6-6 Linna, Väinö: *Under the North Star* (sc)
US $19.95 CAD $27.95
ISBN 0-9689054-0-4 Linna, Väinö: *Under the North Star* (hc)
US $31.95 CAD $44.95
ISBN 0-9689054-3-9 Tuuri, Antti: *A Day in Ostrobothnia*
US $18.00 CAD $24.00
ISBN 0-9685881-0-9 Vähämäki, Börje: *Mastering Finnish* (textbook)
US $18.95 CAD $23.95
ISBN 0-9685881-1-5 Vähämäki, Börje: *Mastering Finnish* (cassettes)
US $13.95 CAD $18.95
ISBN 1-57216-030-6 Väänänen-Jensen & Vähämäki: *Finnish Short Stories*
US $18.95 CAD $25.00

All Aspasia Books titles are available from UTP, Inc.
Toll Free in the US & Canada
Tel. 1-800-565-9523; Fax. 1-800-221-9985
Credit Cards Accepted.

For further information, please telephone 705-426-7290
or fax 705-426-5690 or
e-mail aspasia@aspasiabooks.com
URL: www.aspasiabooks.com